THE BOOK
OF MEN

New York, 2023

THE BOOK OF MEN

Book One

ORIGIN'S EDGE

A. C. COELHO

ISBN: 978-1-6653-0697-3 – Paperback
ISBN: 978-1-6653-0698-0 – Hardcover
eISBN: 978-1-6653-0699-7 – eBook

These ISBNs are the property of BookLogix for the express purpose of sales and distribution of this title. The content of this book is the property of the copyright holder only. BookLogix does not hold any ownership of the content of this book and is not liable in any way for the materials contained within. The views and opinions expressed in this book are the property of the Author/Copyright holder, and do not necessarily reflect those of BookLogix.

Library of Congress Control Number: 2023913152

Printed in the United States of America

♾This paper meets the requirements of ANSI/NISO Z39.48-1992 (Permanence of Paper)

072423

To Lorenzo, Ian and Martin.

When empty; remember.
When sad; my warmth.
When fallen; my shoulders.
When lost; just follow the River and you will find me
running wild with the wolves.

Thank you for your sparkling eyes and love of life.
Your strength continues to save me.

Love forever lasting.
Dad

To all my incredibly faithful readers who have stood by me
throughout this improbable journey.
This story holds no weight without you.
Thank you.

***

And to all of those who still dream like a nine-year-old.

About *The Book of Men Saga*

The Book of Men is a contemporary thriller series adapted from the original film scripts *The Book of Men, Book One (Origin's Edge)*, *Book Two (Ashes), and Book Three (Ascent)* written by award-winning author A. C. Coelho. This is Book One, *Origin's Edge*.

The conversion from script to narrative was executed through a process he created called **Beat-Narrative**™.

About *Beat-Narrative*™

My interest in screenplays began inside a New York, dungeon-like, public library while shuffling for a weekend book to distract my anxiety from my finals. I checked out what I thought was a book on Freud. It wasn't exactly a "book" in the conventional sense. Behold it was *Freud: The Secret Passion's* original 1962 screenplay, a film directed by John Huston.

I was instantly hypnotized and consumed by the format, the style, and its structure. The cryptic messages. The showing without telling. The blanks. The speed. Everything. I was hooked, and from there on I'd read pretty much any script that came my way.

However, three issues constantly frustrated me. The first, was the lack of conciliation of the media – "Narrative *versus* Screenwriting" seemed unfairly binary. I would dream of traditional fiction benefiting from screenwriting's rhythm, mood, plasticity, soundtracks, senses, and most importantly the visuals, the picture in the mind. The second, regrettably, hundreds of thousands of extraordinary scripts never make it to the screens and are shelfed. Why retire wonderful stories? And the third, I wondered: how could any script reach the general public?

To address these issues, and to brake industry rules, I developed this hybrid writing style called *Beat-Narrative*™ – essentially a process to fit a script's soul into a narrative's body. For everyone.

Grateful for your eyes.
Keep your heart true and the soul warm.

Fade in.

PROLOGUE

The human condition - a spell unworthy of absolution.

Great Plains, Unknown Date, Long, Long Ago

The red Sun retires, burning the tip of a mountain peak as a last act of defiance.

It is that ambiguous moment when we can't distinguish day from night - where the wolf cheats the dog. That singular crack in the universe. Dusk.

It is Fall.

Dusk settles in, reluctant to allowing anything plural. It does however grant Native American rhythmic rattles, from afar, to echo through the air - granted in benign solitude.

A massive bonfire. Tiny specks of flickering, ruby flames journey deeper and deeper into the heart of this full-fledge beast. It is a Ceremonial Cheyenne Bonfire. The apricot moon takes over and meets the sky, unassumingly. Purple-azure sunset fills the horizon and stretches across these virgin plains as far as our eyes can reach.

The day finally punches out.

A gathering of tribe members in traditional Native garments dance rhythmically around the massive bonfire. Some are tuned to observing silence.

The bonfire replaces the cardinal Sun as steward of light. The chromatic salmon narrative keeps afloat coating all that moves.

Cheyenne music picks-up. No voices. Mostly rattles and drums.

A massive ten-feet-tall, rectangle-shaped, oyster-white boulder centered inside the bonfire. The boulder alters from its original, rustic, ivory-white to flame orange throughout. It entrusts purpose to mesmerizing.

Seven Natives dressed in buffalo skin dance tangentially to the bonfire while others revolve clockwise around it. They cry a newborn's chant while pitching large cerise oak seeds into the belly of the bonfire. The oak seeds travel on altered velocity. An odd arc they draw; none paying reverence to the laws of physics.

The boulder turning orange prophetically inside the fire.

Cheyenne music stops hard.

Night settles in, at last, and one can touch the stars if one tried hard enough.

Some do.

Great Plains, Same Ceremonial Bonfire

Next Day.

Dawn is just as confident as it is hopeful. There are no ambiguities here to be made manifest. The Wind owns these plains by deed. A timid stream of glacier freshwater cuts through these far lands producing an aria of its own.

Smoldering logs, glowing embers and reminiscences of yesterday's Cheyenne bonfire take center stage. Now empty of tribe Natives.

Same boulder - dressed by crow ashes. Light ash-smoke whispers softly at the boulder defying an unwarranted, however hopeful, chilling breeze that amasses in the thin crimson horizon.

Seven Thousand Years Have Elapsed. . .

It is Spring.

The seeds of time have surfaced.

Our slate boulder is fully surrounded by tall, fresh, green grassland.

Wind whips the silence.

Our timid stream flourished into a striving fast-current Aegean River.

The elements, natural or not, in this world do not play second-fiddle.

A little Cheyenne girl dressed in kimono tribe ensemble stands firm, eyes locked straight at the imposing boulder. She has short legs for her age. She wears a turquoise oak-seed necklace.

She takes pleasure in admiring the surrounding Great Plains' impossible landscape, its wild prairie and majestic glowing mustard mountains. Who wouldn't?

The little girl stands still in front of the stately boulder.

Strong wind rattles her ensemble, but not her determination. Her hair has a temper of its own and rather takes to sparring with the Wind.

She firmly holds then snaps off her leather necklace string as she softly mumbles an ancient Native flute offering ensemble. She kneels in front of the boulder, and, with her tiny frail hands, digs down into the Earth's gorge, burying the necklace deep under it. Her curiosity is just as expressive as it is welcoming. It has an assigned place in this world.

Her displacing of such an imposing object does not feel unnatural. Not the least.

She just may be the only soul on this Earth. And probably is.

Her view is only of the boulder.

Wind picks up. It performs its role proudly.

The morning's red Sun comforts her face while setting the stage. It also keeps her company. After all, this is no ordinary day.

A tiny step back. She slowly backpedals while staring at the boulder and waiting for a reaction. Any. But nothing still. She turns and walks away opposite from it.

The Wind stops and commands mute. A long beat. Her little bare feet halt.

A rectangle shaped shadow emerges in front of her.

She is not alone.

With a relieved half-smile, she turns her head back. Her untamed hair in opposite direction. She is maternally tolerant with it.

She looks back and transitions to a broader, warmer smile. Her body follows suit.

With confident chin raised, she looks fixedly, straight, at the boulder.

A long beat endures as the Earth spins slower. And slower. Then halts. An eternity takes turn. Time follows suit with cordial virtue and extends its nuclear width. What mastery.

She graciously nods towards the boulder.

Our Wind steals a tear from her eye. The tear accepts gravity and falls to the ground splashing onto the virgin Earth. Her wide, innocent smile outshines the red Sun's in depth and warmth.

Mission accomplished, she turns and resumes joyfully back towards the foot of our mighty mountains singing a primeval Cheyenne birth ensemble. They melt into one.

The purity of innocence can and will move mountains. Or even create worlds. This innocence - a window into the unnatural.

A new world is now to be.

Chapter 1

The Plains, Shortgrass Prairie

Unknown date.

Open country. Dawn.

Native victory song - drums, chant, rattles.

Wolf's feet running in hunt-mode across the Plains. Intense breathing. This is no ordinary wolf. This is a robust, a vicious barbarian.

An American bison's feet galloping. Stomping hard in visceral desperation.

It's a one-on-one hunt. For survival.

The wolf's full, charcoal-like face. Its athletic body running monumentally. How it moves takes us to rethink beauty. Wide-opened eyes, gasping heavily. The wolf's body in hunt mode contrasts with the bison's muscular form - both exercise their genetic programing and run for their lives, leaving no license for ambiguity.

The animals speed across a shallow creek as if it weren't there, splashing water and dirt from the riverbank. Both animals come out wet and equally committed. The overconfident wolf in relentless pursuit gains ground.

Downwind through green willows, the bison zig-zags but can't shake the beast off its heals. It knows what's in store.

A hard stop.

Dirt fills the air.

The bison turns and the creatures face each other.

The mist is cold, and the animal's breath cloud the surrounding air.

A standoff.

A last breath before the storm. They grant each other occasion to fill their lungs of fresh air and to appreciate the revered surroundings.

It is time.

The elements want nothing with this feud and step aside.

The wolf grinds. Its genetic instincts kick-in and it charges like nothing these Plains have ever witnessed.

An aggressive clash unfolds.

The bison is no stranger to a fight and rams the wolf down, hard. It launches its one-ton mass at the pursuing carnivore with Wakinyan will. It stomps over the wolf as an avalanche into a distracted canyon. The wolf tumbles, but is back on its feet, committed to the fight, and counters.

Twilight approaches accompanied by seven resplendent stars.

Our herbivore takes round two. And three.

Night sets in quietly not to disturb or get caught into the fight. Time has no place here neither. Hours, if not days, go by.

A melting aurora borealis keeps the lights on.

Duration favors the agile - our carnivore is a long-distance hunter engineered to endure the long haul.

The night is put to rest and dawn leans in.

The first rays of light coat the animals in a deep, rich orange.

Our rivals are bloodied and on their last breaths, their lives on a silk string.

The bison limping backwards. The wolf doesn't flinch and knows this is its last chance. It charges with everything left and some more borrowed. The kill is predictably ferocious.

The towering bison dropping to all fours.

The Earth's chosen Bison lays helplessly down for the count; gone to reward. It lays prone, immobile and moans uncomfortably loud. The wolf, covered in blood, stands erect, incontestably, on top of the stout bovine while catching its breath. It does not, though, feed on the bison.

Time resumes in scene, faintly. The Wind tepidly steps back, along with the downhearted red Sun. All in sorrow.

The Earth bleeds.

A last rattle.

The Barn

Unknown date.

Pre-Dawn.

Darkness takes hold of the Barn with little, if any, empathy for shadow.

A typical, pre-war, mid-west, large Blackwood barn built with enlarged Byzantine-like perpetual windows. Its wood-beams are impotent, just as the cast-iron machinery spread across every square-inch. Inside, a comprehensive, Victorian-age, Science Laboratory filled with biology, chemistry, botanical experiments, and equipment. It is a homy lab with an odeum-like composure.

Built-in apothecary cabinets walls and custom shelves are populated with animal specimens and botany abstracts.

Metal tools clanking from afar. It becomes progressively louder.

At last, an elvish speck of balmy light wants to stretch. And it does, in the quiet. Next to it, a man's oil-greased hand gripping a pipe-wrench fastens a large, rusted bolt. The flickering light from the kerosene lamp covers the man's hand as it runs its business.

Nelson Senior's half body, legs only, laying on the cold floor while repairing a Nineteen Century rotary, 660-V, cast-iron, traction rotary Power Converter he simply calls "DINA." Nelson is a mid-age, well-built, cowboyish, fatherly man with scrubby beard and thick mustache, wearing beaten-down jeans and leather boots. He possesses an oak-like core and unassuming intelligence that noticeably resonates beyond these lands. It is to doubt anyone who claims knowing where Nelson was born. Or how. A mystery incomprehensibly not debated among files of men. This is a man of few words, banking on actions. Tales of his heroism are spoken about and venerated across generations.

By his side, a dark hickory-wood toolbox and a kerosene railroad copper lamp. The toolbox affords the initials "N.S.C.D" engraved in Carolingian script. The copper lamp is all that lights the barn.

Two small children's papier-mâché crafts hanging out strapped onto the toolbox - a red heart that reads *"love my Popz"* and the head of a green fox.

Tools still clanking.

The morning's first rays of light hit Nelson's hand as he struggles to reach a monkey-wrench hanging on the toolbox. A short upset gasp from Nelson, and to himself. "Darn cramps."

Nelson's full face lit by the Sun's golden beam reveals he is by no measure an ordinary man. Nelson is grand.

He emerges from under the power converter, stretching his back, then neck. He grabs the copper lamp and walks towards a massive Westinghouse 250-V DC power panel. The elaborate vintage copper pressure gauge marks *zero*. With a red craftsman's pencil placed behind his ear, he looks at the power converter's panel attentively.

To himself. "C'mon DINA. We got this."

He presses a copper button, turns one massive panel knob, and finally whirls a hand-cranked start-engine. No go. He clears sweat from his forehand with a white linen handkerchief and repeats the sequence, this time slowly. Finally, a muffled bang and we have light. Lots of it.

White spooked wild pigeons – and anything with wings – burst out from the high birch beams. A full blow of thick steam and ruby lights behind the power converter.

The copper gauge reacts and pushes up. The barn fills with abundant warm light. Sunbeams laser-cut across multiple sections. All aspects of the barn and its equipment come to life.

A relieved Nelson. "There! Light I say."

Boots being cleaned in the backdrop. Dr. Hooker, aka "Red," enters the barn strolling in Nelson's direction. Red is a red-bearded man wearing a red Persian turban, white shirt, a red scarf, and a long cloth blue overcoat. He carries a small leather backpack, a barrel Colt rifle and a gun powder goat horn slung around his back. He has been around. Never tires. Red is Nelson's physician and Science man. They have been through thick and thin together.

With a light British-Persian accent to Nelson. "I think."

A beat. No reply from Nelson. Perhaps he is too distant to hear Red. Unlikely.

Red again, louder as he hangs his Scottish cap on the head of Hippocrates' bronze bust. "Need a hand?!"

A beat.

"Yes, you do!" Nelson back at him, referring to Red's initial proclamation (*I think*). Following with: "Early, hum?"

"Data, Nelson, it's all about the data." An analytical pause to examine DINA. "Glad she's still huffing. The town can't handle darkness." Red referring to DINA.

Nelson goes about reorganizing his tools, many of which are un-conventional. He licks the tip of his pencil and makes a few notes into a decent-size, green, leather notebook that sits on top of the Lab's cedar countertop. Red shares the Lab side of the Barn with Nelson.

Red draws five small, Bohemian clear lab bottles containing live tadpole specimens from his jacket inside-pocket. He places them next to a shining brass Watson double-lens microscope and scat-tered Abulcasis-like surgical instruments.

"Yep, had to run them-fishing lines down by the old Reverend's Lake and came across something you oughta see, Nelson."

Note Red tries his best to lessen his foreign accent, sometimes pretending to be local. Not always successfully.

Nelson sketching notes, this time on a Gothic book.

Red turning the old stove fire on.

More notes from Nelson on the book. These "notes" come alive, then fade still. Red holding a loud, simmering, old Ottoman copper pot, pouring freshly made Persian coffee into two light-green enamel mugs.

"Couldn't sleep neither hum? My mind is getting at me. Tired. Where exactly?" Nelson asks.

Red holding the red-hot Ottoman pot. Its bottom plate blazing orange-red.

"By Small Stone's Creek. Remember?"

Nelson's shrug eyebrow is enough to indicate he can't remember.

"Where you got stung by those pesky black-jackets?" Red continues.

Nelson tilts his head embarrassed, a half-smile, however still spaced out.

Nelson hands one mug to Red and takes the other; both carry the same "N.S.C.D." initials.

"Where your most-beloved sister-in-law caught you and Amanda. . ." Red's last attempt of being understood.

Nelson raises his eyes in full alert, his thick eyebrows command a *got it, stop there*.

A beat. A distraction. A bulb pops. Pigeons fly upwards from behind a cabinet.

The Ottoman pot falls from Red's hand. Nelson grabs the pot with his bare hand by its bottom metal plate. His left hand burns a notch. He holds it as if immune to pain. Which he is.

Nelson slowly hands back the pot to Red who is equally indifferent to the phenomena.

"Getting old, old-man?" Nelson mockingly.

Red carefully grabs and holds the pot by its wood handle. He does not want to burn *his* hand.

Red is smirking, in reference to the unnatural phenomena.

They sip and enjoy the hot coffee as if it were their last.

With a turn of head over his shoulders, Nelson nods in the Farm House's direction in reference to Amanda, his wife. Then back at Red. "She won't like me missing bread; again. Let's haul."

Red takes a long, silent sip of coffee, then placing the mug on the bio countertop, next to reptile fossils, on top of notes from The Marsh Expedition.

Nelson slides a hunter's knife into its leather belt holster.

Both men exit the Barn in silence, but Nelson stops half-way out the door for a quick second.

"Hold-on, Red, forgot-there Henry." Nelson says.

Nelson tiptoes quickly back inside, grabs a shabby pocket-size Old Grand-Dad whisky bottle stashed inside an Eskimo's fur-boot and pours a splash into his coffee mug. A quick sip to the bottle. He tries his best to be unnoticed. He grabs his 1860 Henry 44-40 Trapper hanging by a sling behind the door and jitterbugs, just as fast, back out the door to resume with Red. The Henry has an extra leather load of ammo hand-crafted to its wood stock, which is telling in its own.

Red pretends he didn't notice the extra pair of seconds (and back noise) Nelson invested in grabbing the Henry and proceeds to double-check his own 1855 Colt revolving rifle's chamber for ammo.

As they are out the door, they notice it is unusually windy. Some black clouds on the horizon.

Both men walk to the creek admiring the breath-taking, early-morning, Great Plains landscape. They see Nelson's Farm House at a distance on their way to the Creek. They also notice the kitchen's light is on and the heat-smoke flowing from its chimney.

By the Dirt Road

Gusting wind.

Tall corn.

Men walking.

Red kicking river stones.

Their friendship reaches far beyond the numbers, while words are not always necessary in a conversation. In most cases silence bears plenty.

Parallel to the men, a large creature rattles the precious silence through the shuffling of corn stalk and leaves. They extend their eyes but can't see any physical being. The men snap their cara-biners, cock them, and aim towards the moving creature. Their scopes follow that of the creature as it fades deeper into the corn field.

The velocity by which they react is astonishing. It seems age has not affected these men in any capacity. With cautious, fixed-eyes, Nelson lowers his rifle's hammer steadily. The men lower their rifles slowly.

Their eyes meet before they take to their immediate task – the Creek.

Farm House Kitchen

The sound of burning firewood.

A soft humming.

An old English cast iron stove emitting flame light.

Amanda writing in a white leather, bio-chemical cook book.

Amanda is Nelson's self-assured, caramel-eyed wife. One can't distinguish her genetic heritage. She is the daughter of humble Andalucian beekeepers and a blend of all races. All that is beautiful. Subtle in her perfection. She is the mother of all things and is wiser than Nestor. She is kind, but not fragile. Astute and compassionate. It is said she can pitch her voice and speak with bees.

Table

Hand-crafted wood bowls with seeds, fresh greens, and half-cut persimmons.

Amanda's hands knead bread dough on top of a mahogany dining table. She has beyond pleasure in tossing up cooking flour. She could do it forever.

A *Tree of Life* canvas hangs in contrast with the abundant, floating flour powder. A big recipe-book sits fully opened on the wood table next to loads of color pencils scattered all around.

The red Sun is anxious to start the day. It almost wants to cheat to get ahead.

She looks out through the window and notices Nelson's copper lamp fussing in the darkness. She follows it with eyes only. A long stare.

She carefully places a small log into the cast-iron's wood-burning belly, flips a page from the recipe-book and resumes to the window.

A Delphian grey wolf stands firm outside her window. They stare at each other. An empty swing set behind the wolf.

An indifferent, yet defiant Amanda stares cold back at the wolf. Without contempt.

Dirt Road

Early rays hit the farm's cerulean-purple Lavender fields.

As the men pass by the Farm House, they look towards Amanda's amber lit kitchen.

Red looks to Nelson with the corner of his eye waiting for any reaction. None. Silence as they walk. Military pace. Clearly, there is something not to be discussed.

The Creek

Early Morning.

Our Bison lays dead, prone. Its body mostly intact apart from vicious deep kill lacerations.

Nelson and Red take a knee next to the bison for closer examination. Nelson uses his Henry to support his crouching. He runs his hands along the bison's body and fur. His fingers compassionately caress through the open wounds. A disconcerted Nelson gently caressing the animal as if he could bring it back. "These other wounds; they're old. This wasn't the first time these two went at it. No one creature could've alone brought down this buffalo." He looks to his side. "Can't think why this creature would pursue this doing. Not in this particular."

"Above my practice. Can you undue this?" Red asks.

Nelson indicates a sad *no* with head. "We're tardy. Again."

Nelson finally sees an identifiable mark on the bison's back leg – a healed arrow wound. He holds the leg and salutes at it with kindness. Nelson speaks softly. "This animal is an old comrade from a time men could not roam these fields. I know this one, Red." A grim beat. Nodding. "I know this one."

"Don't look random to me." Red says.

Nelson points to the dirt road. "Tracks, Red. One fella. Solo."

"Hunter. Raider!" Red back at him.

Still on one knee, in towering rage, Nelson hammers hard his Henry by its stock onto the ground. An unconventional loud stump echoes violently across the Plains. The elements bow aside, letting the echo make its point. His anger travels the Earth and back. The heaviest stump ever heard.

An upset Nelson. "*Darn-it*! I can't remember ever seeing such a magnificent chief like this one here."

Red pulls out from his leather utility patch a pair of Victorian cobalt apothecary jars and collects two blood samples. After a few seconds shaking them, he raises the cobalt jar against the sunrise light to check for viscosity.

"Might be one of the last true American bison left, Red. Can you fathom?" Nelson says.

Nelson looking at the horizon supporting his crossed hands on the barrel of his Henry, sadly contemplating. "These American bison once commanded these plains. Nothing got in their way. The

Earth trembled with their stomping. That magnificent sound that was. And now; now they face extinction. They ain't deserving of this predicament. This is their land. What have we done?"

Red's concerned, wide-opened eyes express sadness as he manages a long glass dropper. He pours a clear beryl reducing liquid agent into the second jar. He shakes it and waits a beat. The jar turns orange. Then purple. A surprised Red. "A wolf! Definitely a runner."

"Ours?" Nelson posed the question.

"I'll only know the tree-sequence after more lab tests. Data, Nelson. Data. But I wouldn't be surprised it's not from here. Methodology. Methodology matters more than all else." Red observes while kneeling next to the bison.

"Darn, Red! This isn't in the books."

Nelson puts his hands on the bison's forehead, closes his eyes and mumbles something softly in Cheyenne dialect. "Am sorry chief I can't undo this. Trust it won't go in vain."

Nelson raises from his knee, and the men slowly scout the horizon. An echoed thunder pierces the silence, crescendo until reaching the men.

"Looks like we're in for thick-storm by day-end." Said Red, placatingly.

The most diminutive green grasshopper lands on Nelson's forearm. He looks at it with ease and reacts pessimistically. "More than that, Red, much more than that. A curse to be."

A wolf's howl.

Nelson touches the bison one last time; inconsolably.

The valiant Nelson otherwise known for his bravery and

gallantry in the thick of battle, is also well-known for his actions rather than words. Essentially, he will not conform.

The men head back walking side-by-side to the Farm House. Behind them, a huge bonfire where the Bison lays to rest.

The men's elongated, thin shadows follow them back on their seven-mile contemplative, hushed hike.

Chapter 2

The Farm House

Dirt Road.

Tall corn. Unruffled leaves.

The men arrive at Nelson's bucolic Farm House carrying unfinished business faces. An all-embracing Salisb tamarind tree shade welcomes them. The Farm House is still well-kept but clearly needs a coat of fresh paint. Or two. Its better days have fallen behind it without avail – a venue with little, if any, fancies.

Long unmown grass.

They walk by an empty swing and halt at the mailbox. The white rusted mailbox – overflowing with mail – reads *01 Aboro Street*.

Anguished by Nelson's silence, Red dares ask, "How's she doing, Nelson? How're you both doing?"

Nelson takes half a beat to engineer a believable answer. "It's a process. A day, a day at a time, I suppose. It hasn't been easy on my lady... Hard, real hard, Red." He pauses. "I remember the first second I saw that woman. Boy, it was like seeing light." In a deep voice as means to avoid choking in sorrow. "And now... I love that woman. Darn, she doesn't deserve this."

"It's the science. Talk to her about Hanna. It's part of healing." Red says.

"Science? Healing? C'mon, partner."

As Nelson walks towards the Farm House, he assembles wild garden and Lavender flowers and crafts for a makeshift flower bouquet. He pulls a stretch of thin rope from his pocket and fits a lace. Senior is a bit clumsy in the bouquet business. He looks down and to the side before crafting an obvious lie. "I try every day. It's just... let's retire inside and fetch some bread before it *coldens*, and I get in hot water."

Farm House, Porch

They lay their rifles by the porch column, clean their muddied boots on the porch steps, and fall in.

Amanda greets them at the porch door with commanding voice. "Thought you boys didn't know I baked bread this morning, hum?"

Nelson places the plethora of letters inside an opened Inca-wood trunk, already full of previously sent letters. He knows better – these are either requests or complaints dressed in recommendations. As the Town's leading founder, the local populous proclaim him as a type of fixer-of-all-things. A rank he refuses to accept.

Nelson unfastens his brace of revolvers.

Nelson and Red look at each other like twin nine-year-olds trapped inside a principal's office.

"Morning, Amanda, sorry we're tardy. My blunder, pursued Nelson to abet in a matter."

Amanda pointing at Red. "You are excused, mister. And Suzan?"

"Anxious about the baby, and eating the pantry, gross. You know." Red says.

"Now you stick close by her. Real close, understand there, Master Red?!"

"Yes, ma'am."

They proceed inside through a squeaking door. Nelson systematically annoyed with the noise, mutters to himself. "Darn door."

Salon

All three walk past the House's main salon in silence towards the kitchen. A heavily used bowl back mandolin, a kamancheh, a small octave mandocello, and a kid's butterfly net rest by the hand-carved, masterful, double rocker.

By the Coffee Table

The Book of Men rests on top of a dusty coffee table. It is lit by warm golden light, and Nelson looks at it with discrete disdain as he walks by it.

"Boy, something here sure smells irrefutably good." Red says.

A shy and robotic Nelson hands Amanda the flower bouquet; an odd physical distance between them. Amanda looks him straight in the eye, and he catches hers and moves his reposing eyes downwards.

So close, so distant.

The tips of their fingers touch one another in the process. It's a rare moment. They are equally lost but in different realities. Both grieving.

All three move into the kitchen area. Amanda goes in first. Then Red. Then Nelson.

Kitchen

The kitchen is country by claim, Mediterranean by heart, dressed in honey tones, an English wood stove. There is abundant light, large double-hung Queen Ann Sash windows, botany books, and an old children's tall seat.

At the table, Amanda's receipt book, a bonsai persimmon tree. Pomegranate dried seed splashed across the table. A pomegranate tile section covers one kitchen wall. Baskets of seeds spread out – wood utensils and white baking flour everywhere.

Red's eyes run through random family photos hanging on the kitchen's walls. Although he's seen these photos plenty before, his heart takes to the act – once again.

One photo stands out – Nelson and Amanda's inner family. The couple and seven kids: six boys and a nine-year-old little girl, Hanna. Pictures can lie. This one does not. It tells us what we understand as happiness – such simplicity.

They stare at one another uncomfortably. The couple's silence is telling.

Amanda snatches a steamy Challah bread out from the oven to lessen the awkward climate. She puts it on top of the table next to assorted flatbreads.

"More wood! I'll get more outside." Nelson shouts to himself.

Nelson exits via the kitchen's back door. He stops for fresh air out the door while supporting himself and his sadness on a great Bur Oak tree. A bucket full of logs rests under the kitchen's cast-iron stove proves obvious.

Behind Nelson, a white-framed glass greenhouse and over-flowing birch buckets of persimmon surround it.

"How you guys doing?" Red speaks hesitatingly to Amanda.

She looks outside the window into the vague horizon while re-arranging the flower bouquet. She sees Nelson. "It's been, darn hard." Taking a long, deep breath, she continues, "I've been trying to reach out to him. He pretends nothing happened."

"The man is up before the chickens and *ghets*. Back home, same distance." She pauses, looks at another family picture, then re-sumes. "Loving Nelson has been my life. Now, I'm alone in this empty, this very empty house."

As she walks closer to the window, she hands him a bucket of persimmons and a small goat-horned knife and commands. "Slice these."

Red takes to slicing the persimmons, but with attention else-where. From the kitchen window, they observe Nelson outside as they go about the persimmon goat-cheese caprese.

Outside Garden Area

Nelson pretends to look for wood-burning logs. He can't find logs any more than he can find himself. A masquerade into the lost.

Kitchen

A supportive Red. "Yep. He's practically living in the barn. Sometimes he fixes the same machine twice in the same day and doesn't notice it."

A darkly dispassionate Amanda replies. "It's like that sort of dream when you scream, and no sound comes out. No one hears you. Only that vile echo." A long pause. "Like drowning in your own voice."

"Give it time, Amanda. Give him more time." Now more affirmative. "This here is Nelson Senior we're talking about. He brought light and life to this dark piece of nowhere. DINA, the Springs Well, and pretty much everything else has his signature. Gave stop to the plague. Forged them flatlands and, inevitably, it came with a price."

Amanda is not conceding.

"That's the whole point. He didn't see it coming. He feels guilty. *My doing*, he says. Nelson is no ordinary man. Grief?! (She shakes her head) Did Nelson ever feel pain? Does he know what pain, grief is? For him, it's like dealing with an emotional conundrum."

"I look out, and I can't see the horizon-line anymore, Red. I can't see *him* anymore."

"It's the same old hard-headed, big-hearted Nelson, I infer." Red speculates.

Amanda, with determined sad eyes, however politely upset, remarks. "No-sir. He's changed. His heart is shattered beyond fixing. And he *certainly* never wrote this chapter." A quick pause, she looks to the side. "Have you not seen his mandolin? Look! It's been lying there, rotting. Nelson used to be funny; he'd make me laugh from sunrise to sunset. His smile: bigger and warmer than the Sun's. The world convened on his shoulders. And there wasn't anything he couldn't do or constitute."

"C'mon Amanda."

"We speak of a man who never lost." Amanda says.

"Well, that is true."

"Have you forgotten as well, Red? Look at that bastard-book over there." Both turn their heads towards *The Book*. "You see his watch on top of it? It's been laying there since. . ." More gently. "He sits there night after night looking out the door, waiting for a miracle. Nelson! A Goddamn miracle, Red! No Red, Nelson lost. . ." Another eerie pause. She breathes deeply, then exhales. "Faith."

She turns slightly, looks down at Hanna's picture (portrait on top of the table), and repeats it to herself now softly. "Nelson lost, *faith*." She leans into herself. "How could. . .?"

Red, to himself. "Hanna. The book."

The Book on the coffee table.

Amanda peeling a persimmon.

"The book? Yes, *the* book. That damned book. No one really comprehends its powers. Some think it's magical." She laughs. "But there ain't nothing magical or mystical about it. This is Nelson's *book of beginning*. Mark zero. It answers only to him, and to him only, until. . ."

Amanda stops speaking. Brings her head down.

"Until. Until?" Red asks softly.

She raises her head and walks to the window.

Outside, by the Kitchen's Back Steps

Nelson by the oak tree, taking a breath. He looks back and sees Amanda at the window. He knows what they speak of.

Kitchen

Amanda continues. "Until he changed it. He wrote what he called a *retraction prose*. It was meant for Hanna. He wanted his children to take on his work. He felt he let humanity down, that only the eyes of an innocent child could make up for his short-comings. He was self-aware. His love for our little Hanna was something different, new to him. She broke his back. And that love changed him. Forever." A beat. She resumes. "Remember, Red, we speak of a man who never met his father, or mother. Family is everything to him."

Amanda tosses baking flour. "Greed. Self-pride. The pursuit of violence. Selfishness. Indifference. The natural balance of things, what we call humanity. He felt he couldn't square it all. Science. Evolution. Materiality. The contradictions of the species. Then. Then Hanna came along."

"But the boys? Big-Pants?" Red asks.

Amanda with a gentle shake of the head. "Big-Pants. Inevitably, boys are boys, Red. You know. Big-Pants is the sweetest, the most loving of them all. Probably the smartest. But over-shined by his sister Hanna. It was hard on him. He would take it on his older brothers. I tried to fill in the gaps, but that made it worse. You remember, Red. And Hanna. And how he competed for her heart with his father; but loving her equally, to bare. She was our light, and when she went away, all became dark."

22

Amanda turns her back towards Hanna's photo, and her goofy smile.

"*The Book* will only answer to Nelson and to his, now, youngest son. *The Book* will answer to no others."

"And what if we can decommission it?" Red asks.

"Only Nelson's blood can destroy it. But you knew that already, hum. . ."

"But what if? What if? Let's not split this atom."

Amanda looking deep into Red's eyes. "Then, science-man, all is lost. All of us. Everything. No exceptions. And as you know very well, we have very little time to turn this around."

Amanda extends her right arm, with her delicate hand leading the way. Her opened hand shuts into a fist. "Back into infinite darkness. . ."

A dark beat.

"Time then is of the essence, Amanda. Of the essence. . ." Red back at her.

He holds a grim face and calls the conversation over.

Nelson blasts in with a few shabby pieces of wood and places them inside the oven without commenting.

Amanda clears a tiny tear then pointing at the caprese. "Boys! Red's favorite."

A persimmon caprese about to enter the oven.

Nelson looks at the small goat-horn knife while cleaning his restful hands in the sink.

He notices Amanda's tears, and he stands firm. In pain.

Chapter 3

*** This chapter is my depiction of New York in the 70s ***

*** The narrative resumes on Chapter Four ***

What does New York look like (and feel like) in the 70s?

New York City, 1972

Pre-Dawn.

The year is 1972 and faith stands thin.

New York Seventies – a metonym for violence.

Our visibly reluctant red Sun reconsiders punching in ahead of schedule. The best it will do is shine a shallow, mustard beam at the top edge of the North Tower of the Twin Towers. And no more. It is not to blame.

A white pigeon fades into a depressed, meager, raw, and beaten-down, realistic Beame-Koch 1970's New York City. There is nothing allegorical or fictional about New York, its place in time, or its characters. It is the real deal. It is everyone for oneself.

Neither the Jets' underdog Super Bowl title nor Harlem's pivotal 1969 Summer Cultural Festival are plenteous to keep hope afloat. Those lifelines fade off by Fall. An honorable decade sign-off. Dusk, most likely. But then again, we hang on, onto Reed's Knicks. Yes, we do. A thing of beauty in this haze of sober misery. And we keep holding on to it.

What is left of The Bronx is – literally – burning, and the city is fiscally bankrupt along with any shade of pride. Self-abnegating firefighters put out insurance fraud fire arsons by the minute. A special. A rare breed.

The pimp-paradise Deuce (Times Square), with its millions of glittering incandescent lights, counterintuitively comforting, normalizes the scene. But pay no tribute to the Deuce alone. New York has hundreds of similar corners - just as or grittier - but less glamorous. However hidden. However, under the shades. But always open to business.

Unemployment sits at a steady twenty-one percent. A trip to the pump will either foreclose a working man or treat you to a gunpoint carjacking experience on a good day. Some take refuge through the White Flight - city population moving to the suburbs searching for jobs.

Under-staffed and under-gunned, Fear City police can't curb crime or take a scratch at it even. The tit-for-tat mob holds firmly tight. Ghetto and gang culture are disciplines tested in public school curricula. It's statistically a survival of the fittest game. Run your numbers. Darwin had it coming.

The *Out of The Gate* decade starts with unabashed fraction - Kent State and Jackson State killings draw an incomprehensible bleak line, one that calcifies social division. Our zealous super-intendents *do* cross that line. Yes, they do.

Watergate Silent-Majority "Dick" Nixon is the nation's legiti-mately elected barmaster. In tandem, in supporting role, an old-order squadron of out-of-touch myope zookeepers roam in a parallel reality, enforcing an aging script. But they do speak well on the screen.

The country is bankrolling the senseless, data-driven, Vietnam War and a slew of flat-out lies - routinely. And they lie, to all, to themselves, to babies in cribs, to Irish twins, to any available ear; shamelessly, expeditiously, admittedly, in adoration, standing on bucket-loads of fossil pride - a pedestal of the unimaginative, the ordinary. The establishment crumbles through the lack of game - a measly pair of sevens. They sink. Fast.

Bone-spur deferred fortunate ones, enjoying fortunate continental breakfasts, with fortunate fathers, at the fortunate Palace, over-looking Central Park's fortunate landscape, while a carriage horse takes a fortunate dump on all the unfortunate - poor - ones. No privileges spared.

Fifty-eight thousand, two hundred and twenty American casualties. Thousands more wounded and scared. In addition to hundreds of thousands of perished Vietnamese. The neutralized Phoenix non-combatants. And millions of broken hearts - mothers, fathers, sisters, brothers, wives, husbands, sons and daughters, lovers, and friends. And grief.

It will take more than sunlight to close these scars. And they never do.

Divine Madness - Saigon signing off.

The Great Lakes' economic, industrial miracle finds its grey marble tombstone memorial carved with *Rust Belt*. Ohio and Michigan, especially, taking much of the beating. Decadent manufacturing output triggered through low productivity, asymmetric labor dynamics, the lack of innovation, and low-cost international competition. Many take to the bottle. Hard.

New York - also known as The City of Strikes. The decade of *fair is fair* Rank and File. The Strike Movement. Unionization. Trade Unions. Wildcat Strikes. Picket Lines. Sit-Downs. Recurrent Stoppages. The US Bureau of Labor Statistics registers 5,716 strikes involving roughly three million workers in 1970 alone. From postal, sanitation, and MTA employees to the police, municipal, and telephone workers. From TWA's pursers and stewardesses to UAW/Chrysler's sixty-seven days strike.

New York - more ghettos than barrios.

Didactic Sip-Ins at chiaroscuro Waikiki and Julius'. In the shadows, oblivious Waverly Place and West 10th Street, Julius' Bar patrons, supporters, and the *Mattachine Society* advance challenging New York's S.L.A. - democratizing the principal idea that all-are-created-equal. And, naturally, the likes of Genovese-supervised "disorderly houses" such as, but not limited to, Christopher Street and bottle-club, sign-the-book, *outed*, Stonewall Inn; *ceteris paribus* above-average ROIs justify the endeavor - shielded by the runners of *famiglia e tutto*.

Faraway lands and across the country don't fare much better. From the streets of bubbling Compton to Bowie's South Philly. From the rioting, multiethnic Brexton to the brutalistic concrete South Kilburn in London - Krays, Yardies, Scutllers, and the penny dreadful copy-cats, all about.

Juxtaposing New York, Detroit's notoriously vicious ghetto gangs Y.B.I., hand-pumping Errol Flynns, the Black Killers, Chambers Brothers, challenging *Detroit Partnership, Inc.*'s established order and rackets.

Further out, Munich-72', Ireland's complex Long War. Bogside Bloody Sunday. State-sponsored, financed, supported and widespread cowardice torture in Latin America. Communism - a multiplier at work on a global scale. A thoughtful insight turned absurd pretense for unity. An Iron Curtain that wants to expand to the attic.

Complex algorithms ante Berlin, North Korea, China, Cuba, Cambodia, South Africa. A shift in the balance of power and weight in the Middle East. Genocides - not an uncommon denominator in Latin America, Eastern Europe, Africa, and Asia.

The world is busy. The world is in pain.

Every country has its fair share of dilemmas, blood, and embarrassments. Advocating time and energy to someone else's backyard brawl or global affairs is shuffled down the toilet or to the farthest end of the stack. The Seventies - "I got my own problems, mind you." Might as well dedicate your 401k towards a nuclear fallout shelter. Many do.

As for corporate greed, look no further - Valley of the Drums, Parkersburg, New Idria, Three Mile Island, Times Beach, Stringfellow, Love Canal, Hinkley, among other finely tuned operations. Just swell.

Beyond Rowdyism. The coming of age of modern-day guerrilla pirates, some more idealistic than others. Each fighting for the cause it deems justifiable. From derivative political factions, nationalist dissidents, and ethnic, religious zealots to domestic right and left-wing paramilitaries. All couplable. All violent.

The likes of such maternal commingling's as the Sendero Luminoso, New World Liberation Front (NWLF), Sandinistas, FALN, Symbionese Liberation Army (SLA), TFP, PLO, IRA, ETA, Soledad Brothers, Weatherman, Zvonco, INLA, Ernest 2X, FARC,

GRAPO, Jane Alpert, Red Brigades, Baader–Meinhof RAF, Japanese Red Army, KKK, Afrikaner-777, Argentina's and Chile's Dirty Wars, DOI-CODI/OBAN, Libya, plane hijackings, and so much and so on will occupy your evening Tele news.

Theia Mania. God. Religion. Faith - in the absence of *it*; the search for *it*. Wide-spread religious cults call the Seventies theirs. In the house - the Sapir-Whorf hypothesis.

Call them what you want - cultism, fanatism, altruism, non-dualism, utopianism, charlatanism, false prophetism, *con-man-ism*, *sex-predatorism*, rogue preachers, self-proclaimed gurus, rainbow shamans, a legion of literate unemployed, rebel runaways, carrier criminals, small-time crocks, vaudevillian street pimps, bigots, the insane, the sane, idealists, and plenty of malnurtured hearts, souls and minds finding their feeding ground in this dusk decade - a vast hunting ground to recruit susceptible young adults and wounded buffalos.

And it spreads like wildfire. We speak of thousands of new-age cults thriving across America and the world. It is thought to be a global pandemic of sorts. From code-switching Jonestown People's Temple, Heaven's Gate, Sullivans & Fourth Wall, Rolls Royce Rajneesh to Blood-Atonement Mormon Manson, closed doors Laws of Sarah, Church of Synanon, Moses' Children of God, Yonque's Twelve Tribes, Manson Family, Hale-Bopp Heaven's Gate, UK's WRP, out of space spoon-bending "erase" Uri Geller, and the list goes on. And on. And on.

You name it. The Seventies had it.

The pill provides options. Sex is loose in this pre-HIV, cathartic decade. Hurray for plush bathhouses, hanky-codes, and swanky swing ateliers. Heroin, cocaine, grass, LSD are game - anything to keep you numb and strip your predicament from certain death transits the city unceremoniously. And don't forget the fur, the skins, darling. To keep you warm, of course.

New York in the Seventies – I dare you call it The Big Apple.

Fifty-three thousand heroin addicts in the city of New York alone by 1971.

Narcotics. Scholars will argue economic justification - it puts bread on the tables of thousands of unemployed men and women. And best of all - the taxman can't stick its thirsty *manos* inside your Levi's denim pockets and strip its cut. Although, in due fairness, that levy is funneled correctly down to the Five fiscally austere commissioners along the church-going corridors stretching from Brooklyn to Queens, Long-Island to The Bronx and Newark to Yonkers *et al.* And not to exclude *forget-about-it*, Ban-Lon wearing, Staten Island and Harrison. How could you? An exciting light on Marx's social distribution of labor. A heterodox version of alienation.

The *French Connection* is not just a fictional blockbuster.

CIA-backed Khun Sa presides the Shan State and the profitable Golden Triangle opium operation, supplying high-quality *China White* to the U.S. – Harlem its port of entry. One argues that the heroine epidemic in the U.S. is a direct byproduct of the fight against Communism.

The Civil Rights movement, via its Second Revolution, in full swing.

Unapologetic Seltzer Roller Derbies keep amusement current on the TV or at the Garden. Plasticity. Colors. Movement. Violence. Not even Madison Avenue South's advertising jetsetters can reproduce such splendor.

Perhaps the radiant junk dealer, failed schemer Fred, in Sanford & Sons, sums it all. We take refuge in Fred's bigotry and whip-quick-comedy, worn-out fashion, maze of indebtedness, and useless machinery. All of it immersed in every each one of its forty-nine-and-a-half shades of mustard tones. But it keeps us smiling at ourselves, at our own degraded condition. There is nothing like comedy - or sarcasm - to remind us of our state of affairs.

New York in the "Me Decade" resides in an algorithm beyond dusk. It is plain dark.

Things are so bad here it is told that the Redeemer applied for early retirement during that summer - intentionally or not. The request was processed and stamped expeditiously at the 7th Floor of City Hall's Human Resources Department. Our eyewitness, lotted at Old Slip Street and Water Street, the *Famiglia* actuary - best known as Franky Tree Toes - is sure the Redeemer has an inside man on the roll. The story goes our diligent protector, also known as *Loose-Ax,* pre-paid for a non-forwarding P.O. Box over at the 43rd Street and Sixth Avenue's Postal Office. Bought a decaying log cabin far (very far) beyond the Eastern hills of Guadalajara and is enjoying a long-earned sabbatical break from this shithole.

New York in the '70s is the only one. Such contradiction. A decade of dusk.

We can't produce nukes fast enough. The world can many times implode itself over if, by mistake or dark sarcasm, a buffoon sits his official despot Freemason's heinie on the red launch button. It takes only one stooge to get it going (*my money on Curley*). It is that close. Life is that thin. Really. In parallel, a profitable business flourishes - fallout nuclear shelters.

With three World Cups on his shoulders, the masterful Pele tries his hand at boosting soccer in America through the stylish NY Cosmos. That goes nowhere. But good try.

Friday night boxing is the religion - naturally. And the bee-stinging, human satellite launching, undisputed, Louisville Lip holds the microphone. Tightly. And will not return it. That magic. It's all about survival here. Pretty much.
This is a New York like no other.

The subways. Yes, the subways - a riotous sphere in its own right. A dark and incredibly ear-piercing kaleidoscope of the unnatural. Something else. Not a pretty something else. Far from it.

It keeps the can spray-paint business from going under. If Big Spray Seymour is producing two-hundred-and-seventy million cans a year, probably two-hundred-and seventy-one million is unrestrictedly *décor* over tiles deep under the city's under-belly through *ne'-names* et al. *Rusto* for the purists. And *Kry* for budget rebels. All of this in a stew of wilding.

Payback is delivered through Schumpeter's creative destruction - human street art. By the laborious hands of frustrated rag-and-bone street shop-owners and, in some cases, the police. Here we come to the involuntary cangiante sprayed faces of young rebellious artist-defacers. Some more artists. Some more defacers. All poor.

Graffiti - New York seventies' signature *signature*.

The subways. Good luck there. Run your numbers. And just to be clear - Fear watches its back here. Seriously, it does.

Police officers are targeted and assassinated by the hands of the Black Liberation Army. Wide-spread Apads and *scores*-style corruption among the corporation creeps nationwide. The Knapp Commission/ISU in full swing. Not exactly a dream job.

And the filth - anywhere a dime can be spent. By definition, every street trash can must overflow. Albeit in some instances, streets and dustbins are a combined self-ruling entity. These streets. It's a dump. *Walk on the wild side*, one claimed. Which side? Every side is wild! Kicking rats and garbage is left for words. And routine.

This New York. What a party. What a party.

And the rats. These are not your ordinary urban rodents tepid under the shades. No, sir. No, madam. We speak of trail-blazing rats the size of small dogs with intentional disrespect for *no soliciting* signs. They follow no master. To the more street-savvy domestic animals - and everybody else - J-walking to avoid an unwarranted encounter is part of the balancing act. These nineteen-seventies hooligans share this town with every New Yorker on an equal basis. Pound for pound. What sets us apart - taxes. Rodents are, unfairly, exempt.

*** With inexcusable apologies, due to the author's katsaridaphobia, a relevant New York protagonist has been omitted – the New York cockroach. ***

And if you think Forty-Deuce and honeymoon Bowery are gritty, well, sling your groovy rainbow rollers on and disco down - *JB skating* style - South Bronx or Bed-Stuy lane. Or, for the risk-adept, take an August Friday night boogie-stroll through those unassuming folksy blocks along West 163rd Street, between Amsterdam and Broadway, more specifically, to jack your adrenaline fix.

Yes, New York City, the one and only.

Commission Studio 54 car valets to park your Cadillac Seville, Pantera, Porsche 924, or Lincoln Continental. New York discotheque valets - their tips come in more ways than through five-dollar powdered bills. They know the scoop and don't mind the customary white powder on top of the dashboard; it's just coke, blow. They are masters in uncovering the usual secret stash - start from under the carpets, move to under the seats, glove compartment, jack the ashtray out; you get the picture.

Not even Sesame Street's Prozac-Elmo will endure attitude from street punks, and especially from his co-star, the hypersensitive Oscar.

The Seventies. The Son of Sam and the Torso Killer spice things up a notch around town. Or two. Or more. Although in fairness, we are exempt from Haight-Ashbury Mason, Little, Corona, Phoenix de Silva, Beatle Bundy, Club Chaplin Pogo Casey, Casanova, Bondage BTK, Atlanta's Williams, just to mention a few of the seventy's serial delinquents. Such horror. Just a crazy. Violent. World.

New York, a symbol of existential angst.

Equally important is to pay recognition to the regular *filler*, who will mug you, daily, on cue, if not for hard cold cash or sport, just to keep his tab up. Those street warriors. Those young denizens in scarlet coats. In their best wolfpack *colors*. The best in us. But not by choice. Rather - just a bad hand.

This unmatched New York. What a sight. Try rubbing your fingers. You can't. You are desensitized.

Life feels binary as if every Kodak reel can only spit out one outcome - Black & White stills. Not all in frame. Not all duly focused. All blind.

For reference - this is the New York I speak of.

Chapter 4

New York's landscape viewed from Brooklyn Harbor.

613 Wall Street

The Firm's facade, an imposing office tower

Zhain's Office

06:13 AM. Still dark outside.

A lasting French Horn D-Flat solo fills the air.

Twenty-seventh floor. A caliginous, exquisite, mid-modern office. Sfumato paintings. Floor to ceiling windows. Long, suspicious, red velvet curtains.

A dim figure of man viewed from behind, in the shadows by a window. His hands rest comfortably behind his back, holding a pomegranate. His eyes stare outside, contemplating peacefully. Fitting time into account.

This is Zhain Hamour, the Firm's sarcastic, cutthroat Chairman.

He wears a 180's Italian-cut suit and bears a visible scar on the left side of his face. If he could, he would rewrite the laws of physics and humanity. His genuine sarcasm reveals he is intelligent and articulate. He can fluently speak, with little if any accent, seven languages, including Latin. As a member of a secretive, rare books guild, it is believed he is the world's undisputed Master Bibliophile. His unpaired eruditeness will often annoy and sour everyone around him. He is obsessed with immortality.

This man has a plan.

By the Window

Zhain is standing up, looking out the window a few feet from his massive Brazilian-Ipe bankers' desk. Composed, he looks down at the silent grey city.

Behind him, in full focus, Diego Rivera's "Man at the Crossroads of the Universe" painting stands out.

Juan Feist halfway inside Zhain's office door. Feist is Zhain's bouncer-looking, greasy-haired, hatchet-man. "Sir, Missis Alexandra outside."

"Excellent." Zhain soberly replies with eyes transfixed out the window.

Two muffled intro-knocks on the door, and Alexandra enters the office in a confident rhythm.

"God. . ." Zhain softly to himself.

Alexandra is The Firm's #2. She is an articulate, tall, squared jaw, impeccably dressed banker. She is the Firm's grip-of-steel Head of Investment Banking. She is in her mid-thirties and can make an iceberg melt with her stare alone. Firmly to Zhain. "Good morning, Sir."

Zhain looking out the window, still contemplating. He glazes at the Twin Towers being built. Days until completion. He replies, rhetorically, without facing her.

"God. . ." Zhain expels.

"Sir?"

"What if God lost faith?"

"Faith, Sir?"

"In us. In his so-called creation."

Alexandra looking outside to hopeless grey streets. "There certainly is evidence."

"This city; so much light still." Zhain whispers. "Perhaps an equilibrium act. Perhaps a novel social-economic light into Marshallian economics." He turns to her. "Good morning, Alexandra, and thank you for coming this early."

Zhain walks in her direction, pomegranate in hand. He passes by his banker's desk and blandly swipes the tip of his long fingers on top of an opulent Renaissance manuscript. Next to it, a newspaper cover reads "NEW YORK REJECTED BAILOUT" and an opened Flash Gordon comic book, page 13; Emperor Ming gazing at planet Earth.

By many accounts, Zhain's wealth is beyond measure. His is also a man of taste.

Leather Couch

Zhain and Alexandra at the office's leather couch chamber.

A large Gothic coffee table with a crystal bowl of pomegranates, a smaller crystal bowl containing red lollipops, a chessboard, and a dark, rectangle, Akasa wood box in its center.

"Of course, Sir."

Zhain with hopeful eyes and a gentle tilt to the head to Alexandra as they both sit. "Any lead?"

"This, this book! Sir, it's a ghost. We have nothing, unfortunately. Feels an impossible. . ." A frustrated Alexandra.

The chessboard - a game in progress.

Zhain candidly professorial. "Impossible?" Now laughing. "Alexandra, look at you. Are *you* impossible? My *book* is out there. We will find it, and when I do, I will have it my way."

More composedly. "My Dear Alexandra, for the sake of us all, time is not in our favor, you see. We need to find this book. . . the window is closing. . . fast. . ."

Alexandra tries her best to acknowledge.

"Do you believe in our existence, my Dear? In us, this creation?" He looks at his own body.

"No." Alexandra quick as a whip.

"I didn't think so. Would you scrape it all and start over if you had the chance?" He asks.

"Just scrape it. No prisoners." She counters.

"I see. I see."

Zhain contains himself. He takes a long, thoughtful breath while moving Horse-Black on the chess board. Their eyes locked. It is always a match between these two. Perhaps of survival. Perhaps just genetics. But never by chance. The term "casual" has no significance in their lexicon.

She stares at the Horse move. Her eyes jog quickly back at Zhain.

A massive painting of a blue butterfly behind him, by the back wall.

"Perhaps then your wish may just be realized. My book, my Dear, my book. . ." Zhain nodding slowly.

A beat.

"Tomorrow is special - our induction ceremony. The future of this firm stands on our ability to recruit new partners. Our culture is by no measure conventional. You, Alexandra, have given this outfit incomparable pride." Zhain explains.

As he speaks, he slowly peels the pomegranate with both hands, extracting pomegranate seeds. Zhain cleans his red-stained hands with a white handkerchief - monogram embroidered "Z.H." - as he stands up and goes for a rare 1950's *Wolfschmidt Kummel* bottle stashed inside a dark Art Deco mahogany wall library-style cabinet file, just behind Alexandra.

Alexandra patiently observes with legs symmetrically crossed. Her hair is combed to a Spartan millimeter; or less. Everything about her is in place. Calculated. Precise.

As part of their balancing act, Zhain tries to find any crack in Alexandra's composure, character, professionalism. A blink. Anything. But this is Alexandra, and perfection is her birth name if she didn't already have one - which is a mystery in itself.

From behind, Zhain takes a subtle glance at her neck as she sits steadfastly. He sees the tiniest edge of a tattoo running down her pale neck, and her bluish pulsing carotid gives life to the tattoo.

Zhain takes his time to appreciate the beautiful *Wolfschimidt* bottle and its years'-old label against the sunlight.

Now back at the couch he holds three crystal glasses and the old *Wolfschimidt* bottle. He picks some pomegranate seeds and tosses them into another crystal bowl.

"Tomorrow. . . make us proud." Zhain with enthusiasm.

"Yes, I will, Sir."

Zhain nods in agreement. "Notwithstanding exhausting discussions during Executive Committees, I still want your final verdict on all names. No restraints. And I'm especially interested in your last-minute doubt regarding the lively Josephine."

"Doubt, Sir? Respectfully, when did I ever express doubt? She is without question the most talented in my group and will be an exceptional Partner. My concern is explicitly related to timing. She's just too fresh. She has just made Director and skipping ED, MD straight to Partner is a risky ask. We throw her to the wolves too soon and she'll perish."

Zhain paternally "No! No. You're wrong. It is precisely that singular primal selection gene that will kick in and butt-fuck any *mother-fuckin* Wall Street predator that stands between her and her catch. Understand: Josephine is no half-breed. She's the real deal, *zhebu*, like you, and we need her kind."

Defiant, Alexandra uncrosses her legs vigorously and projects her body forward. *Finally, a crack!* Zhain thinks to himself, revealed only by his bulging eyes.

"Zhain, listen. . ." Alexandra starts.

Zhain cuts her off and raises his voice. "This *is* her predicament!" Back in a normal tone. "Josephine will be thrown into the cage, and you will be there with her. And that is that. You'll see to her becoming what you were once. The difference here lies on one tiny detail: she, unlike you, my-dear, was deprived of the Ninth Avenue's gratitude."

Alexandra holds her fire. She does not blink.

"Do you remember not, your first days here? When you stunk of greyhound, and I don't mean the four-leg sprinter." A contemplating beat. "Zhain took you in!"

With no urgency, he cuts the tip off a fat Cohiba, lights it with a long Red Wolf match, blows smoke upwards. The cigar burns strong and the flames are a mix of red and purple. Thick pinkish smoke leaves his mouth as he speaks, now sarcastically telegraphic.

"Yes, my child: Port Authority paradise-pimps. Cheap, hot, A/C-less motel rooms. Cockroach-infested communal bathrooms, Urhg." He shivers. "Heroine junkies knocking your door in the AM. Oh, yes, and let's not forget that unmistakable scent of despair. Do you NOT remember? Be thankful for those privileged days, Sue-Anne. They shaped you. They carved Sue-Anne into mama bear. And we certainly need more of that raw grit here."

A stiff Alexandra still holding her fire.

Zhain holds her right hand with malice. "Here, let me see those hands." A gentle pause to focus on the hand. Then his eyes on hers. "Soft? (teasing) Alexandra, have you overdone the Lan-come?"

Alexandra holds and gently pulls his navy-blue *Pierre Cardin* tie into her direction for a whisper. His head tilts in. Her lips are next to his ear as she whispers firmly. "You have deluded yourself in your book *obsession* and lost clairvoyance."

She takes a few pomegranate seeds from Zhain's hand and gently squeezes them. "I will put you down the day your alarm clock fails to buzz, and you are late for life. Give me half-a-beat or less, and I will rip out your black liver with these soft, fifth avenue *Lancôme*-treated hands." More cordially. "Respectfully, my *descendo discimus.*"

With eyes locked on Zhain, she moves Queen-White diagonally forward across the board. Queen-White is now tainted in rust red.

He nods lightly in appreciation and smiles jubilantly. Paternally jubilantly. A shy tear from his eye wants to burst out. "My girl! My girl. If everything fails, then there is you. Just look at you! If only the old Charles could witness such evolution, my dear. He'd be self-sentenced to rewriting *The Origins*. Perhaps even scrapping it. (softly) It would break his heart, wouldn't it?"

Office Door

Elegant and silent Steampunk-Woman, Ninah, - in her late 20's - enters his office, escorting Cole. She is Zhain's direct assistant. In every way. She is so exuberant. One wonders how floating in such tall stilettos and swaying hips is possible.

Cole takes one step inside Zhain's office and halts. Notably sharp. "Good morning, Sir." He then nods to Alexandra. "Alexandra."

Cole Guntram is a succinct, handsome, tall man equally well-dressed in a two-tone black suit and black English tie. He is Partner #3 and the Head of Treasury and Global Markets. A graduate of New York University's distinguished Courant Institute of Mathematical Sciences, where he lectures in a fellowship capacity every other Fall, Cole knows numbers. Notably, his IQ is off the charts, beyond conventional calibration. As a side effect, he never sleeps. Our Cole is cold. Cole is calculated. Cole is cool.

Zhain and Alexandra greet him back with a routine "good morning." Zhain taps the couch seat to welcome the wonder kid. "Here, Cole, we were waiting for you."

Cole sits comfortably next to Zhain, pulls an exquisite silver pen out of his dark suit, and commences his staple pen-spinning between fingers. He is a pen-spinning master. Literally.

Zhain capriciously pours the aniseed-and-caraway *Wolfschimidt* into all three crystal glasses. He appreciates the bottle, the smooth felt-like amber liquid, and the ruby seeds whirlpooling inside the Aristocratic glasses. A spectacle of will.

"To our seeds." Zhain toasts.

"Sir, the City Treasurer is desperate for an answer," Cole says.

Zhain moves Black-Horse-2 next to Queen-White. Cole nods slightly at the move. It seems Cole is beyond playing Chess. It would feel overkill - and disproportionate - if he ever did.

"Good," Zhain notes.

Cole still uncomfortable. "Will we extend the bailout loan facility, Sir? The odds are less than half-and-a-quarter percent we ever see a nickel back, and it decreases by the hour."

"That high, *Descartes*?" Zhain in mocking tone.

They all smile composedly.

"Cole, keep their dream alive. Tell the elected dignitaries of the EFCB that we will come to their aid, naturally," Zhain instructs.

Alexandra's hand goes for Queen-White. She hesitates. She holds it for a beat. Cole stares at her, waiting for a pulse. Alexandra's eyes at Cole. Alexandra's hand pulls Queen-White back to its original position. Zhain's fatherly eyes fixed at both, sensing (knowing) the fraternal plot against him.

"But, Sir. . ." Cole says.

He delivers Cole and Alexandra an evil smile with a slight nod as in "do you really think I will come to their aid?"

"Nonsense. I want to see this city on its knees! Eating itself up from its guts, its insides. I will set it on fire! And until its demise, let us just. . . just play with it, shall we? Then I will collect the ashes and scrap it at peanuts on the dollar." A short beat. "They will come to me," Zhain whispers.

Cole, smirking, speaks with the side of his mouth towards Zhain. "Most effective, Sir. Most effective."

He smirks back at Cole with the side of his lips. They drink up elegantly as Zhain goes for the wood box. "Here, let's discuss something substantively more pressing now. Although tomorrow is, of course, a big day for the Firm; it bears very, very, special meaning to both of you."

He slowly turns the unassuming wood box to face Alexandra and Cole. Anticipation. The apprentices look at the wood box in unusual suspense - this is new ground for them. Zhain looks at both and soft-spoken. "Zhain liberates you."

Zhain opens the box to reveal its content. Resting on century-old thick Caspian blue velvet, an Indian dagger, and a long brass tailor's shears in full detail. Alexandra and Cole are stunned and struggle to keep their poker-faces from expiring.

Zhain, in mocking British accent "I now expect your true animal-selves take you forward. Let the life cycle run its course. Let's throw our extraordinary old-chap Charles a bone, shall we? Make the good lad's case."

Cole split-second glimpses at the Indian dagger as Zhain speaks and then back at him. Alexandra performs the exact same act, but with the brass shears. However, although Cole's eyes follow Zhain's, his mind tunes to a different frequency. As a floor trader, Cole can multi-task and process indiscriminate amounts of data simultaneously with absolutely no loss of quality.

Two micro flashbacks. . .

Cole's Flashback - Texas, State Reform School - Years Earlier

Loud, rattling, desk fan noise. A teenage Cole thoroughly soaked in blood, holding a man's carved out liver in his left hand. Blood dripping slowly from his hand onto his flat white detention sneakers. A bloodied Flash Gordon comic book inside his trousers.

Zhain's Office - Present

Back to Cole's eyes. He looks at Alexandra with the side of his wide-opened eyes. Queen-White being moved back to its "earlier" position. Alexandra catches Cole's eyes then proceeds to her own micro-flashback.

Alexandra's Flashback – New York, 9th Avenue Sweat Shop - Years Earlier

Loud helo-like ceiling fan noise. A young Alexandra covered in blood, Cheyenne warrior-style - blood across eye-line - holding the brass shears as she looks outside a window into the 9th Avenue wild street hustle. A pool of blood circles her bloodied feet.

Back at Zhain's Office - Present

Dagger and Shears serenely inside the wood box. Cole and Alexandra snap back. Cole still pen-spinning.

Zhain's eyes are locked into Alexandra's and Cole's. They notice that Zhain was "with them" during the flashbacks. Zhain hands a Flash Gordon comic book to Cole as he speaks, and Cole thanks him with a slight nod.

Zhain with a victorious smile. "Your move, darling." A pause.

"Now back to business. I understand we're having some hiccups closing the *Media* acquisition. Hum? We absolutely must get it through. Whatever the cost. Sacrifice. Whatever the risks. Brief me, Alexandra."

A last look from the three at the dagger and the shears

By the Window

Minutes later.

Zhain by the window, contemplating.

New York's daily life viewed through Zhain's eyes.

Chapter 5

The Farm House, Dirt Road

The Stoic Porch

A windy afternoon.

Nelson and Red outside on the porch.

Red on his way out holding a brown paper bag, a cake inside wrap-tied in foil, and thin white leather rope. Written on the bag. "Enjoy, Suzan."

A rusty old truck packed with Awakening Folk drive by the Farm's front dirt road, leaving plenty of dust behind. Inside the truck, an eerie-looking, little boy, with terribly mean eyes, locks eye contact with both men as the truck drives by them.

"They keep coming. By the hundreds, every day, looking for salvation," Red says.

Nelson nods negatively with hopeless shoulders. "Let me know your findings. We'll have a small window to react."

"Should have the tree-trace by tonight," Red says, followed by a contemplating shrug of eyebrows.

Red pats-and-holds Nelson on the shoulder in a warm goodbye. As he attempts to speak, Nelson hastily but politely side-steps him. "And my best to Suzan, we sure miss her around the house."

Red understands a man in pain, and nods in agreement, leaving with his rifle. Nelson turns to his right, searching for the storm to come. Wind picks up. As he turns back to it, he notices Amanda exiting the kitchen back door towards the glass greenhouse.

A light green grasshopper reposing on the porch's window frame, as Nelson enters the House. It holds stubbornly against the sudden wind gust.

Amanda's Green House

The McIntosh tube radio is on.

A soft Kamancheh folk solo.

A wide range of persimmons and dried seeds are hanging in strips on the table and on trees.

The greenhouse also enjoys a botany, experimentation lab section. Tons of science books and equipment scattered with seeds, raw nuts, and wood samples.

Table

Amanda wears a wide brim Panama hat and garden gloves. She works inside her greenhouse. Amanda's relation to nature is evident, and a good part of her life has been invested in nurturing these vast lands. Most of which lacked life, green, and beauty. Through her hands, the Plains became a habitable installment.

Amanda hums a Cheyenne tune to herself while writing one last remark on her receipt book. A farewell note to Nelson in the making.

The note rests inside a Hand-and-Frog pine bowl, on the greenhouse's table, just next to a Paracelsus wood bust. Next to and under the note, a series of dichotomous florae template sketches.

Her farewell address to Nelson follows an *iambic trimeter* structure, and is written in purple, Saka-ink, fountain pen, printed onto light peach kozo Washi paper.

Amanda's distinctly pleasant voice reading the note:

> *It's time, Nelson.*
>
> *Change needs a chance. I will head down first with the Manuscript and will not be alone in rewriting it. Clear your heart and wait for the wall phone to ring. Our kids, Little Nelson. The one to come. They all need us, and we have work to do.*
>
> *Be the man I fell in love with. The one with mighty shoulders and an infinite heart.*
> *And when empty; remember.*
> *When sad; my warmth.*
> *When lost; follow the River.*
> *I will wait for you. In any world, I am Amanda.*
> *Carry on and see you on the other side!*
>
> *Love lasting. My love. Yours always.*
> *Amanda*

Amanda exits the greenhouse, dance-maneuvering in and out through hundreds of files of hanging persimmons stretched vertically to dry. This is where the red Sun finds true pleasure - beaming its sparrow light in and out of persimmon files, and it enjoys every little file.

Kitchen

Amanda prepares a persimmon-ham sandwich, wrapping it in brown paper. Persimmon seeds surround the sandwich package on top of the mahogany table. The paper wrap reads, "don't stay late, love-ya."

Farm House, Porch

The old McIntosh turntable spinning at precisely 45.0 rpm. It doesn't skip a beat. It can't. It reproduces Segovia's *Capricho Diabolico*. The grand descant travels far and reverberates enchantments onto the dwelling's venerable timber frames.

Amanda dressed to travel - scarf, straw hat, leather backpack, and a Hickory walking stick with solid, silver extremities.

She exits the House's front door, then the porch. Her steps are determined and possibly calculated. She halts for a half-beat and hesitates to look back. And doesn't. She can't. She is on a mission.

On Nelson's coffee table, *The Book* is noticeably missing. Clean space where it once sat, plenty of dust around the shining rectangle book-shaped surface.

The sandwich packed in brown paper sits alone on the kitchen-table. Seeds and raw nuts on top of it.

Amanda's legs carry her out, towards the porch, as she looks to the horizon.

She spares a minute to tie a white-and-blue silk scarf around the porch's front birch beam – it sails in the air like a flag. A beacon, rather, which is meant to be. Perhaps of hope.

She sees from a distance an old pickup on the horizon driving in her direction. It leaves enough dust behind to announce itself plenty, and Amanda knows it is Suzan at the wheel.

Chapter 6

Farm House to Dirt Road

Hard Sun. Dirt road. Bumpy ride.

Suzan, Red's mid-age, brown-haired, wife at the wheel.

Amanda inside the old single-cab Ford pick-up driving out towards the Plain's train station.

Amanda surrenders to admiring the dramatically grandiose Great Plains terrain.

Two dusty Awakening Folk nineteen-forties pick-ups jammed with home furniture drive in opposite direction. Their trucks dressed in patina-over-patina coats and double reinforced springs. A subtle indication they have been searching far and long. They are heading towards Town.

Suzan observing Awakening Folk. "They come in hordes; all soured. And going the wrong way. Salvation is in no one place."

The Plains' original settlers refer to the influx of incoming religious awakening people as "Awakening Folk." They have been coming for decades in hopes of more fortunate life and the arrival, or revival, of a Messiah, a savior of sorts. It is known that these lands are developed and offer promising living conditions. However, it is unclear what they have been running from – or after - for so long.

Amanda follows with eyes only. "You-sure about this woman? It's sure-hell gonna be strange-here without you."

Amanda nods affirmatively. "A storm is coming. It's something I need to do."

Her chapfallen eyes contemplate an abandoned, languishing, Drive-In. A sidelined, decaying, roadside, ice-cream truck casts more than the unsolicited dust it dons – it reveals better days.

"Anything I can do for you here?" Suzan asks.

"Well, there is. Don't let Nelson sleep in the barn. The furnace is rusty-old. . . It can get incredibly cold there. And the fumes. *Darnit*, I love that stubborn man."

"And Big Pants?" Suzan asks.

"Big Pants. My little prince Big Pants. (nodding heartsick) He is a party to all this mess."

Amanda looks out the car window and sees the Train Station's corroded water tower to her right approaching. She whispers to herself. "Breaking away from my boys, the hardest part."

The tower reads "The Plains * Home to Dreams."

Rusted Water Tower

Midday Sun.

A desert Hawk scouting for pray.

The rusted copper tower serves as a dry lighthouse, sentinel observation post, and water tower. On its spire, a rounded light-green glass cube functions as focal lens, protected by a bronze dome.

A spotter wearing a sleek cattleman crease, long dark beard, holding up an expanded sniper rifle, with scope, stands on top of the water tower. He delivers a salute at the car with his hat, signaling "the coast is clear."

The women extend their arms acknowledging through thumbs-up out the truck's windows, and a double-honk.

Suzan's Truck

Amanda places one of her signature, blue-stone-seed necklaces onto Suzan, over her head. A last strong hug, and Amanda is out the car and into the sandblasting tempest.

"See you on the other side!" Is Amanda's last, signature, goodbye.

The Plain's Train Station

If nowhere had a face, this would be it.

Dark blue crows scootched on the station's terracotta roof observe in silence.

A typical Great Plains, wood and glass, 30s bantam train station. No surplus here. It sits in the middle of nowhere, and there are no other constructions in sight other than the water tower.

Amanda alone on the platform waiting for the train.

Train approaching from a distance

Amanda looks at her wristwatch, scanning the horizon. She sees the train conductor's head, engulfed in vapor, out from a small train window as the train approaches.

This is Captain Fritz, the train's pragmatic, tough-as-nails, Scottish conductor. He smiles at Amanda, and she smiles back. His salt-and-pepper hair dazzle in every possible direction. The Captain wears a Red Baron style, green lens, aviator's goggles. Their friendship reaches back, way back.

It is believed he was raised inside the British Museum, where his father was the antiquarian chief superintendent (and Lead Primitivist) of its secretive *Reading Room*; hence, his bibliographical erudition.

Fritz is an omnivorous reader and renown collector of rare watches. He possesses retentive memory, sober manners, and is the dedicated Steward, Keeper of Time. He can shoot too, when necessary.

The train comes to a complete stop, unsurprisingly on cue; after all, this is Captain Fritz - and his punctilious manners - at the lever.

Station Platform

Awakening Folk, loaded with everything possible to conquer a new world, and more, off-board the train in a hurry.

Fritz comes out from the front car, stops to stretch his back, and walks in her direction.

The wind blowing Eastbound.

A long hug.

"You haven't changed a bit, Amanda. I got your ciphered message. We're all set."

"Great to see a good, old face again. How long-zit been?"

"Old? We don't wanna count now, do we?" Fritz embarrassedly.

"Senior?" He probes about Nelson.

"Just me." Amanda firmly.

Amanda's millimetric tone of voice is enough to spot a loose bolt in the order of things, and Fritz's refrains from exploring further. His facial expression reveals he is uneasy.

They walk inside the train's car. The car looks Constantinople-like inside.

"I see. One-way to the City?"

"Yes. One way."

"Traveling alone?" Fritz asks just for the sake of it, probably knowing the answer.

Amanda with a friendly smirk. "Hardly."

"Cargo?"

"Me and a dusty old manuscript. Will need any and all the help I can get." Amanda speaks in her smoky, coloratura mezzo-soprano.

Fritz doomed eyes. He was not exactly expecting such commission. The short notice left him obtuse and clearly unprepared for the expected undertaking that is to develop. And he knows that the task demands more than he is equipped for under these circumstances.

"We better get going then." Fritz says politely.

Amanda's Train Car

A concerned Fritz hesitates and does not dig further, adding. "It's Nelson's old car. We'll try our best not to draw attention.

Things aren't the same out there, Amanda, not the same as you remember. The city is dark and wild."

Fritz looks at his pocket watch, then at his two wristwatches, hands Amanda a leather wrap and departs quickly back to the front car.

"Let's haul!"

He signals a thumbs-up to the water tower sentinel. His action is duly reciprocated by the Tower Spotter.

Fritz's Conductor Car

Fritz inside working on the car's exotic command cockpit, where steampunk meets futuristic, meets Constantinople.

The cockpit's main dystopian clock alerts (blinking) they are "ON TIME."

His companion is a dog called "CD"- pronounced *See-Dhee.*

On Fritz's belt holster a patch of keys. An elongated, five-sided ward, gilt-iron, Medieval red one stands out – its ornamented bow functions as a celestial cipher compass.

He inserts the exotic red key into the control panel and turns it. Green lights flicker. A plethora of incandescent bulbs saturates the cabin's interior along with Fritz's apprehensive face.

Fritz to New York's Grand Central Terminal "Tower-A" on the radio. "Car 6-1-3, Southbound, at The Plains, departing O.T. over."

Grand Central Terminal Tower-A Operations - and its masterful 30s luminous panels. (radio comms). "Copy 613. ETA status?" Tower-A on radio.

"ETA: 613, on time, over." Fritz on radio.

Amanda's Car

Amanda sits in the middle part of the car, by the window staring outside as the train gains its first two feet. It halts unexpectedly.

Train Platform

Legs and feet in motion, three Yoldas: Janis, May, and Buffalo Shannon rushing, gasping to catch the train; Amanda's car. The three Yoldas hop in as the train regains motion.

Fritz's Car

Fritz looks at his cockpit clock as it reads a *-171 second's* delay. It has a distinct gadget that measures lateness/O.T. He grabs the comms mic in a hurry, presses the receiver's red lever with excessive force. "613 Southbound to Tower-A." Fritz on radio continues.

"Go ahead 613." Tower-A (Grand Central Terminal Command).

"Technical on converter-line: new ETA. 6:17, over."

"Roger 613. 6:17 NTA." Tower-A.

"Crap, lost my cover." Fritz, upset to himself.

The train resumes and pushes away.

The Three Yoldas

These fighters have a sacred pledge to defend and protect Amanda - in any dimension, at any cost.

Janis is a Janissary-inspired warrior with long, silk, black hair. Her tattoos indicate she specializes in fencing, daggers, swords, and martial arts.

May is a Mongolian-guided combatant ordained in the elusive art of crusade archery and heavy weaponry.

Buffalo Shannon is a Cheyenne-ordered commando and an infamous master of cavalry warfare and gun powder.

Our Yolda warriors are Amanda's long-time, battle-hardened companions, and are not allegorical characters. These young, tough-looking women bear salient, dark green, feather-like neck tattoos and visible facial battle scars.

They dawn gear according to their respective military regiment *arms*. They have been through multiple battles in other well documented, and not, ages.

The trio will escort and protect Amanda on her journey – the transition.

Amanda's Car

Janis enters Amanda's car first, followed by May scouting her six.

Buffalo Shannon enters from the opposing door to close the loop.

Amanda greets them one by one with a gargantuan warm smile by holding, with both hands, each of their faces, individually, eye-to-eye. "Was hoping for an uneventful passage," Amanda contends.

"The tower spotter signaled us. We came as fast as we could. Wouldn't miss this for anything," Janis replies with impartial excitement.

"Woman. So good to see you. Why-the-hell wouldn't you reach out? Unless. . ." Shannon interacts.

"What are we in for?" May adds into the convoluted mix.

"Hold on those horses there. This wasn't planned, and understand: I can't give you safe passage once we cross White River," Amanda ponders.

"Still," Janis says.

"You alone?" Shannon asks.

"Not exactly. . ." Amanda tenderly.

Fritz on the train's loudspeaker. "Be advised. We're expecting stormy clouds ahead. One-thirteen."

"Hush! That's Fritz's one-thirteen," Janis intervenes, assuredly.

Amanda and the Yoldas hear the announcement and ready up. They scout the car and take defensive positions. Shannon to the front and May to the end of the car.

Janis dresses Amanda with a light Samurai chicken-plate.

As the train pushes Southbound, they see a little Cheyenne kimono-girl outside - at road level - standing composed and smiling at Amanda as the train is sucked into the vast horizon.

There is more to what the eye can meet about Amanda - something more significant. Her past holds evidence of an astute warrior. A true combatant. One with command and determination. Wisdom and compassion.

But there is more. . .

Chapter 7

New York, Grand Central Terminal, Track 37

Dawn.

Routine coat-and-cash commuters exiting a Metro North train juxtaposing footsteps approaching.

Generous steam in the backdrop.

Sean Whitaker exiting Platform 37 from the below stairs enters Grand Central's magnificent lobby. Sean is a young, pale looking man. He is frail, shy, and walks awkwardly in short mechanical steps. He wears a green trench coat, green Fedora hat, and green Adidas Franz Beckenbauer sneakers – completely hairless, blueberry lips, eyes like glittering emerald gems. Due to his congenital hypotrichosis, Sean is envious of men with thick hair, and especially those with long stout mustaches.

He walks from Platform 37 into Grand Central Terminal's vast main concourse area. He stops and looks up at Grand Central

Terminal's majestic frescos for half a second, to Orion and its aqua Uranometric celestial ceiling.

Grand Central Terminal is engulfed in early-morning sunbeams cutting through its enormous interior body.

It's brass concourse clock reads 6:13 AM.

Vanderbilt Street

Sean exits Grand Central through Vanderbilt Street, dodging customary fast-paced New York routines. Sirens, clunkers, garbage, the hustle.

The nihilist, graffiti-infested city saw better days. It is tolerantly abandoned, punitively dirty, and unselfishly hard. Trash and pigeons succumb everywhere. Most corners smell like an opened latrine. Others smell like the darkest of desires. It's a societal manmade cesspool. Perhaps it's not all that bad, and the sizzle may just be glazing on the surface.

An allusive junkie rests inside a mundane, metal street-garbage can. He wears no borrowed robe. Only the proper attire – poverty.

A Rasputin-like Street drifter holding a sign that reads. "IF NOT FOR REDEMPTION, WHAT GRACE IS THERE IN SIGNING?"

Sean fends off hustling pigeons using his self-made kid's bicycle, leather-banded ring-bell as wristwatch. "Beat it! Get! Damn pigeons!" He directs. The man hates pigeons and does not intend to hide it. He walks straight towards a blue-and-yellow pretzel and hot-dog stand on Vanderbilt and 43rd Street.

A street manhole exhaust puffs outbound the city's massive underground vapor. Sean piercing purposely right through it and exits blind. His ring-bell joins the egalitarian city sirens. Our bellman makes an abrupt, unexpected turn. He acknowledges two hitmen - Essex and Eone - standing by his favorite pretzel stand. Not an encounter he is keen to challenge.

Vanderbilt Street, South Corner

A third man, Tracker, in his mid-twenties, stands on the opposing South corner and follows Sean's every step with hawk eyes. Tracker is a fresh-out-of-Vietnam veteran. He wears a G1 bomber flight jacket, Amber Matic Ray-Ban, Dingo boots, a long ponytail, and a thick mustache. A pronounced West Texas twang closes the bill. A DOUBLEMINT to the mouth.

The three hitmen are athletic, unshaven, and tattooed. They wear paramilitary outfits, are armed, and in reckon-mode - detailed eye contact as they go about their business.

Essex and Eone-Ixi exchange notes with a stout Turkish stand owner. Tracker is inside a half-glass phone booth speaking to someone on the phone.

Phone Booth

Theatrical posters of Bertolucci's *The Conformist* on building facades.

Poorly taped onto the phone booth, a hand-written cardboard reads "DONT BOTHER OUT OF ORDER."

By the phone booth, two men and a women interact in a game of three-card-monte, a New York civil staple.

A fancy looking, jittery penny-stockbroker approaches the phone booth and repeatedly gestures to use it. He is in a hurry and oblivious to the associated risk he is about to inherent.

Tracker makes laser eye contact with the jumpy private banker. He frees his left hand and shows the agent his left pointer finger and mouths "give me a second." Three seconds go by.

The insistent broker gives two quick knocks on the glass booth to draw Tracker's attention. Still on the phone, Tracker calmly pulls a chrome .44 Desert Eagle out of his inside pocket holster and points-knocking it onto the booth glass, only two gentle taps.

A beat.

The TAP-TAP on the window is enough to tender expectations. The Master of the Universe scrams to live another day and push another worthless stock.

Hot Dog Stand

A teenage busboy dressed in MTA pinstripes uniform running to deliver Essex a paper note. He hands the note to Essex and waits.

Essex gives the busboy a tap on the shoulder followed by a Dr. Pepper soda can, then reads the note to himself. The message reads "PLATFORM A #37F, SOUTHBOUND 613 RUNNING LATE @ THE PLAINS." Essex reads it a second time, this time out loud. "The-fuck. Fritz is never late. Never."

Note in hand, and oblivious to heavy traffic, Essex sprints towards Tracker. A yellow cab avoids hitting him by inches, followed by the stock exchange of gentle words.

Tracker reads the note and is equally distressed. He inserts a dime into the phone and dials a number. He decorously re-reads the note into the phone. The men look unusually agitated.

Tracker hangs the phone and counters with a shoulder shrug. "Nothing. Feist said to hold."

"Hold!? For what?! No. This is Fritz's 613 we're talking about. And he has the key to Zhain's book. No holding. Lock-and-load, gentleman," Essex dictates.

As an ex-CIA operative in Vietnam, fielded under the Phoenix Program, Essex has extensive experience in the so called "non-combatant intelligence gathering and neutralization" - not particularly vetted by the Genebra Convention. His specific assignment was to liaise with South Vietnam's infamous score-settling PRU/Plan-F6.

Such wrongful borrowing of the immortal Phoenix symbol – a mythological Arabian lone bird that represents rebirth, youth, immortality.

Such crime.

Essex looks at his commando watch and directs. "Grab the beast; we'll intercept them at the White River bridge. Once in the city, it gets dicey. It'll be a crapshoot. Grab your shit, wilco."

The Firm's Boardroom

A half-read New York Times newspaper on top of the imposing boardroom table reads "A Friedman Doctrine: The Social Responsibility of Business Is to Increase Its Profits."

Zhain explaining to the Executive Committee Members the importance of the *Media* deal.

Ninah stands behind Zhain as he speaks, explaining, argumentatively.

". . . and if we can't get it by the book, via a standard market tender, we'll just have to pivot to a hostile, bloody, painstaking take-over. Whichever way, I really don't care, we will get this deal through, gentleman, and as always, I completely trust your support. Now, Mr. Williams here has considered an alternate route. Is that correct, Hank?"

Feist, trying to be invisible, enters the Boardroom carrying a small note. He hands it to Zhain with apologetic eyes.

Zhain looks at it and tries to conceal his concern. He quickly turns back to the meeting and addresses the committee members.

"Gentleman, with apologies, I'll need to step aside for a minute. Alexandra will brief you on the *Media* deal. Please, do listen carefully to her."

He steps out of the Boardroom in a rush.

Zhain and Feist, in the corridor, discuss the note's content. Behind them hangs a dark, sinister Flemish painting of *Homer and His Guide*.

Back inside the Boardroom, Alexandra stands in front of a whiteboard explaining with confident hand motion where exactly the *Media* deal fits within the Group's strategic priorities.

Cole drinks a glass of goat milk.

A group org-chart and the empty box space that reads "MEDIA" are on the board. The whiteboard org-chart makes the deal's importance crystal clear to the Firm's future. She turns back and forth repetitively to ensure constant eye contact with Committee Members. She is concentrated and professional. Explaining to members: ". . . and as we see, *MEDIA* and all its specific sub-sectors will be critically important into the next century. You name it, global reach, cable TV, international-linked network, fiber-optics, data-base-analytics." She purposely tempos her speech. "Influence through technology, gentlemen, will more than ever play a decisive role in global corporate dominance and. . ."

The brash Vice-Chairman Williams abruptly interrupts her. She is not surprised.

The Vice-Chairman is a hefty, tall man, with white dentures, wearing a white-stripe gray suit, gold cufflinks, a light-blue hand-kerchief, and a shiny Harvard ring. He is in his early sixties and has visibly skipped the gym.

The Vice-Chairman looks to the door and is careful that Zhain is nowhere near the meeting room. He carries a four-iron golf club with him and closes the room's door with it just as Zhain exits. He then immediately turns to Alexandra.

"Misses Alexandra, that is impressive; however, as you know, and notwithstanding your worthy track record with the Firm, you still haven't been able to bag this deal, am I right?"

Alexandra is single; hence the "Misses" is intentionally misused.

"Correct, Sir." Alexandra composedly replies.

Vice-Chairman peels an orange with his bare, well-fed hands. Emphasis on his board director paraphernalia, then in barbed tone.

"In light of the narrow window and the possibility of either the Anti-Trust delinquents and-or our neighbors down the street threaten our deal; would you still feel fit to lead this transaction, MISSES Alexandra?"

"Yes. Mr. Vice-Chairman, if you recall. . ." A second attempt is forcibly bull-dozed.

He stands up and condescendingly interrupts her once more. "My dear, look, would you not agree that for the firm's best interest - and naturally considering the materiality and complexity of this transaction - we have someone with a *pair* and wide-shoulders?

Someone umbilically associated with our most elevated social clubs and political backdoors to hammer away? Please understand that this is neither personal nor - to the least - prejudice. This here is no Fulton-Street-nail-parlor, darling." He fills his lungs with the toxic air that surrounds him. "What we really need here is a big, hard, swinging dick to close this transaction. *Vous comprenez?*"

The energized Vice-Chairman now assiduously sucks on a slice of orange.

The attending Committee Members observe in Socratic silence. Paulson and Cole shake their heads gently while looking at each other. They know how this ends.

"Sir, respectfully, long were the days I'd pretend to have a pair, or a corky poodle-banker's *chale* in pretentious Aspen. However, as I made ground and bagged some of the Streets' most noteworthy M&A deals, I think I feel perfectly confident to close this mandate, like all others."

"Are you sure, young lady? Look, these are not your usual puppets-and-suckers you are accustomed to." The heckling Vice-Chairman in doubtful tone.

Alexandra goes for an orange bowl on the table. She aligns her hair with calculated reason. She grabs a knife and an orange. She evidently enjoys the moment. Perhaps, she had been waiting for it, even.

"Yes, Sir, I am sure. And, oh, I do recall front-running a mandate, not too long ago, that led to the take-over and compromising *demise* of your old shop. *Nes Pa?* I also recall that it was I who referred you to Mr. Zhain, granted your invaluable mutualistic relationships with some of our finest regulators. And, lastly, as for the hard-swinging dick, Sir." A beat to instate the desired dictum.

"I suppose that would most certainly exclude the both of us, wouldn't it? Another pause to retouch her Venetian red Channel lipstick, then stoutly unabashed. "I will produce this deal. Count on it!" A planned pause. In mocking tone, *"Hank. . ."*

She cuts the orange firmly in half in one vigorous stroke. The blade stops hard on the table's lustrous surface, and its after-shock echoes viscerally across the room and violates through any shed of misogynist pride left within these conservative mahogany walls.

Bam. The Vice-Chairman's face is filled in red regret. Furious; he seats himself - and his tarnished pride - curling into a ball in his preferential seat.

Some of the Partners smirk silently. Others, in instinctive self-preservation, produce a cohesive, a fine-tuned silence.

Crickets.

The Firm's compromising Legal Counsel, Mr. Paulson, stands up and intentionally interrupts the slaughter as Zhain flashes back into the room. "Did our dear Alexandra brief you on the deal's details, gentleman? (he looks left) Hank?" Zhain asks. His eyes moving side to side searching for any answer, then lands on Cole.

Cole answers with a light shake of the head.

More crickets, now joined by wide-opened, petrified eyes.

Zhain senses - knows - Alexandra must have. . . just been Alexandra. He needs to end the meeting and finalizes with a polite, but still authoritative. "Gentleman, and Alexandra, let us bring this meeting to an early close. As you know, tomorrow is a special night for us, and I am looking forward to seeing all of you plenty refreshed, in your best tuxes. Meeting adjourned. Thank you, gentleman. Alexandra."

By the Door

In soft voice, Zhain calls Alexandra, "one last topic, my Dear. . ."

Zhain and Alexandra, face-to-face, discussing from afar as the room's classic Byzantine doors close slowly.

Alexandra's head is down, listening.

Zhain's soft voice. "Patience, my dear, patience. . ."

She nods gently.

Zhain mockingly, with a childish smirk, changing his tone of voice. "This newspaper deal is absolutely necessary (a pause, his eyes on hers), Mr. Thatcher. I want my rosebud!"

He breaks her composure. A relieved laugh from both.

Love – so many palettes.

Chapter 8

Alexandra's Office, IBD

Moments later.

Alexandra in her corner office closing the partition shades. She proceeds to the round, working side table.

Seven dozen deal tombstones decorate her office – evidence of accomplishment.

The Investment Banking Department - IBD

The loud Investment Banking Department is divided only by a glass-wall partition.

The glass-partition shades descending.

The IBD is a crowded, loud, and busy department. Mostly fitted with the traditionally privileged WASP Society & Sons. Tons of deal tombstones and college sports trophies. Assortments of green Mardi Gras beads necklaces.

Office Table

A newspaper cover on the table reads, "President Nixon creates the DEA (Drug Enforcement Administration) under the Justice Department."

A red-lit Duncan Imperial yo-yo moving up and down against the sunlight.

A small woman, seen from behind, playing with her yo-yo, sits at Alexandra's office table. This is Jojo, Alexandra's twenty-something snappy, Bronx-raised, wise-cracking, street lieutenant. She wears a secondhand U.S. Marine's coat and a silver crucifix necklace with dog tags.

Jojo pulls a round, light-blue Coleman cooler out from a canvas army backpack. She twists the cooler open. A beat and dry-ice smoke flows out.

Alexandra's eyes are locked into the cooler's soul.

Jojo takes out three bio blood tubes with pink serum. Simultaneously, Alexandra pulls out a syringe kit from a small medicine pouch.

Jojo, chewing gum, in heavy Bronx accent. "This is all I could get, Boss. But get this: the girl is only sixteen. And there's a kicker. Watch this! She's from The-Bronx! (lacing a big smile), so it has to be some high-quality potent PEP shit here. I got the estrogen and protogen from the same source in Jersey, though. But. . . Got nothing on your book, Boss."

Alexandra is calm and soft-spoken.

Jojo takes off her coat. She wears a black A-tank which holds her fit muscles and tattooed upper body.

"The book can wait. But good, this CRH cocktail will do for now. Good job, Jojo-girl." Alexandra says as she prepares a syringe.

Jojo showing off her toned biceps. A contemplating Jojo wanting to bond with the boss she genuinely admires. "I only wish I could get something for myself. I mean, you know, something real heavy-metal to strip the pain out of this misery. You know, to cope with this revolution in the air."

"For that, my dear, I'd refer you to Mister Smith and *Misses* Wesson. They've never failed me." A politely sarcastic Alexandra.

They exchange a warm smile.

"Boss, you know me. I ain't that classy; I'm more of a Colt-girl. That *steel*, baby That steel! But boss, what's all this hocus-pocus shit about this book?"

"It's an obsession."

Jojo's eyes point and look up to Zhain's 27th Floor.

"Yes. He believes it can change our condition. Something big. Something. He wants to re-write it his own way and control our fate."

Jojo laughs innocently. But stops just as fast. "Ha! Ain't that some crazy voodoo-mamba-shit! What do you think, Boss? What do you think?" Still in scoffing tone.

"You'd be a fool to doubt him. I've seen things, Jojo, I've seen things I don't comprehend. Yet."

Alexandra looks up. "Never, ever, bet against the house, darling."

"What house?" Jojo asks.

"Zhain! Of course." Alexandra replies creepingly.

Alexandra hands Jojo one thick brown envelope containing cash and another with thin light-blue packs of Frank's blue-magic heroine.

Jojo tucks them into her pants (from the inside), not pockets.

Alexandra strapping a rubber tube tourniquet around her arm, then injecting the serum into a blue vein. The vein welcomes the serum, and she sweats. She experiences a deep rush. The back of her eyes turns purple for a beat.

A speck of blood on her arm. She carefully swipes it with tip of a finger then spreads it onto her lips, in lieu of lipstick.

Jojo follows Alexandra's reddish eyes and her reinvigorated re-assurance. She blushes. Her left-hand turns into a tight fist. Her jaw muscles tremble. Her pupils dilate.

She grinds her teeth, opens the office door, and looks out with her chin raised to the noisy IBD.

Josephine, her entrusted protégé, is outside by the door.

"Living. Simply an act of risk-taking." Alexandra whispers to Josephine while looking straight into the IDB.

Alexandra stands firm, then snaps her neck loudly to the left, takes a deep breath, and to herself in pleasurable whispering tone. "Which daddy's golf-playing, frat boy am I going to fuck in the *culo* now." The woman does not blink.

She opens a broad smile and walks confidently into the hus-tling, opened floor IBD, adjacent to her own.

It's hunting season.

Investment Banking, Trading Floor

Traders sitting down by the corridor file looking up at Alexandra as she walks down the corridor.

Her sight on a tall Wealth Management Advisor (aka Puppy-Banker) sitting next to a real equities trader. The fashionable advisor, wearing a Newport, light blue Polo hat, orange tan, with his feet on the table, and a *Jackie O's* Hustler Edition on his lap, speaks comfortably on the phone.

Alexandra's scope eyes are focused on him like a lioness on a gazelle. She despises men (or women) who don't take risk. The *followers* in her clavis. Who fluff their way forward, banking on *networking* with the establishment. Who operate in the edges of capacity – the majority in Corporate America.

The IDB becomes silent.

Her prey senses something is not right. He turns and sees Alexandra closely behind him. His blue eyes bulge. His heart beat races. His lips turn blue. His hands sweat. His Hampton's suntan turns milky white. The curly hair is still blond. There is nowhere to escape.

Josephine closely follows Alexandra's steps in conjugating silence.

Chapter 9

Vanderbilt Street

Same day.

Moments later.

A 1972, all-black, two-door, badass, Chrysler Cordoba thunder-striking the corner of 42nd and Vanderbilt Street, Tracker on the wheel. The massive Cordoba pays neither tribute to reality nor to the marching all-out Oil Embargo.

The men fall in and dash North.

They audit their weapons inside a black military duffle bag as they ride North through FDR, passing under Brooklyn and Williamsburg bridges.

Inside the Cordoba

"What did he say?" Eone asks.

"He didn't. Feist told us to hold." Tracker replies, shrugging his shoulders.

Eone, in disbelief, looks at Tracker, then at Essex. "*Fuckin-fobbit.* My call. If we wait, we'll miss the window. It's a dick any way you cut it. Man, I really hate guardsmen. . ." Essex fills in melancholically.

The eighteen-plus foot long steel monobloc Cordoba thundering northbound through FDR - New York East flank scenery.

A bus surfer rides on the back of an up-town city bus.

Arm out the window, hair surfing the wind, Tracker holds an equable smile while looking out the car window. The guy is in a happy trance. "Man, what a fucking city. Love the grey. The drunk pigeons. This stench of depression alone marinated in a sea of fake aspirations. Gotta bottle this shit!"

"Hooch, what's wrong with you, man!?" Essex asks.

"Yeah, can you fuckers imagine this city all clean and tidied-up like a Susie-house? (contemplating) Maaaan, it's just perfect the way it is. Makes me feel like out of this place." Tracker back at them.

Essex and Eone look at each other, nodding at the uncanny remarks. Tracker looking out the window to a stripped and orphan 66' Windsor Chrysler by the road, facing the East River. One can only guess what color it originally left the factory. It takes a double coat of rust as primer and finish.

The Windsor

Three ten-year-old boys jumping on top of the rusted Windsor. The elder juvenile custodian sits placidly on a pink beach chair on the Windsor's hood. The pre-teenage street lad is fishing while contemplating free river views. His legs are calmly crossed as if he were in his Park Avenue corner office taking stock orders. This one is the boss.

Tracker honks to the boys in solidarity and floors the gas pedal down hard. The beast of the Cordoba bulldogs North loudly, pulling in five miles per gallon.

The grey city under a thin haze from his rear window, like a smog mist.

A flock of two dozen ravens escort the men North.

The Plains Border Limits - White River, Riverbank

Dusk.

The Cordoba parked by the riverbank near the long bridge.

The Cordoba's trunk door fully jacked. Inside, two fully loaded military seabags on top of three shoulder M-60s, multiple caliber ammunition, grenades, donut wraps, Hustler magazines, ropes, and helmets.

On the grass, by the beast, the dark green sea bags wide-open loaded with more guns and ammo.

Essex, Tracker, and Eone beside the car crouched on the dirt floor.

Essex giving instructions. "Fritz can't steam beyond five miles per hour through the bridge. It's our only window and slow enough to bail-in. Eone, you take down Fritz in his front car. Tracker and I will transition from the back and meet in the middle."

Tracker and Eone in unison. "Copy that!"

"Eone, you must pin Fritz down. No matter what, that fucker cannot leave his car. You hear me?!" Essex orders.

"That bastard owes me one. I got his number," Eone replies.

Eone pulls his charcoal Damascus knife and licks it sordidly. A number 731 tattoo printed on his neck is exposed. He also works on climbing harnesses and ropes.

Tracker slips into a chicken plate vest.

Essex works on the unit's radio comms. They hear him test it. "Radio-radio. . . Kilo-1. Kilo-2. Backer, backer, backer. . ." Essex on the radio.

Eone to Tracker. "You're not going to need that chicken plate, dude. I bet it's a dud."

Essex peril eyes disagree.

Tracker neatly assembles his chromed Schmidt-Rubin M1889 with precision scope. He also loads his Desert Eagle Long Ruger and adjusts its sight.

Essex hands each a pair of radio-comms and loads his Winchester 1897 shotgun with perforated barrel, then loads his Mauser MP-57 pistol, extra mags as always.

Eone handles his Nambu Type-14 and loads his Type-100 sub-machine gun. Eone carries a Damascus Subhilt 13-inch Tsavo knife.

The men take genuine pleasure in handling their weapons.

White River Bridge Edge

A red sunset to the West.

An orange full moon to the East.

Frogs croaking.

Tacker's drumsticks clicking arithmetically on the trail tracks.

The men gear up while Essex busts open an electric-train, nickel-plated switch box parallel to the tracks. He aggressively pulls a red cable off from the box; it short-circuits. The sparks and loud pop scare the curious wild rabbits, along with Eone.

"Jumpy-bunny, hum?" Tracker looking at Eone with a smirk of pleasure.

"Smart-ass. . ." Eone back at him.

Essex on binoculars, searching for the incoming train.

Tracker holding an *Angelus Roll Call* shoe wax polish tin and smudging his face with black wax. A DOUBLEMINT to the mouth.

Fritz's Car

Fritz flooring the train's speed throttle down to max speed in a last attempt to override the auto-speed limit.

Train Windows

Amanda and the Yolda's heads are out the window gazing at the sunset. Their long hair surfing the wind against the sunset.

A flock of one-hundred Carolina Parakeets escort the train.

White River Margins, The Last Passage Sentinels

Five-hundred meters before the White River Bridge crossing.

Two files of cowboyish sentinels in full black rice bags over their heads, white roses on their jackets, lined-up with their long muskets raised upwards, saluting the train and its passengers.

Exactly thirteen on each side of the tracks.

They bow as the train zooms ahead to the White Bridge.

The women observe in silence.

In reciprocity, Fritz actions the train's steam whistle.

Train's Windows

The Yoldas' heads are still out the windows.

May looks at Buffalo Shannon and nods lightly. Then Shannon

turns her head, looks, and nods at Janis. Janis nods back at both May and Shannon.

It is time.

Their heads follow the covered-head cowboy men as they fade into the skyline.

These are the glorious Last Passage Sentinels of the Great Plains, once revered as the most formidable warriors of their generation – the very ones who served Nelson so very well in countless battles. Once an army of thousands, they are now confined to twenty-six strong.

Inside the Train

Centuries of deadly perils have tenured a level of perceptual sensory awareness no ordinary human could ever fathom - the Yoldas embrace for what's to come.

Fritz on the radio. "Tower-A. 613 Southbound to Tower-A, over."

"Go ahead, 613." Tower-A back.

"Requesting manual override White Bridge speed limit to 10 MPH. Over."

"Negative 613. Negative! Fritz, what's wrong? Over. What's your. . ." The line is cut. Loud static noise on the other end gets Fritz jacked up.

By the Bridge Edge

Tracker cutting land communication cables by the bridge entry. Train loses full comms with Tower-A.

Fritz's Car

An amber panel light inside Fritz's car blinks a WARNING sound loudly. It reads "TOWER-A COMMS." Fritz quickly presses the button to shut it off, then grabs the train's comms microphone.

Fritz's voice on the train loudspeaker. "Car-3 be advised of technical circuits-jam: Code 7-21. Repeat 7-2-1 imminent."

Car-4R

The Yoldas double-check their weapons with urgency. They open their respective small leather backpacks and unveil their game. A disappointing hand. Janis holds a repetitive English OSS Little Joe bow and a dozen Persian long arrows.

Shannon carries iron daggers and a Gurkha Kukri sword.

May musters a collection of Damascus Kunnais and a Ming-era blue-blade sword.

"This is it, girls! Mayhem is upon us. Take defensive positions. Amanda, you're with me. Stay on my six." She turns to May. "May, cut lights! Shannon, you got tactical!" Janis instructs.

May and Shannon in unison. "Ready-that!"

The Yoldas ready their weapons and take their positions. Amanda firms her grip on her cane and secures her back-pack in front of her body. She hands the leather wrap to May.

The Yoldas cut a slit on each other's wrists. They follow by swiping their finger on the exposed cut, and blood. The sangria fingers smudging blood under the eyes and malar area of the face, in preparation for battle.

The train speeds aggressively.

May investigates the small package's content: one gun-flamethrower to signal Fritz and a Colt .44 revolver, extra bullets. Her eyes reveal she is not exactly enthusiastic about its contents. The Yoldas short notice reveals their under-preparedness. They are audibly outgunned and will need to scramble. Improvise.

White River Bridge

River embankment.

The train approaches the White River Bridge. It decelerates automatically to comply with the bridge's hard-wired 5 MPH speed limit. There is nothing Fritz can do; it is out of his hands.

Essex looking at his Ranger wristwatch, while on the radio. "Two mikes, boys! Two mikes."

Tracker in soft voice to himself. "Boy, do I miss Bangkok. . ."

Fritz's Car

Fritz sees the train's traffic signal blink "SPEED CONTROL 10 MPH" inside his car, and it blinks "MAX SPEED 5 MPH - AUTO" two seconds later. Fritz handles the speed-control lever down to "AUTO - 5 MPH" position. A loud cracking lock sound.

The Train

The train decelerates brusquely.

Men in positions along the bridge readied-up for assault.

Train enters the bridge.

Men running to engage train.

Eone runs and jumps between Car-1C (Conductor's Car) and Car-2E (Economy Class Car).

Tracker and Essex run and jump between Car-4R (Restaurant Car) and Car-5F (First Class Car).

Tracker takes sniper position on top of Car-5F - the train's last car. From Car-5F's rear, he has a full view of scope of all cars in front of him. He uses an anchoring gun to set two supporting hook-nails and runs ropes to secure himself. Then readies his pristine sniper carabiner and puts on yellow motorcycle goggles. A last calibration of the rifle's sight while enjoying the wind in his face, then on radio comms. "Kilo-two in position. Surface clear. Over."

Eone is in position, on the radio. "Kilo-three in position."

Essex in position, on the radio. "Kilo-two. Engage!"

Essex enters the Restaurant Car. He shoots one warning shot and yells. "Everybody out! Move to the back car! Now!" Essex orders the mob of passengers - a crowd of three dozen scared passengers runs out to Car-5F, to the end of the train.

Essex pushes ahead towards Car-3E (Economy Class Car).

Essex and May engage in the crossfire.

Shannon, who was in the back part of Car-3E, hears the gunshots and proceeds to engage at Car-4. Bullets scud everywhere – no China or crystals are spared, the air producing a shower of cutting fragments. May realizes she is outgunned. She cuts the lights inside the car.

Car-4R

Car-4 under dim light.

May launches three kunnais successively but at futile effectiveness.

One hits and sticks on a plank of wood trim an inch from Essex's face. Another hits him in the arm, but equally ineffective.

Essex blasts his Mauser, reloading many times in rapid repetitions. He is moving forward. "Moving!"

May's weapons are little match. She takes heavy fire and retreats to Car-3E, where she sees Janis from a distance. May to Janis. "We need to push back to Fritz. Now! Go!"

Bullets burst and explode inside Car-3E. Wood chips from train car scatter everywhere.

"Everybody out!" Janis orders.

Amanda tosses Fritz's leather pack to Janis, revealing the .44 Colt revolver, then Amanda shoots the flame gun out the window, then runs to Car-2E.

Shannon secures Amanda and keeps her umbilically with her. They duck and run. Run and duck.

Fritz's Car

Fritz spots the flame fire trace against the deep coal sky from his cock-pit window.

Eone attempts to unlock Fritz's front car door with an iron rabbit hammer-jack. But the steel outer door is impenetrable. He shoots a few times at its lock, but no go. He tries other corners of the door, but nothing penetrates.

Eone yelling to Fritz from the door. "Open up old-man, or I will blast everybody inside! Counting. One!" He doesn't get to "two" and, visibly frustrated, shoots and kills a suited-up male passenger, point-blank, merciless with four consecutive rounds in the torso. The man's suitcase blows open and pink and white penny stock order slips flow up in the air.

Eone on the radio. "Kilo-three, securing Fritz's car."

Fritz now fitted with two shoulder cartridge bandoliers, pulls a Colonel Lewis long gun out from a reinforced steel secret wall cabinet.

Car-2E

Meanwhile.

Amanda pops her cane in two, revealing its silver spear on the tip. She launches it at the car door, precisely at the hand-knob to hold the attackers from advancing.

Along Car-3E, Car-4R and Car-5F

Essex tries to open the jammed door repetitively, only to conclude it has been purposively jammed. He blasts it with three consecutive shotgun rounds.

May is trapped in the shootout and goes out the window of Car-3E. She is instantly hit on the shoulder by Tracker, punching backwards, then losing her balance by the edge of the car's roof. An inch from death.

Tracker on the radio. "Kilo-one, roof secured. Moving!"

Essex takes Car-3E, then on the radio. "Kilo-six, Car-3 secured. Moving."

Tracker releases Car-5F, knowing passengers are all confined there, and pushes forward to Car-4R to meet up with Essex.

Car-5F comes to a stop, and passengers inside are relieved. One young female passenger making the cross-sign repetitively.

Eone intentionally shoots a second passenger cowardly in the back just to make a point. He yells at Fritz and, frustrated with no reply, cuts another passenger in the face.

Meanwhile, Janis and Shannon exchange violently with Essex and Tracker.

Tracker is shot in the chest twice by Janis's Little Joe crossbow. The arrows ricochet onto his chicken plate.

Janis pitches Shannon the Colt and runs with Amanda to Car-2E.

The women are clearly losing the wrestle. Overwhelmed, Shannon ducks and stays behind to hold Tracker and Essex. She unloads the Colt at the men, then tosses it over to Janis.

A pinned-down Shannon in the back of the car takes two direct rounds to the upper torso and one to the neck. She is dead on the floor; her lifeless body falls sideways into the corridor. Essex shoots her one last time, execution-style, while stepping over her.

Amanda's still eyes. Her tender voice heard from another dimension. Her pale hands holding Shannon's hand as her soul parts this dimension.

Inside Car-2E, Fritz is shot in his abdomen and bleeds. He returns fire and shoots Eone twice. One bullet hits his comms radio, the other his neck. Eone is KIA.

Tracker hears the static BLIP on the radio then to Eone. "Kilo-two? Eone?!"

Static comms noise. No response from Eone on the radio.

Tracker goes out the window of Car-3E.

The train is off the bridge charging furiously at full speed.

"Kilo-two?! Do you read? Over." Essex on the radio. Static noise. No comms from Eone.

Five terrorized passengers proceed from Car-2E to Fritz's front car for cover.

Amanda and May side-by-side with Fritz.

Janis tossing the .44 Colt to May.

Fritz's Car

Fritz pulls out a large Gothic painting off the car side wall and opens a secret cabinet door fully loaded with heavy weapons.

May reloads the .44 Colt and provides covering-fire with the last few rounds. Outgunned, May thinks Fritz is distracted with train details. "Am outta ammo! What-are you doing, Fritz? Get back in the fight, man!" May yells.

Fritz out loud, almost to the world. "Quit the Robin Hood bullshit!" Fritz surfaces, blasting with a mean-looking shoulder-strapped MK1 automatic machine gun. Emphasis on Fritz's angry satisfaction and uncontrollable body vibration. "NOT-IN-MY-TRAIN!"

He lets it loose. A massive haze of bullets from the MK1. His trembling body sweeps forward. Burning gun casings drop everywhere. He can hardly handle the intensity of the gun's massive recoil.

Gunpowder smoke, glass, and wood splinters engulf the train car as Essex runs for cover, taking a non-lethal bullet to his arm.

The men retreat.

Tracker is behind Essex and takes two rounds on his chicken plate. He punches back. He also takes wood shrapnel to his face and neck, and his face bleeds.

Tide has turned.

Janis indulged in Fritz. "Show them whose' boss, old-man!" She grabs Fritz's Action Gun and reloads it quickly. She fires it violently.

May grabs a Walther WA2000 sniper from the gun cabinet and

runs furiously to join Janis counter the gun exchange. She provides cover over Shannon, not realizing she is dead. She checks for a pulse and follows with a bleak face.

Fritz takes suppressive fire position behind a connection door at the end of Car-2E until he runs out of ammo. Janis, then May blast their way through him with additional overwhelming fire entering Car-3E in total defiance.

Janis and May keep synchronized movement and eye contact as they counter-attack.

Overwhelmed, injured, and under fire, Essex and Tracker inevitably pull back to Car-4R, returning fire. Then to its far end.

Amanda alone with passengers inside Fritz's car. She bleeds from her chest - Samurai chicken-plate exposed - while applying a tourniquet on one injured woman.

Car-4R

On his way back to the last car (Car-4R), Tracker tosses a military, green haze, smoke bomb at the end of Car-3E.

Car-3E is fully engulfed in whirlpooling green smoke.

Tracker's view of the train speeding Southbound with a green haze smoke tail behind it contrasting with the full moon.

Car-3E

From the end of Car-3E, Janis yanks the car door down with her battle boot, releasing Car-4R.

A long silence endures. The train needs to breathe.

The exchange is over.

Car-4R is released, and it slows down tiredly.

Janis sees Tracker and Essex catching their breaths, looking out from Car-4R as it fades away and comes to a full stop.

Janis chaotically reloads her smoking gun, then turns and runs back to the front cars.

Amanda patches up May's left shoulder from buckshot wound.

Tracker goes for his pants pocket and erects an exquisite red train key with leather strap. He, somehow, stole it from Fritz's front car. It's one of the train's access ignition keys. Tracker smiling. "Got us a souvenir."

Chapter 10

New York Noir

Hours later.

North Edge Landscape.

Southbound Train Tracks. The hazed-in-bullets train arriving in New York via the Hudson River. George Washington Bridge approaching. It looks tired.

The City's intense lights suddenly fade-off in domino-effect - New York's 1973 August mini blackout.

The train cockpit panel's red alarm lights up. Various siren sounds overwhelm the space.

The deep darkness makes the sirens sound more aggressive. More necessary.

Train, Conductor's Car

Tower-A's monotonic radio voice. "Advise all cars, energy outage throughout all major metropolitan areas. Emergency back-up Yonkers generator on. . . (static noise) Run cars as per protocol RED-17. Repeat: blackout in progress adopt protocol RED-17."

A bandaged-up Fritz speaking to Janis and Amanda. "Shit. Do you have a safe house?"

"Yeah. We secured one with. . . (a pause) better you not know." Janis says.

Fritz to Amanda. "Good. Hop off at Harlem and use the subways. Grand Central will be swarming. The blackout will give you enough cover. Amanda. . ." He speaks with eyes. "Book?"

Amanda nods positively. A relieved-looking Fritz.

"See you on the other side, Old Man." Amanda says.

Harlem 125th Street, Train Stop

A Dantean hot night. New York under blackout.

A dozen police cars, ambulances and firetrucks await the embattled train.

Amanda, Janis, and May disembark on Harlem's 125th Street platform, then down the dirty stairs to the subway token gate entrance.

125th Street - #2 Green Line Subway Entrance

A pungent odor of abandonment.

New York hosts one-hundred-and-fifty thousand heroin addicts. And Uncle Ike's AWOL bags keep coming.

Our women descend Harlem's 125th Street's North-West entrance.

Graffiti take over.

Theatrical posters of *A Clockwork Orange* and of *Dirty Harry* wheatpasted on tile walls.

Vagabonds, pushers and homeless anywhere a pigeon hasn't already claimed.

A vandalized Marlboro tobacco add.

A solitary Little Kimono-Girl, dressed in light blue, passes by them swiftly up the stairs. Behind her a sign reads: "SAVE ME LORD."

Subway Car

The tired women ride the #2 Green to Brooklyn in silence. A nun sits opposite them in the bumpy subway car.

A regular shopping-cart junkie urinates on the opposite corner of the subway car. He holds a brown bag in one hand and his wiener in the other. He makes sure the passengers can listen to the affair.

A long-haired Vietnam Veteran plays and sings a crestfallen tune to himself on his mandolin. A theatrical poster for *Sweet Sweetback* behind him.

On one end of the car, a Ukrainian Orthodox priest holding a long hickory wood stick, dressed in full black and gold crucifix necklace. On the other end, a modestly dressed Imam stands firm, candidly observing the Yoldas. Both men nod at our Yoldas. Between the two clerics, a young woman wears a white T-shirt with the red cover of TIME's 1966 edition "IS GOOD DEAD?" serigraphed on it.

Brooklyn, Lefferts Street

Moments later.

The women arrive at 1223 Lefferts Street, Brooklyn.

Next to the three-story Brownstone a worn-down light-blue neon store sign flickering "WINNIE SHOEMAKER" is all that lights the street.

Chapter 11

Financial District, Delmonico's Restaurant

Same day.

Night.

The Firm's Annual Induction Party in full swing.

It's a big day. It's a comprehensive, lavish Wall Street event to induct new partners.

Inside Delmonico's massive, busy, and noisy kitchen: tall fire-blaze, steak, and smoke. Busboys fighting for space.

Prominent well-to-do men and women enter via Delmonico's main entrance steps: stretch limos, fur coats and Tuxedoes.

A waiter carries a smoking semi-raw steak out the kitchen door and into the event's main dining hall, maneuvering across The Firm's well-dressed employees.

Pomegranate seeds and rose champagne indulge the guest's tables. An enormous red velvet cake stands out in the middle of the main room.

A massive Zeus ice statue at the center of the herculean table.

On stage, an artsy band performs *Mr. Bojangles* to the awe of thrilled guests.

Inside Zhain's Limo

Zhain inside his stretched black limo reading the newspaper – front page the "train shootout."

The sumptuous limo approaching Delmonico's entrance.

A whopping tomato explodes loudly and aggressively onto his side window. A street protester. "You mother-fuckin sons-of-bitches!" He holds a sign that reads "NO JOB. NO FOOD. NO GOD."

Zhain hardly pulls a muscle and speaks to himself with a roll of eyes and a shaking of the head. "Do I *really* deserve this? Hey, Joe, you'll be thanking me when you realize my full work. You're welcome!"

Delmonico's Rooftop

Moments later.

Zhain on the asphalt rooftop.

Like a cosmic monolith, he observes Cole sitting calmly on the edge of the tall building, legs crossed yoga-style.

Cole looking out to Manhattan's infatuated noir. The usual city sirens, canon lights and liminal edge as backdrop.

Zhain's paternal preoccupation revealed through his concerned eyes. He cares, after all. He cares deeply. But can't change the past - at least for now.

Zhain cautiously approaches a dazed Cole from behind. Zhain holds a red, James Brown-like cape on his left hand, and a glass of goat milk on the other.

"Pain everywhere." Cole softly whispers out to the crowded skies.

Cole holds his signature pash dagger in his left hand. It is dressed in fresh, uncoagulated, possibly warm, blood.

Cole speaks to the infinite sky, knowing Zhain stands immediately behind him.

"Does existence proceed essence?!"

A beat.

"Son, it's time. I need you by me." Zhain very gently not to disturb the writing.

"Answer!" Cole asks firmly.

Zhain chooses not to.

A necessary beat.

"I can't. . . stop, Zhain." In unbearable pain. "I can't let it go. It's too vicious in me. If only Mathematics. . ."

Zhain sees the bloodied dagger. He looks to Cole, knowing he needs to act incidental. It's an act of selfless theatrics. A microsecond. Cole's faith hangs.

An unshakable inquiry from Cole. "What is the essence of existence?!"

"We'll sort it out, Cole. I promise!" Zhain empathetically, exercising causality. "Come on, son, let's go back inside before our steak *coldens*." He tries to contain his unfathomable resentment; however, not at Cole but, rather, at the human condition. At every tune leading to Cole's construction. The scramble of humanity. The limitations and imperfections of the built.

He offers Cole the cape, conducting every single instant of the act. His last card. "Son, I need you."

The elements hold life into account and prepare to intervene if summoned.

Cole lets the dagger accept gravity. It falls to the ground unashamed.

Cole replies. "Not today. Not this day."

Zhain pleading with doting eyes.

Cole in a trance, looking abashed at the Dagger. His eyes draw reality deep into a murky tunnel. A tale of existential angst at work.

Cole's Flashback Begins. . .

West Texas, State-Run Reform School of Boys - "White House"

Day. Late 1950s. Infernal hot. Humid.

A place for the unwanted.

Office Hall

An authoritative 1930s wood-and-glass door hands us "State Reform School."

A standard secretary's office desk excessively well kept. The cover of a 1958 "GLAMOUR," January Edition, reads *How you can be more Beautiful in 1958.* Not exactly a place for nostalgia.

An indifferent office Secretary, in her early 40's, caring for her polished nails and sprayed Marilyn *updo* curls. Her eyelashes are combed to millimetric perfection. She is willfully oblivious to the school's abstract reality. She simply does not care.

Cole's juvenile eyes screening through a Flash Gordon comic book. He waits outside the Warden's office hall sitting on a Blackwood bench in meditative silence. He is next.

To his right, a twelve-year-old awkward-looking kid with flushed dark military haircut, unleveled eyeglasses, and rumpled uniform, exiting the Warden's office. The kid stares at Cole with long floored eyes. It is unclear if they know each other. But this wouldn't matter. It is the sum of all parts that Cole comprehends. As proved.

The Secretary notices the excessive odor of nail polish and turns the desk fan towards her nails. She looks relived with her ingenious undertaking. Another glance at the wall clock.

The starry-eyed kid, who looks sixteen, and Cole stand lodged face-to-face. Cole slowly elevates his left arm and settles his hand on the kid's right shoulder. Cole stately nods half-degree down. The kid nods back. Cole takes the rolled Flash Gordon comic from behind his back pocket, and hands it to the crestfallen minor. The kid takes it in reverence, nods back in accordance, and leaves depressed with his head down.

"You can go in now, Mr. Guntram," the Secretary addressing Cole with eyes fixated exclusively on her pink nails.

Cole's gelid, iron-willed eyes beam into whatever holds inside the office.

Inside the Warden's Office

A rusty sounding 30s desk brass fan blows hopelessly loud at full speed trying to lessen the excruciating Texan heat. Or impunity. It can't. Neither.

The fan is joined by an alluring, possibly rare, Art Deco Streamline Desk Inkwell contradicting the remaining want-to-be-elegant memorabilia. Perhaps an unconscious (or conscious) attempt to abate the horror that lives true inside these reform schools' walls. Or, possibly, a manhandling assault on sanity. Such pride in men. Bottomless.

The Warden's vast office smells of cheap whisky and eucalyptus.

The ego wall behind his desk is decorated with plaques, awards, club memberships and yellowish attendance diplomas.

He wears a light-beige suit, blue tie, and thick-framed squared black glasses, and sits behind his prominent, neatly fashioned, mulberry banker's desk. This is the Warden, the school's impresario. By definition, he inherits poor hygiene. Bad teeth, of course. His shining, spotless, black-and-white Oxford leather shoes close the bill.

Young Cole is dressed in spartan detention uniform, except, unlike others, he wears a white cotton "A-tank." He takes to pen-spinning. His white denim pants are at least two inches short. His weight diligently supported on a second-hand pair of beaten down flat white detention sneakers. Sockless, for the concourse. The man is himself, the epitome of confidence.

The Warden sluggishly pours blue ink into his collectors' 925 Gold Meisterstuck Montblanc fountain pen. His gruesome thick fingers and gold graduation ring struggle with the act.

In befriending tone to Cole. "Come in. Glad you could make the time to review your papers, Mr. Guntram." A beat to impose his cachet. "This is your first week here at the White House, and I want to personally give you my warm; my most warmest welcoming." Another boss-like pause. "I understand you're some kind of numbers whiz-kid and ball-player, yes? . . . I'll tell'ya, I've seen one or the other, but never both, not in one graceful soul. Praise the Lord."

"Three." Cole coldly succinct.

A long beat.

"Excuse me?!" Interjects the intrigued Warden as he stands up slowly, now holding a timeworn eight-hole, seventeen-and-there-quarters inch, hickory paddle. The holes crafted for dynamic repetition - performance at the punishment level at its prime. The Chief Disciplinarian brings his prized stick to his shoulder. Then taps it onto his loaf-like palm. Cole can hear, and almost feel, the wood landing on the flesh.

Young Cole takes a calculated step inside the master deacon's office, then halts. He scouts his surroundings realizing the Warden is not alone.

He zooms his eyes straight at the feudal paddle. Mr. Guntram is no stranger to corporal punishment and the hard stick. A twist of faith. Not sin.

Cole advances with: "Three, Sir. Three in nineteen-million, six-hundred-twenty-two-thousand-and, well, (pause) thirteen other juveniles. Or, one in six-million-seven-hundred-and-forty-two thousand, six-hundred-and-thirteen, just here in Texas. Give or take. That is: there might be only one other like me out there, Sir." With torrential eyes, Cole implies in silence - *your move.*

The Warden tries to contain his emotions, countering with a re-hearsed. "Are you special, Mr. Gruntman?"

Opposite the Warden, a college sports recruiter, Arthur, a pale, psycho-looking man sweating profusely. Red handkerchief in hand. Gruesomeness seems to be a common place here.

"No, Sir, like hell I am not." Cole clears his throat and answers politely. Sarcastically but politely.

Warden preaching. "I'm starting to alike you, son. . . more and more. You have no idea. . . If you're a good boy, you'll do just fine here. . . our Lord in heaven, the wholly-spirit, they are my witnesses, and my compass." He holds and points to his East. "Excuse my rudeness - this here is Mr. Arthur (eye-pointing at Arthur), our football assistant coach. Am more than confident both of-ya'll fine gentleman are gonna have a funckin' good time playin' ball. . ."

Arthur's sweaty face turns timidly to his left, diagonally, to assess Cole, toe to nose. They lock eyes, and Cole is cold firm. Arthur split-second turns his cowardly eyes away towards a more comforting object, the Warden.

The Warden, now finally done with the pen business, proceeds to test it. A tiny spec of blue ink falls onto his silk tie, and he is obsessed with cleaning it. The harder he tries, the more the ink spreads.

Behind Arthur, a wall fully adorned in shining college football trophies. A wood cross, some diplomas mixed with photos of Arthur and the Warden celebrating with shirtless young football players, hang illustriously side-by-side, in premeditated synchrony, with the century-old teal grated windows.

"You know, young-man, we measures' no means here to get a win. And I do mean - *no means*. Do you understand, Mr. Guntram?" A closing breather to reimpose his rank in the natural order of species. "Do you like winning, Mr. Guntram?" He asks, pedantic to the end, while hard tapping the hickory paddle on his palm.

Behind Arthur, a cobalt cougar face college felt pennant aligned with a photo of the institution's entrusted board directors (all white men) decorate the insanity, the apparent justification for chalice cowardice - *homo degeneratus*. De-evolution at its finest.

The fan blows harder and louder, to no avail. It has no authority here whatsoever.

The Warden strips his smudged tie off and tosses it to the garbage can, missing it by inches. The tie lands on the floor, immune to rejection. All three men stare at it for a beat. Then eyes back at the Warden.

On his desk, a glass tombstone reads: "GOD IS YOUR SAVER" - irrefutable proof our Warden is the chosen, heaven bound, *Jocko-Homo*.

Cole from behind: a sharp dagger tucked in the back of his short indigo trousers. The Indian *pesh kabz* dagger's ivory hilt embraces gravity, descending *pianissimo* into Cole's full grip. Young Cole is cognizant this is a frame in the making and wants to relish every second.

He continues to pen-spin, with outbound gusto. It's chilling. He hisses softly. "Winning? Naturally, Sir. I have a bit of a killer instinct myself. And yes-sir, I am into. . . (he nods) yes, especially contact sports, Sir."

A beat.

Cole looks upwards and closes his eyes inordinately slow. His hand squeezes the dagger stock hard. Excessively hard.

The dagger is fully revealed.

The air is sucked out the room.

The room turns pitch black.

The elements bolt expeditiously.

School Corridor

Moments later.

Office door sprayed in coagulating blood.

Our Young Cole encased in blood, head-to-toe. He calmly tap-dances out the office, chin up, passing through the wood-and-glass door, dagger in left hand, owning an evil, triumphant smile. A long stride as blood follows his command.

The kid can dance.

And he can slide too.

Cole smiling – a rare break.

He indulges in his cloistered universe. He owns this reality and will not share it. Not in this lifetime.

Around his neck, our danseur dons a make-shift necklace crafted from his victims' four bloodied ears. He proudly wears the Warden's spotless prized Oxford shoes. Remarkably, it does not carry a single speck of blood on it. Not to doubt Cole is a perfectionist.

Corridor

The Secretary's frantic footsteps fill the ghoulish silence.

Cole, exiting the Warden's office, dancing in his own element as if in a saloon of pink dreams. The showpiece Meisterstuck properly balanced behind his ear. To his rear, the bloody corridor ripped by the Secretary's frenzied legs running in opposite direction.

Corridor

Our crowned jovial Cole seen from behind, soaked in blood, dancing, sliding down the nightmarish corridor.

He owns it.

Warden's Office

Desk, brass fan cranking loudly. Helplessly.

The Warden's dead body down on the floor, back to a wall, legs stretched out frontwards. His eyes are carefully blindfolded with Arthur's red handkerchief. Arthur lays dead flat on the floor horizontally, supine, with his head resting on the Warden's lap. Cole's pen halfway inside Arthur's capon neck.

Blood still flows out from Arthur's neck dripping onto his gold and ruby alma mater graduation ring. Except for their socks, and black garters, both men are naked and covered in blood.

Loud, frenetic running steps.

The Warden's Secretary, groaning, runs, in utter terror, towards the office's front door. As she speeds, she slips on the pool of blood left behind by our juvenile Fred Astaire. Still in inertia, she slides ten-feet forward - as if stealing second base - coming to a hard stop beside the dead men. Safe! But not from omission.

She gazes at the men's faces and their wide opened eyes. The Warden has an *Ars Goetia Asmodeus Goat on Bear* tattoo stamped on his chest, by his heart. The illustrious Arthur stores a dark purple *Seal of Belial* reproduced on his forearm. Both tattoos bleed on their own.

Like Kafka's hexapod Gregor, the sedated Secretary tries repetitively and desperately to erect herself but fails every time. Impaired and crying, she crawls her way out to the corridor on her hands and knees. Her apathetic heart, accessory soul, and indifferent consent follow behind her, playing catch-up.

Equally desperate.

Analogously guilty.

She screams worthlessly, but no sound can be heard. Remember, the elements are absent. The airless room gives no density for sound to travel. Sound has left long ago, not by choice, but in justifiable fear.

Faustian bargains have no amplitude in Cole's reality. Cole is just. He carries the raw conscience of righteousness deep inside his core and will not compromise, nor trade. A pure breed, nothing like the invertebrate men that have for long subjugated his constitution.

Indifference - the slow dripping faculty eroding humanity's chance for acquittal. A leap into cathartic death. In sum, it damn hurts.

West Texas, Panhandle Town Police Station

Night.

Young Cole lays, a cappella, inside a damp prison cell. Brittle water drops as Cole pen-spins a plastic prison spoon.

The Oxford shoes, the 925 Montblanc and the Pesh Dagger resting as evidence on top of Sheriff Ed's desk. Also on the table, the Deputy's legs, his died-blue rattle snake boots, a long-barrel nickel S&W 29/.44 revolver, two *MADs* and one Flash Gordon comic book, and a long white pointed hood under a stuffed beaver (with protruded eyes and pronounced teeth).

Two men talking: Zhain's soft-spoken city Lawyer, Mr. Paulson, and the bean-shooting hard-talker Sheriff Ed.

Young Cole lays down on the cell's concrete floor, supine, gazing silently up at the ceiling as water drips down from a ceiling crack into a small puddle next to him.

Police Station, Lobby Area

From afar Lawyer Paulson's voice revibrating around the grey corridor walls. ". . . you don't understand Sheriff, my client, Mr. Zhain, is prepared to conciliate any inconveniences and will be fully responsible for Mr. Guntram and his transition back into society as a reformed and productive member of our community."

Paulson, forcing his hand, places a crocodile-leather suitcase on top of the Sheriff's desk. An oppressive metallic double-click TAK-TAK as he opens it.

Sheriff Ed follows the lawyer's strut movements with immovable eyes; and with the authority of an elected official. "Is this some kind of shaggy-dog Yankee-joke? Listen here, y'all city-folks don't understand the workings of affairs around down here. Did you see the piece of art your *Picasso* performed over at the White House, hum? Look here mister New-York-lawyer, do me a favor and grab your blue coat and thousand-bucks purse and. . ."

Prison Cell

Meanwhile.

Zhain stands inside the prison cell, face to face with Cole.

Both men in silence look at each other, while patiently listening to the intake dialogue across the room from the cell.

A long beat.

Sheriff Ed's distressed voice flows inside the cell. ". . . we follows the law here, line-by-line, and I'm-here officer shit-on-wheels. Do you *compri-en-do*?"

Lawyer Paulson cordially. "Yes-sir. I do. Completely. And I didn't mean any disrespect."

Sheriff's Office

Deputy's cowboy alligator boots still on the desk on top of Cole's Flash Gordon comic book.

Phone rings loudly inside the Sheriff's office. The Deputy is quick to answer it. His boots promptly bail the desk and land hard on a deer-skin rug. This deer rug comes with head and wide-opened eyes. It looks alive. One can almost hear the animal's breath.

Sheriff Ed takes his cowboy hat off. Less confrontational. "Mister. . . look, there ain't nothing I can do or would be inclined to. . ."

Sheriff's Deputy interrupting. "Hey boss!? You oughta get this one!"

Sheriff Ed to Paulson. "Give me a second there-partner. Pardon, my Deputy seems to need his calming elixir." Sheriff Ed leaves to answer the phone.

Paulson's stern eyes follow with indifference. He makes use of this intermission to comb his hair with a turtle shell saloon comb.

Deputy's Office

From a distance, Sheriff Ed standing up inside, talking to the other party on the phone, while trying to contain his aggravation. He clears sweat from his forehead. Obviously, this is an unexpected call. More head-scratching.

"Well, Sir, this is a shit-pickle here and I'm afraid. . ." He is interrupted, listening. He resumes more cautiously. "No, Sir. . . Sir? Not a chance in this world, nor in hell, not even if the Al-Mighty himself. . . or Washington. . ." He is interrupted yet again. "SIR!?" A flabbergasted looking Sheriff Ed hanging up the phone in utter disbelief, but mostly with a bucketload of rancor.

Damped Prison Cell

Zhain offering Cole the Flash Gordon comic book, the one by the deputy's boots.

Cole in prison blues holding and looking at it.

Zhain gently to Cole. "Pack your things, son. We're going home." Zhain slings a red circus-like cape over and around Cole's shoulders. It comforts him.

Corridor

Warm balmy lights.

They exit the cell into the precinct's long winding corridor, roving by the Sheriff's office open door. They halt uniformly, then robotically angle their heads into the inside of the office. They focus on the two-tone Oxfords on top of the Sheriff's desk.

With a milli-second nod of the head, Zhain looking at Cole. "Get your shoes, son. You earned them."

End of flashback.

Back at Delmonico's Building Rooftop

Present.

Cole wearing the Oxford shoes.

Zhain's spellbound voice from afar: "C'mon *mister-Bojangles*. . .

c'mon back and dance." A beat. No movement. Cole inches from certain death, looking down.

Zhain knows he is at his limit and running out of licit tangibles. Empathy alone won't suffice. A last try. "Let me see those old-soft-shoes, hum?" Zhain more cheerfully, however candid.

He punctures a thin crack into Cole's Arctic heart. Cole produces a reluctant smile. He stands up, tip of shoes less than an inch from the ledge's edge and certain death.

Pigeons scram.

A last look at the city, then he swings back to Zhain.

One quick hop and Cole is at Zhain's eye level. His Oxfords land hard. An energized Cole to Zhain: "How do I look?"

Face to face, Zhain fixes Cole's bowtie. "Splendid, Cole, absolutely splendid." A warranted beat. "There is absolutely nothing like you in this world, son."

Cole grabs the goat milk glass from Zhain's hand.

Zhain then blankets Cole's shoulder with the red cape.

Love, a discounted commodity, moves in such unexpected gradients.

Chapter 12

Delmonico's Private Room

This is the Partners' closed-door induction.

Live orchestra scoring airy hearts.

An elegant waiter knocks on the private room's door, then enters. That division of labor. The divide. An abyssal distinction between the *haves* and the *have-nots* narrated in monotone chords. Indifference. Our waiter has no face. No identity. Waives no abstraction other than the blip of randomness – he was born poor.

Ceremonial Table

Zhain stands on the far end of a fifty-feet ceremonial table.

Seven partners-to-be plus Alexandra, Cole, Paulson, and Vice-Chairman surround the table. Ninah stands closely behind Zhain.

An army of faceless waiters and undocumented busboys cater to the exuberant closed-door induction. Loads of Caspian caviar on hand-carved ice blocks.

Zhain is standing up. Everyone else is sitting down.

Raw steak being served. Long, unyielding knives, capacious silky steak, and blood. On their plates, only steak and pomegranate seeds to rest. Lavender bouquets on each seat for enlightenment.

An elated Zhain. "If you are here today, it is because you have earned your way here. For decades this firm has prided itself on one thing, and on one thing only: its people. You!"

Zhain walks proudly around the table, with clasping hands behind his back, looking carefully, closely at each new Partner.

"For centuries our firm, your firm, The House of Accumulation, has promoted excellence and rewarded success. Not decades, ladies, and gentlemen. And I will see to it that we take on the next century as such. In this life, or the next, I expect nothing but everything from you." He takes a long breath, looks to the window. "Eternity is not for the regular pedestrian. Accumulation, though, is, without doubt, eternal."

As Zhain speaks, our Vice-Chairman downs two whisky shots sequentially while keeping his sight on Alexandra.

She welcomes the flirt.

Cole observes in silence, eyes looking horizontally at the events being played out, pen spinning of course. A glass of goat milk in front of him.

Josephine standing by Cole, respecting his silence. She observes with younger sibling attention.

"Trust your instincts. Let your animal spirit rule your bearings. And finally, when in doubt, just simply go for the kill." Zhain continues.

All looking up to, and admiring Zhain as he pulls out a millennia-old Nubian ivory box containing eight gothic Damascus knives.

One is his and he individually hands out the others to each new Partner.

"For now, let us share bread."

A massive, oversized, bread loaf in front of Zhain on the table, surrounded by seeds and dried persimmons. Zhain proceeds to break bread with hand, gently placing them into silver dishes. The army of less-privileged-looking waiters serving the Partners.

The excitement amongst the Partners is evident as they accept their knives, then slicing their steaks.

One young Partner, K. Desmond, tests his knife's blade for sharpness pressing it against his thumb. Blood quickly flows and Desmond is evidently embarrassed, feeling like the sacrificial lamb in the room. Possibly just semantics.

A beat.

All necks turn to, and eyes zoom straight at the blood, then at Desmond's pale eyes.

Another unnerving beat.

Zhain fills the silence with an objective. "Yes, steel, ladies and gentlemen, steel and blood, built this world."

Zhain spates a rare 1937 Dom Perignon champagne bottle. He serves the first crystal to Josephine, then hands the bottle to his dashing assistant.

Alexandra and Josephine looking at each other, then at the elated Partners to be.

The Partners toast with their long crystal glasses.

"Now, let us enjoy this fine meal." Zhain proclaims.

Vice-Chairman delights himself in raw steak showing very little, if any, respect for British manners. He is no more than a schooled brute.

Alexandra raises her glass in toast mode solely to the Vice-Chairman. With egos high, he accepts.

A drop of red wine falls on the Vice-Chairman's Harvard Ring. He cleans it off in a whim, making sure it is shiny.

Alexandra now looks deep into her plate. She zooms in on the steak's blood.

Zhain standing up behind a dazed Alexandra. He tilts his head down at her, and gently whispers into her ear. *"Daydreaming,* my dear?"

A confident smile is all Alexandra has to offer back to her mentor. And nothing else.

Delmonico's Saloon

Zhain walking and chatting joyfully with awfully excited guests.

He takes to the live jazz band. On his way, he halts to speak with Feist, who whispers something into Zhain's ear. His attentive visage reveals it must not be good news.

The Stage

Zhain hops onto the stage. Grabs a microphone. Lights on him.

A beat. He breathes heavily onto the open microphone.

"How does one justify capitalism? *Laissez-faire?* Without wealth(!) there can be no saviors. Without wealth there can be no messiahs!" A beat. "Let the laws of accumulation run untamed, and your animal spirit rule the laws of distribution. Here! A toast to you and to this House - the House of Accumulation."

A short, loud bang followed by sudden lights and power outage as he speaks.

Diesel generator sound winding down.

New York's 73' blackout unravels

Delmonico's is pitch-black for a full three seconds.

Zhain's monotone, sadistic voice over the microphone. "Zhain's gift to you!"

A few seconds in the dark and the generator cranks up.

Engine build-up.

Loud Jazz music resumes.

Intoxicated guests in excitement neither notice the blackout nor the raging nineteen-percent unemployment rate. Every basis point hurts.

The Firm's employees converge on Zhain, like bees on honey, during cake cutting.

He is handed an extra-large slice of cake, only but offering it to the blithe, however computed, Josephine, while childishly licking smudged French whipped cream off his fingers. He toasts peacefully with Josephine. "To our future. . ."

She smiles back at him enigmatically.

Zhain knows there is much more to Josephine than meets the eye but can't quite pin down her bearings. That task he assigned to Alexandra.

CBS RADIO overlaps the scene, officially announcing the 1973 August Blackout.

RADIO VOICE ONLY.

Chapter 13

Alexandra's Condo, 250 Park Avenue South

Same night, moments later.

A sweltering night.

An elegant, mid-modern, minimalist Park Avenue condo with gold and lavender themes, scattered with hand-picked Modern art.

A 1932 Model M Steinway grand piano sits steadfastly. Standing opened on its music rack, Cicero's original *De Natura Deorum* manuscript - "The Problem of Evil" notes as musical score written in purple.

No argument, the lady has taste. And depth. But she wants more. She wants it all.

Within these walls, one will find no reference to the brunette Sue-Anne. This interim belongs to Alexandra exclusively, a string of truth far less comprehensible.

Kitchen

Alexandra in flamingo pink, Gucci high-heels, Arabian Gulf pearls, Dior 999, and black Yves Saint Laurent lingerie – and that is it.

She is on her back, flat on the floor. The entitled Vice-Chairman Williams is inside her stalwart legs with his back to her, gasping frenetically for air. Her arms on a brutal choke-hold. He is atrociously desperate. His skin is turning blue, and his eyes are bulging vermilion. His pupils are dilated, and what is left of hope has retired. Those last seconds before mortem - a particular oracle for Alexandra. Something to live for. Revenge.

Alexandra holds her long brass shears halfway inside Williams' neck. The more he resists, the tighter she grips. His all-bloodied Harvard ring reveals more than plagiarized, fabricated, or acquired social status.

Williams is cross-dressed. He wears a long peppermint wig, black Pacific pearls, Russian green velvet lingerie, and La Diva Plum lipstick. He pleads for clemency.

Alexandra's body painted with William's blood. As she speaks, blood flows out from her lips. With bloodied teeth and a low tone of voice, she asks. "Can you feel my *pair* now, fat frat-boy?"

Vice-Chairman regorging blood profusely. "Please (coughing)...I don't wanna...I don't wanna die." His last bloodied whispers. "You fuckin' street-whore. I'll see you in Hell..."

"Yes. You read my mind. That *is* the plan." Alexandra triumphantly.

Williams is down lifeless, flat on the floor, eyes wide-open.

Condo Window

Minutes later.

Alexandra standing up, looking outside her condo's sumptuous Park Avenue window into the New York's blackout empyrean. As our wolf would, she has one foot on top of her prey.

Her face is painted in blood stripe across her eyes, Cheyenne warrior style. She casually sips Goldwasser served on a small Baccarat crystal ruby tass while zooming her pleasing eyes into the bloodied shears still lodged halfway into her prey's neck.

William's Harvard ring now braced on her engagement finger. She looks at it. Admires it. Her comic, but hair-raising laughs endures, and can be heard across the lightless town.

Blood from her lips joins the Goldwasser and makes a condemned chroma inside the Italian crystal. She raises the tass against the moonlight, and the unbiased full moon's light crosses the tass, submerging into Alexandra's torrential eyes. This woman owns the night.

Touching up her lipstick while admiring the ring, she whispers nimbly. "Always wanted to be an ivy-leaguer."

A beat.

She is happy.

Living Room

A Maelzel Paquet metronome holds time into account and the universe in pacific repose. Its tempo-keeping faculty commands inaction and inducts what's to come. Such an objective mandate. What if life could be this simple? TIK. . . TAK. . . TIK. . . TAK. . .

Bloodied fingers gentle on the Steinway's ivory keys in ways it fears no harm.

Arvo Part's solitude *Spiegel im Spiegel* sonata fills the room and welcomes all senses.

The lament bears absolutely no relation to the deceased corpse in the kitchen. It is, rather, a tenured celebration of Alexandra's rebirth. It is the only occasion Alexandra will allow Sue-Anne to roam the room.

Alexandra in peace.

Embark on Alexandra's flashback. . .

Ninth Avenue, Tailor Sweatshop, Second Floor

Early 1960s. Day.

A punishingly hot and excessively noisy New York.

Two flights above a staple Cuban-Chinese joint and a cramped cigar shop.

Spiegel im Spiegel's monody joins this scene, but not for long.

A large professional *Coricama Pro* tailor's brass shears cutting lilac leather, followed by Mandarin and Spanish cautious small talk.

A young, black-haired Alexandra ("Sue-Anne") wearing an orchid rose bra works inside a low-end tailor sweatshop with perquisite West Side, Inc. views.

The shop's walls are covered in boutique-grade mirrors and are dedicated to tailor-fitting the city's *nuit clientele – des rue courtisanes*, drag-queens, and the so-called *leather punks*.

Sue-Anne is among half-a-dozen young female tailor professionals lined up, in bra only, in silence, inside the cramped sweatshop, which also serves as sleeping quarters – an unregistered corporate perk - evidence of the ruling laisse-faire prominence.

Windows are open wide - a firsthand glimpse of the outside rackets.

Six ceiling fans blow at full speed.

A micro concerto of illegal sewing machines, the debased ceiling fans, and New York's urban slaving ballad offers opposition to Carnegie Hall.

By the Window

Sue-Anne's sewing machine island stands adjacent to the window. She is sitting down and focused on a glittering purple pants project. She is entitled to a *White-761 Automatic ZigZag* sewing machine. Its industrial gauge, punching up-and-down, keeps us in priggish tempo.

The pale and makeup-less Sue-Anne sweats profusely while working on her White-761. She wears her hair pulled up and uses thick-lens metal-framed glasses.

There is little pride in her work, if any. It's a step-up, and it pays the bills for now. Her mind and heart have nothing but attention to and will for upward mobility. The fan, however, has no option – it must spin.

The sound of the brass shears become progressively louder.

With little concern in masquerading his heavy Russian accent, the Fred Flintstone type shop owner Julius walks within work islands supervising his proletarian, non-union aggregation while eating into an extra-large bag of potato chips. He crunches loudly, and his bovine hands are evidently greasy.

Potato crumbs from his hand and mouth fall to the wood floor. His boots purposively crushing them.

He approaches Sue-Anne creeping up from her behind.

He licks his salami-toned fingers and observes her shiny, sweaty neck and pulsing carotid artery. This one has a pulse.

His eyes shift from her neck down to her project's stitching line. He notices a blunt error. She missed a dotted stitch line and essentially spoils the order. Julius catches the screw-up and, with no warning, snaps at her, verbally brutal. "You dumb *striet-horeh*! How many times you're *gunna escrew* me?!"

Sue-Anne perks-up, scared to face the Russian dissident. Yet again.

She takes an evasive step astern, in fear. He leans into her. She takes another step backward, and he leans in tandem. Their bodies are less than two inches apart. Without warning, the grody Julius punches her stiff in the stomach. Sue-Anne makes a muffled sound and falls to her knees.

Mannered societal norms resign forcefully, and the alchemy of genetics assumes the deck and holds the fort. It is Sue-Anne who crumbles; but it is Alexandra who arises. And how she does.

Alexandra elevates slowly while bleeding from the mouth. She hoists her figure straight, firmly, staring at her captor, in the eyes, countering with a fencing, raging, bloodied spit to the face – New York style, of course. Potato chips and any consideration for autocracy fly up in the air like dead feathers.

Julius's choked face is the main act.

With a bank of accumulated rage, Alexandra exerts. "You cock-sucking-lady-boy! Let me get this stitch-line straight!" She follows by grinding as a wolf would, and her bloodied teeth savor the catch.

The elements know it's time to egress. And do. Fast.

Alexandra, back flat on the floor. Julius tangled inside her long-toned legs, his back to her. She holds him from his back with herculean force. Her arms around his neck in a brutal choke-hold. They wrestle loudly on the floor.

The political *émigrés* can only see the ceiling fan blowing hard as a last tune of surrender. His face turns bluish grey and swollens. His eyes bulge outwards. His tongue extends for air. All for nothing. There is no escaping Alexandra's Everest construction. No one has, yet. Her genetic programming is like no other.

Her long brass shears are halfway inside Julius's neck. She barely pulls a muscle as she applies pressure. A light turn of the shears for added terror. Julius yells in horror like a pig attending a castration session.

Alexandra's view is that of the shears entering Julius's carotid artery. Blood splashes everywhere. She is surgically precise and seemingly in no hurry.

The half-moribund Julius struggles to counter her pressure. He rattles his legs and white crocodile boots in all directions. He kicks the legs out of a Parisian wooden fashion manakin that crumbles on top of our wrestlers.

Alexandra's cold eyes.

Alexandra's hand slowly wielding the shears out from Julius's neck.

Julius gasping heavily and loudly for air as it thins out in respect for justice.

Another one hundred and thirteen stabs to the corpse. One could not imagine a man could hold this much bodily fluids.

The Zenith radio plays Eybay's *Victory Song*, drums, voices, and rattles.

The remaining working girls are standing up, sighing, and looking down at the scuffle in absolute shock. Only the fan produces sound, otherwise, complete silence. Stoned eyes ascending. They follow Alexandra in awe as she emerges triumphantly from the floor.

Her silk bra bathed in blood; she cleans her shears slowly with Julius's peach pocket handkerchief.

The overhead ceiling fans now spin tangled with bloodied feather boas, machine-gun splattering Julius's fresh, sanguine fluid everywhere. The room is coated in sangria.

Julius's lifeless body lays slanting next to the ill-legged manakin, which itself is dressed in a black drag-queen wolf skin performance outfit.

Alexandra's right foot nestled on top of her catch, claiming it as a Safari trophy hunter would. She snaps her neck left.

She then clears her blood-drenched face with a white boa as she looks out the window. She throws the boa out the window, and it takes its course, landing on the halted feet of a Little Kimono Girl who looks up at Alexandra.

Street Level

The Little Kimono Girl brings her head down and walks away,

submerging into the hustle. The scene would generally seem sur-real, but this is 9ᵗʰ Avenue, New York 70s, and there is nothing odd, unusual, or out of place in this reality.

Only Alexandra's eye-line area is cleared from blood in a rectangle-shape strip, while the rest of her face is fully painted in blood and lots of glitter. Her face glows.

She resembles a Cheyenne warrior post-battle.

The Mirror

She steps towards a three-panel, rectangular, dresser mirror with golden metal edges, placing herself in front of it. The mirror reveals three versions of Alexandra. The first is the current Sue-Anne dressed in blood. The second mirror delivers a refined Sue-Anne, a precursor of Alexandra. The third mirror gives us the silhouette of a grey wolf with bloodied teeth standing on top of its catch, a Canadian moose. The moose's body is superimposed onto Julius's boor body.

She envelopes a sheepskin scarf around her neck for style, for reference, thinking - *how soothing the warmth of blood*. She looks outside the window and projects her voice to the world. "Am coming for you! For ALL OF YOU!"

The craft is calculated.

Revolting, however, stateless.

Hateless, however, undogmatic.

It is part of her conditioning - an act of survival.

And survival is the prize.

Ninth Avenue Shop, Street Level

Moments later.

Night prowlers. *Book stores*. Sex emporiums.

Fur coat working girls everywhere. Hoards on every corner.

Iceberg Slims running tight ships.

On the opposing corner, a group of three dozen protesters wearing brown bag masks yelling, "Down with the Shah!" One protester holding a sign that reads "U.S. Puppet. Down with the Shah."

Same Street, Police Car

Alexandra cuffed-and-stuffed inside a banged-up blue-and-white. Note this public caboose has graffiti gang codes sprayed on it, a sign of utter disrespect for authority. It is leniently acceptable to taunt the police.

Her eyes look out the police car through its half-opened window. Next to it, junkies and the usual scarlet women curse at the cops. Emergency-red rotating siren lights flash intermittently onto Alexandra's face. Correspondingly, the smudged blood and glitter cocktail painted on her face come to life.

Her eyes are fixed on an outdoor, CAMEL, smoking billboard. The puffed smoke just under Hotel Claridge's sign flows out the mouth of a #24 Giants football player. The sign reads in candy red, *I'd Walk a Mile for A Camel.*

Police radio comms, sirens, and an unkempt ambulance arrive on scene. A gathering of tired-looking cops along 9th Avenue in front of the shop building entrance doesn't spark any unusual attention, naturally.

A slow riding 1968 dark green, two-door, 390 cubic inch, AMC-AMX muscle-machine pulls in and double parks against an unmarked standard-issued NYPD, pearl, Mercury Montego. A noteworthy contrast in police hierarchy.

The muscle-rich Andrew Fleming, aka Hammer, in full black leather, exits the indomitable AMC.

Phone Booth

Hammer speaks authoritatively on the phone inside a graffiti-decorated phone booth while downing half-a-dozen light-green pills from an amber prescription bottle and leather booze pocket flask.

A loud jab to the booth glass to reemphasize his point of view.

His eyes grab a Saint Augustine holy card glued on the phone unit.

The image of Saint Augustine is depressed, saddened. It stares at Hammer.

The conscience-stricken Hammer stares back at the image of his beloved saint in a mix of disdain and embarrassment.

With his palm over the saint card, Hammer pulls his Cuban Link, a gold necklace from inside his shirt, and kisses both the Crucifix and the Star of David pendants, twice each.

When his eyes return to the holy card, it finds the card no longer. In its place, a hand-written message in red reads. *"Give me chastity and continence, but not yet. Not yet!"*

Our emphatic lawman has anisocoria, expressed by his unequal pupil size. A condition considerably more prosaic than understood, but one that produces a reading into his uneasy personality.

Hammer is Chief Francis's eldest bulky-build son, a street cop with a cause, an M9-Beretta, a snub-0.38 ankle throwdown, and hard-to-tame anger. Lots of it. A former Marine who served on the Northern edges of I CORPS' Loc Ninh district and a youth Golden Glove Middle-Weight top seed, Hammer heads New York's newly assembled Street Crime Unit (SCU) - a proactive elite unit tasked to combat violent crime. And they have just the right man for the job.

Thanks in large part to what is considered by the police as the *battle theatre*, cops and robbers keep a running "points table tab" against each other. The rules of engagement are tacitly broad - make it till the end of the day in one piece. By design, the rule of law has precarious range. Hammer's mandate is succinct - keep the running table score tilting towards the men in blue. Darwinism at full range.

Although Hammer's blue eyes are still young, his soul and body are old. He has aged beyond his natural years.

There is still controversy over the origin of his nickname. Some will say it grew from his boxing days. Others will argue it derived from his early years fighting organized *tongs* deep inside Chinatown. A third group is confident it is due to the rap sheet of broken hearts. There is something dark in Hammer's persona that attracts the opposite sex.

By the Blue-and-White

Loud emergency radio shattering.

A beat street cop, Officer Franco, takes notes and interviews one of Alexandra's co-workers; or tries his best to act at it. A department stable, his non-issued, thick, dark mustache completely covers any sign of lips or neutrality.

Besides Alexandra, the resting shop's female workers are illegal immigrants and do not speak comprehensive English.

Officer Franco mutters to himself in a phantom daze. "These streets. . ."

Hammer walking toward Officer Franco.

"What's the number here, Sargent!?" Hammer asks.

A beat. No reply.

Franco is involuntarily distracted by Alexandra's anesthetic exertion. Or life. Or by the fact, he deals with such exponential violence. Togetherness, his emotional state of mind is dubious, most probably by twenty-three and a half years of New York beat. He is still in a trance.

"Officer!" Hammer pronouncedly.

Officer Franco nodding in Alexandra's direction. "Sorry, detective. One-eight-seven. Cutter." Franco in a haze, something unusual even for a die-hard street man of law. "Take a good look at the frail Shirley-Temple over there. Back seat." They both look at Alexandra inside the police car.

"What-a-bout-er?" Hammer asks.

"After gutting the fat *John*, she took the time to sew the poor bastard's lips to each-odder. She then finished a bag of *patatas* and, only then, the broad called the cops." Franco explains in his best English.

"Any other signatures?"

"Yeah, he is missing his pecker too, Sir. One of the broads, the skinny one, said our lady stuffed it inside his mouth before sewing it all up. And she stabbed him so many times, the body looks like a Jersey pastrami and Swiss-cheese roll. Shit man! I'm telling you, Detective, I'm telling you, this one is different. Look at those eyes. . ."

"Does she run a beat? A corner? Have a man?" Hammer inquiring about her street status.

"No, Sir. She looks clean. No credentials."

"Impossible! Hand tattoos?" Hammer asks.

"Nope, nobody's cattle."

Julius's bagged body being lifted by three EMTs into the decrepit ambulance. They need a fourth EMT, the assigned driver, to complete the task. As is every public service asset in New York, the stretcher is on its limits and breaks down like a deck of cards. Julius's black body bag falls to the ground producing a horrendous thump. Pigeons scram.

The die-hard first responders look at each other with doleful eyes and resume lifting the gross corpse. Just another day in the office. The commanding driver EMT yells to the others. "This is our last good stretcher, Man! Wasted on this big, fat pig here!"

Life as an EMT in this decade, in these particular litter-scattered streets, must be an act of insanity. What a job. Wonders how much one can take. These uncredited street angels. No medals. Little, if any, recognition. Struggling to make ends meet. It must; it *has* to be the mandate. What is left in humanity, plausibly.

The human condition – a riddle not for the common.

Cuban-Chinese Joint

Two cryptic-looking men approach Hammer trotting from the inside of the bustling Cuban-Chinese joint, each carrying a white fold-pack box and chop-sticks.

The first man is short and stout and carries a leather briefcase and a notepad in one hand.

The second is tall and slender.

One can tell they are not from around here, nor Jersey - their black-leather, pristine shoes and perfectly combed hair give them away.

By the Blue-and-White

Both men are in dark suits, sunglasses, and Fedora hat. The Tall one hands Hammer a light blue note followed by hush-conversation. A brush of elbows. They whisper. Hammer handing the message back to the Tall one. The men proceed to the ambulance and to Julius's bagged body.

They eat into their fold-packs as they speak.

The Tall one struggles with the chopsticks. Definitely not from New York.

Hammer unzips the body bag. They discuss the case over the cold body.

A more energized Hammer. "Fuckin-A, Man! Our girl deserves a fuckin-medal. Lose the shackles, Sargent."

"Nefarious eyes. This one here is no wounded buffalo. No Sir." Franco to himself while staring at Alexandra.

Hammer commands. "If the address is right, she's done us a favor. In this dump, you gotta pick a side, Officer. And this one just did." He speaks more gently. "We had been on watch. The John is, well, was an alien informant. Fuck, I don't get how we allow this shit to happen under our noses. If these streets weren't enough. Any other country would have kicked this piece of shit out their borders in a heartbeat. We welcome them. Fuckin traitors!"

"Sir, excuse my intrusion, but any lead on that Pen Killer case you can share?" Officer Franco asks.

Hammer shakes his head negatively and walks towards the AMX.

A muscled, skinny Drag Queen, wearing denim shorts, surreptitiously makes it to the police car window. He has title to this corner. Our Drag Queen leans inside the depressed police car's window.

A light-blue Dijon Lincoln slowly strolling the scene unsolicited, offers Burdon's superlative "Spill the Wine" through a compounding 1,000 Watts of Earthshaking bass. It fills the air and claims the unsanitary block.

The Drag Queen's gold and emerald crucifix necklace swings back and forth inside the police car. It formulates its own cadence to tempo the conjuring attention. A last hint of faith, perhaps. Though unlikely. "Princess, you are more than all this inhuman meat-grinder. And you be good now darling, you hear? I love you, babe-girl." The ceremonious Drag Queen whispers gracefully.

Kindness can be universal.

He hands her a small paper note and blows her a kiss as Officer Franco abruptly manhandles him with his ratty Billy club. "Yooow, keister-stash, beat it!"

In earned subversion, our Drag Queen points to his featherweight physic. "Take it easy there, tough-guy. You don't wanna spoil the brandy now, do-ya?" Shifting eyes towards the well-combed Hammer. "And who is that handsome?"

Our Drag Queen gives our salacious Officer the stink-eye - in lieu of the finger - and catwalks away, street-dancing, laughing to mess with by-standing prospective *Johns and Tricks*. And there are plenty here. Under unobstructed bright daylight. Shamelessly confident.

Even everyday lawless street hustles are prone to *de facto* wilding. And humor. Whatever carries you to finish your round.

South Bronx, 41st Precinct, Fort Apache

Dejecting interview room holds more cracks than walls.

Loud casting closing-cell-bars clang.

Zhain alone, from behind, inside an empty glass tile interview room, standing framed in front of the iron door. Overhead flickering white light and moss-like metal grated windows appends to the cold, eerie silence.

Alexandra enters the room barefoot and observes Zhain's sable contour. Her hair is wet and poor. She looks tired and hungry.

As he turns towards her, they establish intense eye rapport.

She is covered by a long, adult-version of a newborn pink-and-blue receiving blanket. He places a pomegranate, a clean glass of water, and a signature hot dog on the peeled table, then speaks serenely. "From the Seventh and 52nd corner Salim's cart. My favorite." He follows, landing a mustard and a ketchup bottle next to the hot dog.

An icy, leery, stoic eye is all she has for him.

Zhain back at her. "We now *do* need to work on that rage, don't we, Sue-Anne?"

She is noticeably hungry and takes to eating unceremoniously. An approving nod to second New York's celebrated bocadillo.

Zhain sits opposite her, unreservedly, with legs corporately crossed.

Alexandra is done with eating and looks less diluted.

Zhain calmy hands her his linen white Navy, edged handkerchief. He is in no hurry in the act.

She takes it and cleans her mustard-ketchup lips with it. She can't help noticing the embroidered initials "*Z.H.*" along with the fine cotton quality feel to the fingers - a touch to the cotton she had never experienced before.

He stands up and walks listlessly, gently, very caringly towards her. He politely lands his right hand on her shoulders. She flinches. He resumes with the necessary surety. She stands up and accepts it. Her protector holds her tight by the shoulder. Her inherent instincts are like no other, and she senses the bona fide confidence in his purpose. She equally cognizes his genuine magnetism and veiled mandate.

"What do you think about immortality?" He asks.

Silent eyes from Alexandra.

"Let's go home, Sue-Anne. We have work to do." Zhain paternally resolved.

He registers Alexandra as no ordinary disciple. She will sense any hesitation. But Zhain is far from orthodoxy, and she knows it.

He slings a James Brown-like, velvet green cape, with gold edges, around her shoulders. She accepts it without reserve. It comforts her. A docile, ephemeral crack in her architecture. It does not last more than a minute, though. She loses the receiving blanket as it falls to the stained cell floor.

Her unadorned bare feet.

Her eyes consciously resume looking into the surrounding reality. A cold prison cell. Poverty. A probable life sentence.

He pulls out a solitary Daffodil from inside his pocket and places it on her right ear.

Spiegel im Spiegel revisits the flashback.

She exits the room in silence. A blend of oscillating honey and ruby gleaming light blossom behind her as she strolls towards a small waiting room. Zhain, on the far end of the hall, waits for her. Receiving her.

A blotched emerald moth lands on her left shoulder.

A fervent bright light invades the receiving space.

Sue-Anne is no longer.

Alexandra is born.

Salve Regina!

An unyielding kinship is formed for the great beyond - and thereafter.

. . . Alexandra's flashback ends.

Chinatown, Mott and Pell Streets

Late afternoon. 6:13PM.

Grey skies.

Opium dens. Prostitution. Gambling. Rackets. Fund the American dream.

Three Young men pacing, "running" the Southeast corner. Notably, foot soldiers of the Hip Sing tong. The smaller framed one, wearing an Elvis-like leather jacket, swivels his metal nunchaku discreetly. Days into his eleventh birthday, he is barely five-feet tall.

A Chinese Bakery

A theatrical poster of Costa-Gavras' *Z, il est vivant!* wheatpasted on the bakery's façade.

Hammer exiting a Chinese bakery. His hair wet. His face sweaty.

Halfway out the street pavement, a sexy woman dressed in more curves than privilege, dashes out the door from the inside of the bakery, her dark hair flying like a dragon kite in the storm, carrying a bag of Macanese egg tarts, and hands it to him. She then voluntarily holds his face with both hands, her toes *en pointe*, chin raised, kisses his lips passionately. He takes it. Then slaps her behind with gusto. A content smile back from the bakery's master-chef.

In a soft voice in his right ear. "Babe, not in public. You don't fool me, I know you have a heart of gold."

She steps back.

With a docile half smirk, he blinks back at her. He then pulls her slim body, with one hand, forcefully against his and retributes with such a kiss that blasts gravity from under her legs. This man can see through shades. He can cross that fine line between life and whatever holds beyond it. He was born and coexists in this dimension.

A beat.

Pigeons in the air.

He is off walking towards his AMC.

He scans the horizon, looks up, South, to the hopeless Civic Fame statue, then enters his green AMC and bulldogs North.

Chinatown, Northwest corner

A proper, routine police shakedown. Nothing out of the ordinary.

Five teenage borough men lined up; legs spread against the graffitied wall of a busy Hong Kong style dim sum joint. Visibly too young to be On Leongs. For now.

Age is irrelevant, means absolutely nothing in kafkaesque streets.

A reality that can't be named.

Cantonese Tea Parlor, Window

A theatrical poster of *Doyle is bad news, The French Connection* wheatpasted on the parlor's façade.

With head halfway out the second-floor window, a notorious, stern face *dai ma*, dressed in red Adidas sweats, calmly drinks black tea, smokes a Camel, and supervises it all from the century-old tea parlor.

How does one judge a person who owns the souls of hundreds of teenage boys? Who will this beast answer to? Few young men will make it to the age of parenthood and fewer will ever escape the claws of poverty.

Greed. Savagery. Survival. All the same. All too thin. Counts for nothing.

An American Insanity painted on a frameless canvas.

A clampdown on social mobility.

Municipal Building Tower, One Centre Street

An August sunset. No rainbow.

Meanwhile.

The once lustrous lady of hope, Civic Fame can't stomach the city rotting under her watch and discreetly rotates South. Her back to Chinatown.

Her once golden skin rusts against the pink crepuscular sunset.

Her once proud eyes bleed ruby tears of disillusion.

Her once purposeful laurel crown crumbles down onto Centre Street's decaying asphalt.

A checkered cab runs it over shattering it into pieces.

A black Rottweiler pissing on the sidewalk's sewer drain hole. Its dog-tag reads "CIVILITY."

Civic Fame's shattered crown pieces are washed away down the filthy gutter hole under dog piss.

No one knows.

No one cares.

No one dares.

Life. As in hell.

Chapter 14

The Plains, Farm House

Kitchen. Day.

Nelson enters the house kitchen through the back entrance, carefully cleaning his muddy boots. He looks at the brown sandwich wrap Amanda left him, then rests his Henry by the mandolin.

Nelson looks at the back of the rocking chair and at the unassuming side table. He sees the empty spot where *The Book* once laid. He looks around the living room, searching, chasing. Although he is alone - and conscious about it - Nelson still tries to find something or someone. He leads himself outside through the front porch door.

Amanda's scarf flapping on the birch beam.

His boots descending.

He pushes to the marching dirt road.

He stops in the center of the crossroads. Dust-wind picks up, sweeping Nelson's clothing as it ricochets violently out of control. The elements witness a forsaken Nelson standing in the middle of the road - of the crossroads – and huddle into a parley. The crossroads configure a perfect cross.

Dust-wind grows more intense as Nelson looks to the East.

There is little the elements can do.

By the Rocker

Nelson, on his double rocker melting into a deep, seemingly endless sleep without a single voice to enable comfort. At this point, the search for meaning, existence, or true essence is irrelevant and holds no weight. Rationalism means nothing. The outer banks of love are the only, of course, singular reality left in store for Nelson. But he is continuously subjugated by inbuilt absence of will - a condition ordinated in perpetual, existential angst. Pure pain.

Nelson's tired, dilapidated hand next to the coffee table is evidence he wants to reach for a particular moment in his past.

But can't.

Time-Elapsing. . .

By the same Rocker.

The unimpeachable elements and the celestial outbound are ill equipped to deal with such pain and fast-forward time itself.

Resting on the coffee table, a big bottle of Old Grand-Dad full, its amber liquid slowly "emptying" itself as Nelson ages.

Another bottle.

A third. And more. . .

Each one sentenced to the same fate.

His hands collapsing, and progressively aging.

The weather changes repetitively in a dawn-to-dusk cycle.

Who knows how many years have gone. . .

Chapter 15

New York, Amanda's Brownstone

Present.

Next Day. Post-Blackout. Brownstone steps.

Ravaged streets.

Amanda sits alone on the Brownstone's steps, looking out at an ensemble of borough girls jumping double-Dutch.

A five-year-old, sable-hair boy on his shiny new Big Wheel making a cracking noise, Tak-Tak-Tak-Tak... A sudden cart-wheel. He smiles at Amanda. She smiles back.

Across the street, another brownstone hosts Janis scouting out the window from the second floor and May sitting on the steps of the same brownstone. Janis mostly patrolling the horizon.

Two third-grade neighborhood boys playing with Chinese fire-crackers. The firecrackers POP...POP. The firecrackers snap the daze, and the Yoldas, joined by Amanda, make worried eye contact.

Winnies' Shoe Shop

Winnie's Shoe Shop shares a wall with Amanda's brownstone.

Our Freud-like shop-owner, wearing a teal bowtie and round-framed, light blue glasses, comes out from his shop playfully charging towards and yelling to the fire-cracker boys. "Darn kids, always playing! You're scaring my customers!" Then to himself sarcastically. "Thank God!"

Winnie and Don are the same individuals. To Amanda and the folks at the Plains, he was (is) known as Don (Donald). Some say he was born in the age of Enlightenment. What is certain is that time seemed to have little effect on him. Others say he sleeps smiling - something out of place in this decade. Perhaps, the riddle to his immortality resides in his mastering of this tightly-lipped, deceitful cast – the smile.

To the neighborhood and the Lefferts Street folks, he is known simply as Winnie Shoemaker. And although he does take care of shoes and *soles* specifically, his real mission is to elevate children's self-being, pro-bono, in any way he can. With a mellow smile most of the time.

His Shoe Shop is a grid maze of the eclectic, the ominous, the cerebral. One wall cabinet is jammed with flashlights of all sorts, all ages. His fear of the dark is yet another amusing tale fabled among adults and children especially. The kids call him "Lamp-Winnie" warranted he is never caught without half-a-dozen flashlights strapped to his self-crafted utility belt.

Don is not particularly religious and has been known for a deep-seated disheartened attitude for priests and houses of prayer.

Either by Revocation or by sheer will, he is convinced of

ecclesiastical abuses, both doctrinal and moral, perpetrated throughout centuries of death and upheaval. In contrast, he is equipped with abundant spirituality, metaphysical magnetism, and love for children, a combination difficult to be matched by bone-and-flesh, titled or self-proclaimed, clerics of God.

It is possible he's been roaming Earth for ages, centuries. But no one really knows exactly.

Winnie comes with the block.

On the Shop's South corner wall, an astronomical collection of mind-bending, hand-assembled "analysis-glasses," a type of apparatus one would expect from a Jules Verne ophthalmologist's assemblage, if there was ever one. He uses these Daedalus apparatuses to navigate deep into the *souls* of children. Into their darkest fears hoping to alleviate some of it through a mix of *play*, care, and a little-known, quasi-extinct commodity, so prohibitive, so secretive, so impossible to extract from inside the human condition – love.

And let us not forget his signature avocado donuts, another staple among innocent fingers.

His primal hypothesis is bare, arcadian. If one can learn to love and care for another being, one may, equally, over time, profess to love oneself in the process - thereby a close proxy into healing. Could it be simpler? Perhaps by conditioning. Perhaps, indeed. His constant contrition, however, stands on the fact that life itself equally requires self-built survival engines to endure perpetuation – becoming an inscrutable wrench in his postulate. A colloquial conundrum beyond mathematical statements. Something, perhaps, not entitled to provincial human resolution. An object, rather, for the unnatural. And this is what Winnie is.

Amanda and Winnie latch eyes.

A joyful Winnie to Amanda. "Thank God. Yes, if anything, God likes to play, am I right, my Dear?"

"Don, you haven't changed. Time has not worn you down, my dear friend. And how is your inner-self doing, Mr. *Soul-Fixer*?" Amanda affectionally back at him with wet, candor, honey eyes.

"Boy, it's nice; it's really nice to see you, Amanda! You'll be upstairs from me. It's the best I could bargain for under these circumstances. A dash tight, but tons of light! And Nelson Senior?" Winnie asks with hopeful eyes.

Deaf ears from Amanda. Her eyes turn to the window.

Winnie with careful words. "Hum, I see. I see."

Winnie approaches closely to her face. He pulls out one of his alien pair of glasses and looks even deeper at and into, Amanda, examining her.

Another crack in time and space.

The ambience turns black.

Winnie's tepid flat voice. "Hum, I see. (examining) I see. Oh, Amanda, Dear. We have a lot of work ahead, my Dear. But then. . . very little time. Am not sure I can fix. . ."

"I have something to show you. Come with me." Amanda back at him, interrupting while holding his hand.

Lights resume.

Amanda turns and walks towards the building's entrance hall.

Amanda's Kitchen

Amanda and Winnie sit at the birch kitchen table.

Amanda looks at *The Book* that lays on top of the table (beside a bowl of persimmons) while clearing the table of flour. Her hands fully veiled in cooking flour. She dusts off some flour from *The Book*'s cover as it rests engulfed with dedicated sunrays.

Behind Amanda stands Aragon's *El Alma de la Virgen* painting hanging on the wall.

Winnie follows her eyes. Once he sees *The Book,* he zooms into it. His eyes now super wide open as he holds his breath in utter disbelief.

The orphan *Book* on the table.

Amanda offers Winnie some chopped persimmons. He is oblivious to the offer and with locked eyes on *The Book.* "Is this, Amanda, is this Nelson's *Cipher Manuscript One?*"

"Yep." Amanda plainly.

Our Panglossian erudite pulls out another analysis glasses from his Scottish dove sweater side pocket and a chromed flashlight from his leather utility belt. He is careful in selecting among seven other flashlight options. He peers in with the pair, lighting purple light onto *The Book* as he flips page after page.

About The Book

This mysterious, *lunellum-scudded,* parchment-bound artifact can hardly be considered a book in the traditional sense. It is primarily a comprehensive, unfinished, 316-page manuscript, bound in limp, sage vellum, ornamented with engraved clasps and woodcut illustrations. Alum-tawed thongs and goat leather holds it all together.

It is sewed with hemp fiber thread onto flax (linen) cords.

Not all the fading tawny-brown script ink is legible by contemporary commoners unless versed in - or in possession of - the equally ominous "dispel artifact" – *the Codex Cipher Unit-71*.

Because this manuscript holds no loyalty to any element or dimension, it is neither bound to submission nor susceptible to revision. On the contrary, Nelson's *Book* is a self-ruling entity, only deciphered by either those carrying his blood or, in rare instances, through the *Codex Cipher Unit-71*. This decipherment tool has been called many things over the ages, including *Cipher-71, Codex-71, Unit-71,* and even *Nelson's Abacus*.

The manuscript's ancient, age-old parchments carry undeciphered texts, vibrant washes in various palettes of lilac, iris, amethyst, jade, emerald, ruby, garnet red, cobalt, sage, basil green, and onyx. There is a clear predominance, or preference, of luminous green and red ink pigments.

His eyes fade into the manuscript's lively images revealing the abstract natural world along with planetoid stars, alchemical variations, biological specimens, astronomical beings, botanical flowers, seeds, distributive mathematical algorithms, DaVinci-like human chassis', metamorphic animal figures, genetic diagrams, celestial systems, electro-mechanical tools, medical utensils, cosmical orientations and random metaphysical notations. There are no specific chapters.

On its far end, the manuscript holds an ubiquitous table containing what resembles cuneiform signs, scripts, and logo-syllabary - methodized and tabulated in positional polynomial arithmetic system.

Another pop-out reveals what appears to be a celestial map, a multidimensional astrophysical, sketch of the universe, with specific coordinates.

Equally, there are references to human sentiments, the senses, and the elements themselves, but unconventionally. These, rather, fall into the category of construction, such as engineering blueprints and architectural drawings.

The manuscript bears no author's name. It only holds one symbol on its longitudinal leather spine – a *beautiful* positional "nfr" with an eclipse-like symbol embracing it.

Amanda's Kitchen

Winnie lingers quixotically. "Some progress. Some progress; indeed, however undeniable angst. Unfinished algorithms. Strangely, uncharacteristic of Senior. Not Red's signature either. Certainly not yours. Whose? Whose? Hum, little hands here, Amanda. Little hands!" His fingers grab one specific page for augmented scrutiny – the page with the kid's crude drawing of the black wolf in bloodied teeth.

His mystified eyes whiz deeper into it. He swipes his fingers on it, then rubs them against one another to feel the ink's texture. He yells, stupefied. "Carbon-Phollium-13! That can't be! It can't transition here. It couldn't have made the passage. Absolutely not! Unless. . ."

He changes the flashlight to an extended, thin, more elaborated titanium flashlight for augmented prospection. A twist on the emerald crystal glass lens for focus, another adjustment on a small metric knob, then a light remark. "Yes-yes! Carbon-P-13! I see. I see. Different hands, different imprints."

Amanda's blunt, unsurprised eyes.

"Amanda, you know what this means, right?"

She nods an indifferent "yes."

It finally dawns on him – this is her plan, her work. She must know.

Winnie resumes flipping *The Books'* pages with awestruck eyes.

His eyes can't but continue to admire *The Book.*

"Oh-boy. And Nelson?"

Amanda nods negatively.

Winnie turns to a stone wood shelf and grabs an olive, enamel bowl. He proceeds to fill that bowl with warm water and green leaves.

"Who else knows?"

Amanda nods towards outside the window, referring to Janis and May.

"Oh-boy. Are you sure about this? Amanda, this is, this is, this is *The Book*, Nelson's manuscript. Why would you bring it here, my Dear?"

Amanda nods positively as Winnie becomes progressively agitated. "It needs a new owner. It needs a clear heart."

Winnie looking downwards and talking to himself softly. "Hum. . . Yes. Yes! Of course! A clear heart – yes, the celestial coordinates for transitional continuum. Of course. Of course. But whose?"

He looks for and finds a kitchen towel.

He throws some more garden leaves and dove crystal salt onto the bowl. He picks up speed. "Did you come alone?"

Amanda, still standing up beside the table, shakes her head negatively. A beat, and she looks down to her belly. She passes her hands softly on her tummy. A light blue and golden aura encircles her belly.

Amanda is expecting.

A beat.

Winnie's shocked eyes bulge. He faints, falling back flat on the ground like a legless ironing board. The enamel bowl floating in the air.

Amanda reaches and holds, with supernatural reflex, the enamel bowl from certain disaster - not a drop spilled. Her hands do not burn either.

A few minutes elapse.

An awakened, but no less agitated, Winnie. "Oh-boy. Oh-boy. I see." Pacing himself back and forth like a soon-to-be father waiting for the revealing of his newborn's gender.

Amanda sitting on a walnut chair with calm eyes.

Winnie kneels in front of her, a towel on his right shoulder. He places the white enamel bowl in front of Amanda's feet and gently takes her leather sandals off and places her feet inside the bowl. Sunrays illuminate her feet. Increasingly agitated, he proceeds to wash her feet.

"Why, thank you, Don."

"Amanda, this is extra, extra-ordinary. This is. . . This is. . . This is something beyond illusion! We have so much to do. So much to do. Little time. Little time. Oh boy, our existence in the line."

"My Dear, you have an important role in writing this story. I will need your help." A beat. "If anything is to happen to me, you must then go on with it." Their eyes jointly zoom into *The Book*.

"Oh-boy. A *not-me* for me." Winnie reacts.

Winnie accelerates, cleaning Amanda's foot faster. Amanda holds his hand firmly. He stops the involuntary rhythmic rubbing.

"Don't be afraid. You've done so much for our children. When the time comes, granted, you will bring light forth and know what to do." Amanda says.

Condo's Front Door

A knock on the door.

Francis Fleming, a tattooed Chief firefighter, who lives on the Brownstone's Third Floor, and his wife Beth open the door.

Chief Francis is a legend among fellow firefighters, never accepting credit for his sacrifices. He is the man you want behind you when attacking a Coney Island, twenty-three-story high, brown-brick development tower engulfed in demon-like flames. Those middle-class brick complexes built under the premise of urban exploitation and unsanitary ugliness.

He will never speak of his days as a Navy Corpsman during the Korea War, where he served side-by-side with the infamous 1st Battalion, 1st Regiment, 1st Marine Division. He shared bunkers with other gallant Corpsmen such as "Jackie" Kilmer and witnessed firsthand bravery in deadly, chaotic battlegrounds. He keeps a flat-head military trunk in the basement, under the darkest corner possible.

The only reference he ever made to his military past was during a cold April night in 1969, after a three-alarm structure fire, in Jamaica-Queens, that claimed the lives - by carbon-monoxide suffocation - of an entire undocumented Bolivian family. His exact, remorseful words being *"the heart of a Navy corpsman is the closest thing to an angel one can ever wish for on the battlefield. And I was just too late in this one. . ."*

Francis dressed in Class-B firefighter's uniform.

A joyful Francis welcoming Amanda. "Wanted to greet the new neighbor. Winnie! You beat me to it. I'm Francis, this is Beth, the boss."

"Francis is one of the good guys, something we need more of," Winnie proclaims.

"It's been hell out there. Seems the whole city is in constant distress, and yesterday was especially bad," Francis says.

"Francis, please," Beth interjects, then to Amanda. "It's great to have you." Beth is scouting the room's surroundings, walls, ceiling, and windows, "and how did you get so much light in here? And this wonderful smell, what is this?"

Amanda and Winnie reply in unison. "Bread!"

"Well, then I absolutely need this bread recipe," Beth speaks, and the Sun shines a rapt light on her David Star gold pendant.

"Amanda, join us for supper tonight?" Francis asks.

"Yes, of course," Amanda agrees with warm eyes.

The first daughter of a Cuban trumpet player and an Iranian Jewish mother, Beth is Francis' enchantingly engaging wife. She keeps her copious tawny eyes and benevolent Baekje smile beamed at Amanda and can't but notice Amanda's characteristic pre-natal glow - she is expecting.

Corridor

Lieutenant Johnny pops in quickly, calling Francis as he rushes out the corridor and down out to the street. Johnny is Francis' second, free-spirited, athletic son. He also wears Class-B Firefighter uniform and carries a Judo *Gi* wrapped in a black belt slung around his sinewy shoulders.

The cleaned-faced, slender at the waist, and fit Johnny is a black belt Judo Sensei. "Let's go, Pops! The Chief can't be late! And I don't wanna look bad, c'mon!"

On Johnny's heels, his older brother, the muscular Andrew (aka Hammer) charges down the stairs and yells a general, "Good morning, all!" and flashes past Johnny. It seems they are racing.

Francis waves Amanda goodbye and leaves out the door.

Outside, Street

Johnny and Andrew sprinting down the brownstone's steps.

Andrew now cranking his custom, stripped to metal, cafe racer, a Honda CB550 Four, aka *Lucky-7*.

At one's elbow from Andrew's Honda, Johnny cranking his custom red Husqvarna 400.

Andrew's jubilant smirk. "Second again, sucker!" and off he rages on his café racer, leaving tire smoke, dirt, and pissed-off pigeons behind. He purposely turns his face back simply to mock his younger sibling.

Johnny laughing, speeding behind, trying to catch up.

The helmetless brothers speed by Chief Francis who boards his beloved 1971, black, boat-tail, Rivera GS, parked in front of Winnie's, white-and-yellow VW Westphalia type-2 bus.

A dissatisfied Chief Francis inside the Rivera. "Damn kids! Always playing. Always playing!"

Such is life.

Such is family. The most sacred of all goodful gifts.

Back at the Door

A soft knock on the door. Feet first. A shy, milky bald head tilts in. It's Sean. A distressed Sean, rather. He eats a pretzel, wears purple lipstick, and carries his Leica IIIc (with yellow 35's) by hand. Apparently, some kid painted a devil's horn on his forehead and smudged chocolate mousse on his fragile face. He wears a white T-shirt with a bulls-eye red "X" superimposed on a pigeon's head. His disliking for the feathered urban creature needs to be expressed very clearly.

"Winnie! Those darn kids are going wild downstairs! And I mean really wild. You better *ghiet* back."

Sean points angrily at his forehead with predictable mannerism. On it, the hand painting of a devil's horn on his milky pale forehead.

Amanda, Beth and Winnie produce a comforting smile.

Winnie's Shoe Shop

Minutes later.

An exquisite, early-century, dentist-style, leather reclining chair. An olive-green, velvet couch. Wood toys and board games scattered around the floor and walls. A deck of Dutch puppets hanging. A lounge *divan* covered in a merlot, Scythian rug. A collection of portrait sculptures on top of his office desk. What is left of space is covered in books. A plenitude of donuts, of every sort, inside a jumbo pink bowl. Under the bowl, an unfinished, one-thousand-piece puzzle of a New England Light House.

Five second-graders play unsupervised and freely inside his shop.

An old black and white, Philco TV yields *2001: A Space Odyssey*.
Winnie and Sean enter the room.

The kids immediately halt and quickly fall into stiff martial attention and silence.

A long beat.

All souls in the room hold their breaths, waiting for a reaction.

Little twilight eyes moving side-ways.

Winnie tries hard to hold his smile, only to break into mammoth laughter, seconded by the kids. "Let us play! Let the children play! Who wants a donut!?" He yells loud enough to be heard across blocks.

The kids laughingly go at him, jumping onto him like a pack of hungry baby wolves.

That innocence.
Can close wounds.
And will.

Chapter 16

Amanda's Brownstone, Garden

A blue, breezeless night. A full Moon.

An abundantly set Mediterranean Levant dinner table sits outside, under a century old Luso pergola housing persimmons and canary bulbs.

At a long white Spanish Cedar table with calm candles sits Francis, Beth, Amanda, Winnie, Hammer, Johnny, little Claire, and Hammer's Fiancé Fatima.

Fatima wears a discrete beige head hijab, and drinks water only. Hammer kisses her frail forehead, and they touch eyes. He smiles at her. They are in love, and this might be the only occasion Hammer ever smiles.

They keep to themselves, just enjoying the beautiful night. That night. No dialogues, only music and woodwind instruments escape the vintage wall 60s *Victrola*, and the music fills all empty spaces, as intended.

Fatima came to the United States with her ousted family as a Palestine refugee, having blossomed into a first-rate ER attending nurse at The Brooklyn Hospital Center (TBHC), on DeKalb Ave – where the couple met under unusual circumstances.

Hammer & Fatima

Their arc began two springs past.

Hammer and his squad killed two and wounded one known cop killer during a Sunday night gang bust and shootout inside one of Frank Lucas' Harlem Cut Houses. One assailant was left for dead in the hospital's crowded ER corridor.

TBHC, ER Corridor

Hammer enters the hospital with a cut to the left temple. Dried blood down his neck.

Once at the TBHC, Hammer finds nurse Fatima and a male doctor performing CPR, followed by the closing of gun wounds, on the quasi-dead gangbanger.

Tasked with concluding unfinished business, Hammer needs to convince the petite nurse Fatima against resuscitating the criminal, while imposing his credentials onto her. "Ma'am, you absolutely cannot save this man." He speaks while flashing his badge. "Excuse *me*?! And who are you to determine one's life?" Fatima, quick as a whip, back at him.

"I'm Detective Fleming from the S-C-U." Hammer in coercive voice.

"Then, mister SCU-detective, until God hands you his job, you can put your G-Man badge back in your jacket, grab a seat, and let me save this soul." She walks away from him. A short beat and she turns back to Hammer with a half-smile. "And that includes you too, Colombo. Sit yourself on that chair right there and I will take care of that graze."

The hard-pounding street cop can't believe his eyes.

She looks him straight into his ashen eyes, straight into the man's iron heart. "And please get going because I have a lot of work to do now. Go on. Go on. . ." Hammer's eyes rally, and his lips void of words. Fatima's assertiveness and genuine caring soul cut deeply through him – such a small frame.

ER Corridor

Moments later. Midnight.

A less crowded, silent corridor.

Fatima stitching a laceration above Hammer's right temple.

His eyes soaked into hers. She can feel his pulse.

They are so close that he can feel her body's warmth. He can smell her hair, her natural scent. The man is taken away.

His guard is down.

He is mesmerized by her energy. Her will to live. Her passion for caring. Such contrast.

He can't take his curious eyes away from her. He feels her gentle and soothing hands on his muscular body. *Who can say that angels don't roam this Earth or that love can't come in such delicate spell,* are his thoughts.

Fatima's eyes toddle patiently through Hammer's body wounds, scars, and tattoos. Then her round brown eyes catch his staring at her. A beat. Their faces, inches apart.

"What? Never seen a woman this close before?" She mocks him.

He blushes like a nine-year old waiting to blow his birthday candle.

The street bull is restful. His soul reposed under the light of discovery.

Lenient desires.

The hard-pounding Hammer falls in love with the life-saving flyweight wordsmith. Just like that.

From that day onwards, Fatima is Hammer's beacon. His alter-humanity. The one keeping him from entirely losing it. And, for that, the Fleming's are eternally grateful.

Contradiction. Antagonism. Balance, nonetheless.

Fatima, doctors, science, and first-responders defying destiny. Cheating the natural order in the name of the preservation of life. Then there is Hammer, a trained killing machine caged by anger. Conflict. The forces of existence stretched by human doctrines. Rage and love – one of the same.

Fatima and Hammer understand that life is fragile. Too fragile.

This world. This dimension. Reality has no compassion.

This city perpetually erases and rewords itself. So too, do people. So too, can a dark heart be rescued from the savages of life. Can it? But for how long?

Back at The Diner Table

At the table, the twelve-year old, eloquent, enticingly charming, Claire sitting next to her father, Francis, flipping a battered "The Tolkien Reader" edition. They are close, as it should be, of course. The pale, sweet, and crafty Claire is hairless and uses a sapphire blue head handkerchief. She undergoes chemotherapy at the Weill Cornell Medical Center on York Avenue. Claire is a bookworm for romantic books, classics, and thrillers – she is known to read a book a day.

Hammer serves his signature sangria at the table, intentionally skipping Fatima. His crucifix tattoo properly printed on his forearm.

Beth attentively takes notes from Amanda's receipts on the far end of the table.

Our illustrious Winnie takes to analyzing Johnny with his dark-green, sci-fi glasses. Johnny feels as if he is a Guinea pig but goes along for the ride – he is a light soul.

Brownstone Steps

Meanwhile, Janis and May outside the Brownstone's front steps playing cards and sipping cold, white Porto while vigilant - intimately facing each other. No Zippo needed here to light this fire.

Janis, now with tight blond cornrow braids, takes off her mule and gently caresses May's toes. May has a toe ring.

Janis wears cutoff jeans and a red-tongue, Rolling Stones black and white baseball T-shirt; she is braless.

May now in mohawk short hair and short skirt. Her legs are semi-opened in explicit untamed intimacy. They are very much at ease admiring the full moon, the windless flamboyant New York noir, and, especially, one another.

Back Inside the Garden

Johnny serves Amanda a huge Challah bread.

A playful Claire competes with Johnny in offering Amanda a loaded plate of Oreos.

Claire glows. Wide beautiful smile. She is the happiest.

Claire's innocent voice asks Amanda. "What are you going to call him?"

Amanda in unsurprised voice. "You knew. . . he is anxious to meet you, Claire." They smile as if partners in this plot. She adds with pleasure in her smile. "He will mean so much to both of us. Life, little ones. Life. . ."

Amanda and Claire interact. Claire's tiny hand on Amanda's round belly. Amanda takes off her blue, oak-seed necklace and puts it on Claire. She kisses Claire's forehead with profound meaning.

"He feels like a daring little soul. Maybe too daring. . ." Claire says laughing.

"Yes, my dear, he will need to be. . ." Amanda laughing composedly.

Amanda whispers something into Claire's ear while holding her hand firmly. Amanda's hand trembles. A controlled trembling, though.

A long commanding beat.

This is no ordinary night, and it makes a case against skeptics in faith.

Claire is fully lit in warm golden light. She looks up to the infinite. The sky accepts her clear blue eyes in solemn grace.

A long, lonely act of love cries a celestial tune.

The elements bow in reverence. To the limit.

Claire will overcome and thrive.

The world needs her.

Chapter 17

The specter of nuclear holocaust still prevails inside our psyche.

Crime Incorporated

The year is 1977, and New York is just as dark as it will ever be. Not particularly your typical Dickensian modern-day cosmopolitan fable.

Half-a-million heroin addicts roam U.S. streets.

It is to speculate if the Grim Reaper itself hasn't yet considered a sabbatical. By fact or by convention, the story goes that it got home one cool, spring day thrilled with his newly acquired *Sansui 8080* receiver purchased, cash, at the Crazy Eddie's Prospect Park commercial establishment, only to find bricks inside the sealed box - in lieu of the receiver. A handwritten note read "not in my town." The Reaper felt disconsolate. His heart, broken. His pride tarnished. His *golden fiddle* handed as prize.

Only those with grit or lack of option are sticking around. Another group just to see it through. And lastly, the true New Yorkers. It's difficult to explain obsession.

Time Tunnel

The elements construct and deploy a credulous time tunnel of events. . . as follows. . .

Amanda's Kitchen

Amanda in her natural element, except she wears bell-bottoms. Amanda is no longer pregnant.

She wears her hair up while baking bread, tossing baking flower up against sun rays. Dough platter going in the oven. Fresh bread coming out of the oven. Repeat. *The Book* sits on the pine table.

Neighbors help Amanda build a small greenhouse in the back garden.

Johnny wears a Scottish Kilt.

A dinky, long-haired boy plays a game of scrabble with Amanda. This is Chris, Amanda's six-year-old, pure-hearted, congenial son. She smiles at him, and he smiles back. He joins her in the "breaking bread sessions."

Chris fiddling through the Manuscript attentively with big open eyes while handing out wrapped sandwiches to incoming building neighbors. Winnie, by his side, keeping close to his new disciple.

Claire on the far end of the kitchen reading *The Lord of The Rings*.

Chris' favorite task of the day is to help Amanda hand out early-morning sandwich wraps to their neighbors. It is when he feels a sense of family - being around the Flemings, Winnie, Fatima, and the remaining Yoldas. And then there is Claire. Yes, there is Claire. And the reason for dreaming of skipping childhood and shooting straight to manhood. He is simple in his objectives - to do good and marry Claire.

That innocence expressed in a child has no bearing – it is the ultimate prize.

His heart transcends anything earthly.

Chapter 18

The Plains, Shortgrass Prairie

Present. Day.

A rebuilt stagecoach.

A perilous Barred Owl on a tall leafless tree stump.

An old, working windmill in solitude. Its blades are our first view of the Sun; it reflects the early Sun's first rays. The sunbeam is particular and guides itself on and off the road; it warms Nelson's back as he walks West.

The windmill multitasking.

Wild horses exercising in the flatland.

A sentinel American eagle supervises it all.

A sweaty Nelson mechanically chops lumber under the intense dry Sun.

Red arrives galloping from the horizon on a brown, Arabian horse.

Nelson clears sweat from his forehead.

Red looks at and notices the excessive amount of chopped timber. He fails to conceal his concern. "Nelson, we need you at the barn. DINA's been down for two nights, and the town folks are flocking."

Red knows all too well that isolation is by far the worst cruelty that can be inflicted on a human being.

Nelson dropping chopped logs, oblivious to Red's words or existence. Nelson's bloody right-hand grabs the Henry with one hand and the encrusted ax with the other. The pouring blood flows between his index finger and thumb - an aftermath of the obsessive wood-chopping. The axe's handle is wrapped in fresh blood.

Nelson finally turns to Red, perhaps by chance, rather than to acknowledge his presence.

His eyes reveal he might have been crying. Possibly for years.

Every part of him says *don't stop.*

Deferral is not a space Nelson is accustomed to. This man was not (ever) given to inaction. We speak of a strong man who can whirl a sword and take no prisoners. Who in many moments did not leave anything to chance. Their faith in him, unwavering. Borderless.

But we also speak of a man considering undoing his mistakes. All of them.

The Barn

Getting late. Not dark yet.

Awakening Folk outside the Barn. They don't look pleased.

Nelson and Red next to the Power Panel.

Nelson caresses DINA, then looks up at it, speaking. "I guess we've gotten outmatched. We used to have a hold on everything. I guess I got tired, old partner. Been having a hard time mustering what's real and what's not."

Nelson takes a beat to look at his reflection on DINA's shiny copper panel. He sees his deteriorated figure, and he understands time has taken away what took him forever to build.

"You promised us!" Awakening Jeremiah yells.

Red and Nelson's roll of eyes to each other.

Nelson crouches and grabs a handful of dirt. He stands up, opens his hand softly, and lets the dirt fly sideways away.

"You gave us the cure!" Awakening Matthew says.

Red's omni-scientist eyes at Nelson.

"You promised!" Awakening Jeremiah once more.

"We came because of you. Your cure." Awakening Abigail howls.

Nelson to Awakening Folk. "Folks, all is gonna be all-right. Go on now. Please go on now. Please go on. . ."

A frail seven-year-old Awakening Girl, with owl-eyes, pro-actively walks towards Nelson's left side and clutches his hand in innocent solidarity. A child's understanding of life and meaning is as clear as day and night, and it reckons no ambiguity. The little girl raises her chin in a demonstration of support and defiance. She is just.

Awakening Folk disperse with small, if any, confidence in Nelson, walking back towards the sunset anchor mountains. These pilgrims, united by prayer and hope, seek the promised land, but only scorched land cuddles them.

The ginger-haired mademoiselle stays behind to let her eyes focus on Nelson then giving him a positive nod with the head. Her gesture signals, *everything is going to be all right, mister,* and proceeds to jog after the devoted Populus herd.

Her older protective brother there to escort her.

Nelson cascades into accidental inertia. He takes a moment to look fixedly at his extended palm and at the vacuum left by the little girl's absent hand. It reminds him of that feeling, one he has been struggling to defer. It reminds him of Hanna.

The little girl fades into the horizon with her brother and all the dirt possible behind them.

A flash of light interrupts the daze, and Red follows gently. "Nelson?!"

Inside the Bran

By the twelve-gauge, cast iron, double-dynamic, Karbatz mill.

Nelson's tired eyes follow the dust on the horizon by the Barn's window.

No reply from Nelson. He is too distracted. Too confused. Nelson is essentially numb, in deep sorrow, with no gradient of remediation in sight.

In his inertia, Nelson mounts an effort and takes to brewing coffee. He assembles his millennia Ottoman pot. A scoop of raw Arabian coffee beans falls to the ground over his aged boots. It would have mattered long ago. But it doesn't now. Nelson is losing his senses. He is thinking through a bleak funnel. He gasps for air, then smells the coffee beans, in pleasure, before the process.

The coffee scent reminds him, triggers so much - of a full life. It reminds him of the man he was; but one he recognizes no longer.

His regrets have matured and marshalled back to claim deed and punish his omissions. His chest is too vague, too lost to equate any decimal of bearings.

In sum, the man is adrift.

One tube valve pops, and he snaps back to the present. Not to reality.

He mechanically measures DINA's panel gauges one by one, and with a copper pressure calibrating instrument, replaces two 25Hz green tube valves. He inserts a third valve deep inside DINA's core command unit; this one is more robust. It is a mesh of alternating mix of blue and purple that glows incandescently as if it were an autonomous being.

"Nelson!" Red exclaims.

A distracted Nelson. "I don't know how to keep going any more than I know how to stop falling into this damned void." A stern beat. "That should do it."

Nelson at the Power Panel's gauge turning DINA back on. It takes a second, and DINA comes back to life.

Nelson asking Red what he probably knows already. "How did we get to this, Red? To here. Remember when we first got to these lands? The dust. The lizards. Dark, crowded with ramblers and the Northeastern plague. Crows. Rattles. Crop wouldn't grow in this miserable Alkali soil."

"Yep. I remember. Empirically dead."

"I failed. And how I did!"

"What do you mean?"

"Wrong. How's that? How could I've have been this wrong?" Nelson to himself.

"Nelson. . ."

"Need to square off this manuscript business. Permanently!" An upset Nelson.

"But at risk, Nelson. Can't turn the clock back now."

"No, Red, that's exactly what Amanda is doing. Fixing my clutter! From day one, she warned me." A short beat. "My lady's been right all along." Another pause. "And Red: I can't carry this town, The Plains, this. . . on my shoulders anymore. My bones are tired."

Nelson pours scalding coffee into the men's mugs. This time, he is unashamed to pour his Old Grand-Dad whisky generously into his mug. Nelson now at the bio-lab part of the Barn, looking into the Watson microscope. He notices the kids' papier-mâché next to it. He holds it up for a second.

Farm House

Moments later.

Night has claimed the day.

Nelson from behind, silhouette only, as he sits in silence smoking his Scottish pipe sitting in his double-rocker. His boots gently take the rocking task as their own. He looks out to the open porch. Henry by his side. There is nothing but sorrow on the horizon.

The coffee table next to him holds his wristwatch, an old bottle of Kentucky bourbon, and the McIntosh receiver, all blanketed in decades-old dust. His left-hand hangs on the edge of the coffee table. A red-turning-orange dog leash is tied to the rocker's right arm. The dog leash has aged and lost its fibers. Nelson's hand holds the watch firmly.

As he sits on the double-rocker, he gazes outside to the horizon, again. Nothing there to focus his sight. Just the empty. His heart commands his eyes, and as they focus on the open seat next to him on the rocker - the red dog leash. His hand swipes dust from the vacant seat. The walnut wood shines a bit, but it too is clotted with dismay.

Everything here: the elements, the senses, the people, the animals, the insects, the tree swing, miss the cherry little girl.

He reaches for the McIntosh and turns the nob "ON," as it, too, is in no hurry to light up fully. It drags. A viola-and-cello duet clears the air; however, it hardly fills any fraction of sorrow.

The receiver's warm orange tube lights take shape and finally glow whole as Nelson glances at his wristwatch - the dial shows 6:13.

Nelson melts into an infinite hibernating sleep while the McIntosh's orange tubes fail to lessen his abyssal grief. Nothing can.

Nelson lost the faculty to dream. His memories and his own voice inside his mind are his only companions.

The elements take turn in keeping an eye out for him.

They better.

Chapter 19

Nelson's Deep Sleep Flashback Begins.

Nelson's Study Room, Second Floor

Years Earlier. Dawn.

The Farm House is in its prime days. Clean, neat, organized, dustless, squeak-less. Lots of light.

Little Hanna's bare feet, wearing a light-green, kimono drapery pajamas (Thayer's version). She sits on top of a massive sepia-red Pazyryk rug, with bovine motif, inside Nelson's Victorian-inspired study room.

She is flipping through *The Book*.

Hanna is Nelson and Amanda's nine-year-old curious and astute daughter. With great, wide-opened emerald eyes, and a sunshine smile she reads *The Book* with careful, analytical attention. She is a compulsive reader.

She randomly flips pages and sees undated ancient scribbles, drawings, and notes written on vellum. These sketches are colored of humans, plants, animals, the solar system in their natural state. Some illustrations are more scientific than others. Notes. Some pictures are unfinished. The last few pages are blank.

A soft spellbound, "And what is this?!" from Hanna (to herself).

Hanna feels the need to engrave her own declarations and draws an imaginary version of a human being on one of the pages. Her drawing brings us to a sketch of a slim, pale man, but in children's tones. Her drawing is a kid's version of Sean Whitaker.

Another quiet remark from our reader, "I must have it. . ."

The Barn

At the far end of Nelson's bio-Lab section, the silhouette of a ten-year-old boy tuning a French Horn.

Nelson's Study

Peter and the Wolf 's French Horn notes invade the Study Room.

Hanna notices a dried-green butterfly as page-marker holding another kid's (earlier) drawing, but one of a wolf, a sinister-looking wolf, a spec of blood drips from its enlarged teeth. She isn't sure who is the "other" intrusive author.

The French Horn stretches progressively louder.

Next to the unfinished wolf sketch, a hunter's knife drawing. She looks curiously and passes her fingers over the wolf's crayon-thick drawing lines to feel its surface texture.

Sensing a dark mist, she swiftly retracts and pulls her finger up and out of the picture. She doesn't like what she feels. She nods assertively to the wolf's image. "Baaad puppy!"

She is mesmerized by this particular "book" and takes to read it in more detail.

Although she has read through files of her parents' comprehensive library (and Red's million-volume athenaeum), this specific one is enigmatically alien. As she flips its mystical pages, her eyes witness a mysterious script, challenging to comprehension, to process. As part of her constitution, Hanna can intuitively understand most, if not all, of the scripts.

But she is less interested in the scribbles. Hanna is transfixed with its vibrant, almost alive, imagery, washes, figures, codex, radiating symbols, ciphers, sketches, pronouncements. Meaning.

With pencil in hand, she draws a grey cloud. A beat and the room's Sun rays fade off instantly. The sky turns ashy grey. She proceeds with sketching raindrops under the same clouds. She looks out the window and witnesses rain. She immediately erases the rain drops, grabs a wood box of Crayons, and draws a rainbow. She looks again out the window. Behold, a rainbow fills the skies.

She comprehends this is no ordinary book.

More pages. More ciphers. More questions.

Another page. She discovers a pull-out that unveils - and rebuilds itself into - a sizeable periodic-table-like empyrean matrix, but one framed with exactly 613 prismatic elements. This specific section produces an ecliptic, four-dimensional elements map. She swipes her finger on the one entitled Carbon-Phollium-7 (an element unknown to mankind).

As her finger swings through the element, a seafoam, greenish, powder-like substance mixes with the air producing a glowing spark. She does not know what to do or how to react and simply claps her hands once. In a micro-second, the shining spark zooms out the window, leaving only a floating trace of light green powder suspended in the air.

Her eyes have never been this broad before. She yells, "hot dog!"

Hanna is ecstatic and speaks cordially to *The Book*. "You *really* have to be mine!"

A few seconds later, a tiny green bird with berry blue wings, smaller than a hummingbird, lands passively on her arm. She looks at it with excitement and follows with. "Aren't you just the most beautiful creation."

She closes *The Book* and notices the arcane solitary symbol on its spine. It is the only clue she will have of its meaning, eventually. She swipes her tiny finger on top of the "nfr" and eclipsed *brevis in long* anceps symbol and notices that there is a second, faded symbol beneath it.

With wide-open eyes, she proclaims. "Quite clever! Quite beautiful! Very clever indeed, my Dear *position placeholder and dot duet*. I got you! You are Mark Zero, aren't you?"

She courts *The Book* and it looks back at her, in silence.

"Boy, wait until you meet my brother, Nelson Junior, he's gonna really like you!"

It just may be possible *The Book* may have spoken to her, but one can't scientifically confirm.

Living Room

Nelson's younger eyes notice the less than random phenomena. He shrugs his eyebrows and looks upwards, to the second floor, to his study.

The tiny, green feathered creature zooms out the house through the front door gazing over Nelson's head.

Nelson's attuned eyes passively observe in paternal silence.

Nelson's Study

Meanwhile, Hanna immediately erases the rainbow, then draws a little black-and-white baby goat, a tree swing, cerulean butterflies, and a bright ample blonde Sun.

She hears Nelson's Mandolin notes floating in the air from downstairs.

Hanna's tiny feet sneak down the stairs.

She is dressed in taffy cotton pajamas and stealthily descends the stairs from the study. She holds *The Book* and wears Nelson's Genovese wristwatch.

Living Room

The living room is filled with bright golden sunlight.

Nelson sits on his double-rocker looking outside the opened doors into the porch. He sees blue butterflies in the horizon.

He can't see Hanna, but knows she is coming down the stairs. He tweaks the mandolin's notes to mimic that of her descending footsteps. Nelson heightens the tone and alters the rhythm with each new step.

"I smell a goat. . .," Nelson cries playfully.

Hanna's cover is blown.

"Come-on, Popz, can't you at least play along?"

Hanna rushes to give him a big hug and kiss, and he turns and grabs her as if it were their last day together. They are face-to-face, eyes locked in love, only an inch separate their eyes. Time is slipping away.

The elements jolt in uninvitedly not to miss such spectacle of life – a daughter and father discussing life in the age of Enlightenment.

"How come you are so beautiful, hum?" He stalls and looks to his right. "Wait a minute there. Did you make an intermission over by my study, young lady?"

Hanna playfully. "Veeeery attentive, young man (mocking his tone). You did notice my new watch, hum? Doesn't it look just right on me? See the matching tones, hum?" They hardly match.

They laugh. She sits next to him on the double-rocker. Her tiny legs can't reach the floor. He leans towards her.

"You can have it when you're fifteen, how-bout-that? But don't tell your mom, she's on my case."

A bossy Hanna. "But, Popz, isn't that exactly the way it outta be? I mean, *I am* the only, undisputed, princess in all these woods, what would you expect?"

They laugh again. Nelson looks at Hanna with melting admiration. Nelson less playful but still warm. "I see you brought my old sketchbook with you."

Hanna speculative. "Never read this one-fella here. Found it inside your *secret* drawer." Hanna mocks the word "secret," using two pointer-fingers.

Nelson swaps his voice back to normal and reflects. "Hum, haven't seen this old companion in a while. A long while." *The Book* is noticeably dusty.

"Something wrong, Popz?"

He holds and gallantly opens *The Book*.

"Was it opened when you first saw it?"

"Yep. Wasn't me, really. Swear."

"Did you like what you saw?"

"Most of it, yes, I guess, but feels unfinished. And that scary black cat, too. I mean talk about scary. . . Can I ask you something, Dad?"

"Of course."

"Why did you leave this one unfinished? It's not like you, mister *who is the very eyes of age.*"

Nelson is careful about his answer, yet truthful.

"Hum, Princess, well, this is no ordinary sketchbook. I worked on it for so, so long, then you guys came along and, DINA, the Well, the Plains. I guess I got distracted, left to finish it some other time."

Hanna doesn't buy it. She insists. "C'mon, Popz, I'm already nine (condescending). You never leave anything unfinished. What's so special about this one?" She reflects. "I can finish it for you, you know."

"Ha! You know what: I think you'll do far better than I have. So why don't we put these two aside for now until you're fifteen, hum?"

Hanna interrupting. "Make that fourteen, mister! Times are changing. . . you know?"

While looking straight into Nelson's eyes, she slowly takes the pencil from behind his ears and puts it behind her ears. Then she extracts *The Book* from his hand and holds it for a beat before placing it back on the unbiased side table.

"Deal."

Hanna gives him another bear hug and whispers in his ears. "If God were ever to have to make a dad, I bet he'd look just like you. I love you so much my-Popz."

He holds her tightly while trying to distract her from *The Book*. "Have you ever thought of the idea that God may just be another one of us? Pretending to be like us?"

An enduring silence.

Nelson tactfully goes for *The Book*, but Hanna holds his hand and wiggles a "no" with her tiny pointer finger.

Life feels just too perfect, like a one-off dream, and he doesn't know how to deal with such abundant, overbearing plenitude.

"Look, sweetie, your mom is baking your favorite cheeseballs."

"Do you think he knows how to cry?" Hanna interruptingly.

"The Maker? I don't believe he does. Perhaps it's time someone schools him, hum?"

"Shoot! Why not?"

"Guess he never learned." Nelson agreeing.

"Hummm. Nobody ever taught the Man how to cry?! He must've had a dad, too, no? I mean, then where did the Man come from? I mean, boy, this is getting complicated; best we fetch our butterfly-boy to help figure this one out for us, hum? Nothing that kid can't square out. Right Popz?"

Nelson nods in proud agreement. They both look to the corner of the room, to a kids' butterfly net by Nelson's mandolin.

"Does he at least feel pain, like us? I mean, like me?"

"Pain. Define pain?"

"Like when your best friend dies, and you wanna pretend she didn't. And you wake up next mornin' only wanting to go back to sleep, kinda-pain."

A gentle but upset Nelson. "Hanna, Dear. That darn plague was mean, real mean to so many families. Darnet that plague! And everything that came with it!"

"Not ours. Not our family." Hanna refers to her inner family and the fact that they somehow had a genetic predisposition to combat the morbid illness.

"Look, we don't have the plague anymore, right? And that's good. Real good."

"Thanks to you and uncle-Red, Popz."

"The Red-guy mostly." Nelson needs to change subjects again. "Do you think the Man knows how to love?"

A puzzled Hanna shrugs, placing her finger on her chin. She looks up, then to the side, then back at Nelson. "Hum. May he not reckon with the meaning of love? He has to, no?! Hold that thought. Let me think about that, and I'll get back to you with my answer."

A kiss on Nelson's cheek and Hanna hops to the kitchen, followed by a black-and-white baby goat on her tail laced on a red dog leash.

The Book conversation got Nelson off balance. He stands up, placing *The Book* on the small coffee table next to his rocker. The wristwatch on top of it reads 6:13. His head looks down at it for a while.

Attached to Nelson's cowboy belt a large Bowie hunting knife, with antler handle, inside a leather holster.

Something outside the house catches Nelson's attention. He freezes, eye-brows arch, he fits a game-face. He looks out the door to the dirt road. His eyes lock on something out on the horizon. He taps his knife's holster with his right hand and unclips its shiny brass safety button with his rugged right thumb.

His boots turn towards the door. He grabs his Henry and walks outside to the front porch scanning the horizon.

Porch door slamming shut.

Nelson scouting on the porch.

The Henry being cocked loudly.

Hanna and Amanda's voices can be heard in the backdrop.

Kitchen Counter

Hanna's voice progressively entering the kitchen. "Mom, look, Popz gave me his watch."

Amanda interacting. "Reeeeally? And good morning to you, too, young lady. I see you brought a four-legged sidekick with you for breakfast." Amanda looking at the baby goat next to Hanna.

Amanda wears a period apron that reads BOSS#1. They stand by the kitchen window.

As Amanda goes by her baking routines, Hanna follows suit and mimics, in perfect detail, every single one of Amanda's moves in choreographed motion, in evolutionary mode.

"Oh, she invited herself, she's always hungry, and she loves your cheeseballs, too, Mom."

The goat by her leg. To the goat. "And whyyyy do you always have to string along?"

Hanna swiftly puts on her apron, a miniature apron identical to Amanda's, which reads BOSS#2 and is loaded with kitchen utensils.

Amanda ducks for a copper pan. Hanna ducks the same.

"She oughta; they're *the* best in all these Plains, note you."

Amanda opens the refrigerator and grabs a giant milk bottle. She closes it with the back of her right foot.

Hanna opens the same refrigerator door, grabs a small milk bottle, closing it like-wisely with the back of her right foot.

"Your fair hair looks so beautiful today. Any speeeeeecial occasion, Madam?" Mocking her.

Amanda goes for a clear sugar bowl on a top-shelf.

Hanna grabs a bench, moves it to the shelf, and stands on top of it to retrieve a milky sugar bowl from the same top shelf.

"It's your father's birthday, remember? But, you know, I wouldn't be surprised he's forgotten. That man. His mind in the clouds, always. Am baking him some. . ."

Hanna interrupts her and inquisitively direct. "Mom, what's the scoop on that book over there with Popz? Why is it so special?"

Although Amanda can't see *The Book*, she suspects what's going on. A cold chill crawls up her spine, and her eyes are wide open. Cornered, she turns to seize baked cheeseballs from the inside of the oven. "You mean the big dark creepy leather one?"

Amanda needs to buy time and starts blowing on the cheeseballs to cool them while placing the hot tray on the table.

"Yep!"

Hanna joins Amanda and blows on the same tray. Hanna keeps

a fixed eye encased on Amanda waiting for her answer. Hanna does not blink.

"*This* book, hum?" A short reply from Amanda.

"Yes. And, Mom, please tell the children the truth."

Amanda cautiously. "Jeez-honey, that unfinished manuscript, you see, it's more than special. It holds the key to *everything*, because it kind-of created *everything*." A short beat. "And how did the princess of hungry Goats-Ville find its tweedy little butter-fingers on to it?"

Hanna purposely doesn't answer the question.

At the table, Amanda shuffles cheeseballs neatly from the hot tray onto a Greek porcelain serving platter. Standing parallel to Amanda, Hanna follows suit and sets cheeseballs onto a blue-and-white smaller platter. A smiley-face cheese-ball version on Hanna's though.

The baby goat follows Hanna around. Hanna thinking with finger on her forehead. "Say you not!? Everything? As in *e-ve-ry-thing?*" A moment to breathe. "Ha! Now ain't that *some-thing* to have, ain't-there, Alfalfa?" While looking at the clueless goat and whispering. "We're gonna have to share this with our Butterfly-boy; only he can crack this one."

Hanna, mouth-filled, munching a cheeseball, to the goat. "Uhmmmm. Imagine that? All the people. All the king's horses."

Amanda less playful but loving. "Young lady, this Book is never to leave this house. And I mean *never*. Whoever holds it can change us all. Our condition can be re-written, do you understand, Hanna?"

Hanna cuts her again, then resumes brokering, "Not to worry, not to worry, gonna be our own little secret, hum? What do ya say there, Madam?"

With the tip of their fingers, they gently smear a speck of baking flower in each other's noses. Amanda in parental tone. "Young lady. . ."

Hanna kneels, opens her hand, and offers a cheeseball to the goat. The goat complies, and she whispers a tune into its ears. "I will undertake that as a *maybe-yes-will-think-about-it-but-reluctantly-concede-in-the-end.*" Hanna jabs back.

Their voices fade in the background.

. . . Nelson's flashback comes to an end.

Chapter 20

Farm House, Rocker

Present. Day.

It rains heavily.

By now, the Farm House has been stripped of any portrait. Nelson has intentionally stashed every family photograph to the bottom of an old trunk, deep inside The Barn. It is just too painful to remember.

His hair and beard are long and aged.

The coffee table is chalky and tired. Remarkably, the McIntosh doesn't light up as brightly. It, too, was built with a soul and is not immune to a father's broken heart. Nelson is shattered in minuscule pieces, held together by an act of unwilful defiance.

He has the desire to end his life. But will not.

The old wall dial-phone rings loudly. It keeps at it for a full one minute.

Nelson awakens abruptly, stands up, and knocks down his Old Gran Dad bottle. Glass shatters.

He goes for the phone, tipsy on his feet.

With a confused expression on his face, he cautiously places the headset onto his ears.

He listens in silence.

The room's overhead light dims slowly. He looks up at it, not at all surprised.

His hollow vacant eyes seek any reason but finds only drained regrets.

Conscience and inaction are all about the same thing.

This is a fight no man can win.

Lefferts Street, Amanda's Kitchen

Present. Same moment.

A sunny morning.

Chris' esteemed turquoise, General Electric portable turntable player spinning.

Amanda's two fingers placing the needle gently on top of Marley's single *Turn Your Lights On*. It echoes in the room.

Amanda sitting on top of the cedar table with phone in hand. She presses the handset close to the record player's speaker. The music flows into the handset. She offers a candid smile. A long loving one.

While looking outside the kitchen window, Amanda whispers something into the phone with the Sun reflecting on her gleaming skin. Only her mouth moves.

Back at the Farm House (same time)

A dazed Nelson with ears pressed on the phone's handset, silently listening to Marley's ballad. A long contemplating beat. He knows. It's time.

He hears Amanda's voice again. This time not a whisper but her warm, congenial voice. Her voice triggers something inside his core. He recognizes a place he misses so much - himself.

Lights slowly dim once again and a soft breeze of air blows Nelson's hair. Amanda's voice flows from the telephone's handset into his ears, straight into his heart.

Amanda's loving, caring words. "We're ready."

Those simple words will save a man from himself. And his life, a new fitting notwithstanding.

Amanda's Kitchen

Amanda in silence.

Farm House

Nelson in silence.

Amanda's Kitchen

Amanda gently hangs up and delivers an incandescent smile out the window, North, to the Plains. To her man. She turns left and sees Chris standing by the door, in patient silence, observing the entirety of the legible sequence. Chris wears a New York Jets jersey, a Kilt, and a *judo gi* slung around his shoulder wrapped in blue belt.

Little doubt – he wants to be a Fleming.

She smiles at him. He smiles back with innocent eyes.

Farm House

Nelson holding the phone handset close to his ear while looking at a photo of their inner family pulled from his back pocket. He places the handset back onto the telephone forcefully, producing a hard clank. He is upset; however, it is unclear at whom or what, or if at himself.

Distance matters nothing.

Time is an illusion.

Love is sovereign.

Chapter 21

The Plains, Train Station

Next day. Dawn. Fall.

It rains densely.

Night is falling.

Owls prowling. Wolves howling.

Nelson standing at the train station's platform, looking at his pocket watch. His Henry slung around his shoulder along with a brace of long-barrel revolvers. He holds Amanda's farewell letter, placing it inside his front shirt pocket.

Train arriving from the East.

Nelson scouts his beloved Plains one last time.

Fritz and Nelson face to face shaking hands on the station's humble platform.

"Got your note, Nelson. Had to change trains. Good to see you." A stern-faced Fritz says.

"My dear friend. How long has it been?" The men take a minute simply to look at each other - a necessary reverence.

"Does anyone know I'm coming?" Asks Nelson cautiously.

"Not sure they even know you. I mean. . ."

The men waste no time and fall into the iron beast's front car.

Front Car

Nelson inside Fritz Conductor's Car observing its standard mechanical and electrical instrumentation.

An uninvited storm approaches from the South. Dark clouds, thundering bolts, and heavy winds shake the Earth violently, unexpectedly.

A flock of ten thousand crows piercing through the skies.

Fritz quickly closes the car's two side windows. He is late in the act, and the men's hair do not escape the wind's furor.

"Heck, where the-hell did that come from?!" Fritz interjects, startled.

Nelson's reply is just a subtle negative shake of the head.

Nyman's *MGV First Region* escorts the train South.

As the train thunders forward, Nelson's face outside the car window looking at the snafu-haired Red by his truck, holding a now useless, blown-out umbrella.

Red can only produce a hopeful nod of the head. This is his beloved comrade leaving for *who knows where*. A nod is all that Nelson can expect. This bond will endure, nonetheless.

Red recons that Nelson's mission is a make or break for life's continuum. Equally, Red recognizes the possibility that Senior could finally make peace with himself, which justifies Red's tears.

Their eyes produce a close-hearted, although silent, goodbye - the type that comes with a beautiful fable of its own.

Nelson's eyes turn more determined.

From Fritz's rear mirror, the men focus on Red's frame fading on the bleak horizon.

Off goes Nelson.

It rains dead, short-horn locusts.

Fritz's Car

Nelson looks at the train's factory panel instruments, then asks. "Amanda?"

"No. She's blended in. Nelson, understand, it's been a while down there. I'm not sure you'll be able to find her. And if you do, remember, she'll be different."

Nelson cocks his Henry to check for rounds inside the chamber. He inspects the inside of the barrel with a one-eye check.

Dead migratory locusts smash the car's head window. Their smashing sound against the train resembles that of ice-rain – a hard solid pound against metal.

"She and her Yoldas put up a high-cost fight to get down there. I trust we will slip in unnoticed this time around." Fritz explains.

"I'm going to end this nonsense and get my lady back. Fix this mess. Bring my boys back home."

Nelson aims at the horizon and shoots a blank. The dry click reminds him of the smell of gunpowder. Of determination.

"For all I know, you've been able to keep this gate safe. You've done well."

A tube panel-bulb pops. Fritz shakes his head sideways, disappointedly.

A short beat. "They have a master key."

"So be it! They don't have you! And they don't have my *Book*. I will leave the Plains for you, Red and the Sentinels to steward. Understood, old friend?"

"I figured. I'm just glad you're here. Back. Look, Nelson, the City is madness. Out-of-control. New grounds."

Nelson acknowledges with a light, indifferent nod.

Fritz resumes. "Once you get to mark zero, reach the Lost & Found and ask for *knuckles*. Anything else, and you'll be exposed."

"Got it."

Fritz shifts his voice to speak on the radio. "8-17 to Tower-A, over."

"Go ahead 8-17." Tower-A back at him.

"We are clear for ETA, over."

Their journey into the city is surprisingly uneventful, thanks to Fritz exclusively.

Fritz turns on the radio: CBS RADIO ON; while train enters New York City - in darkness.

White River Margins, The Last Passage Sentinels

White River Bridge crossing.

Nelson's Sentinels in full black rice bags over their heads, white roses on their jackets, lined-up with their long muskets raised upwards, saluting the train.

Exactly thirteen on each side of the tracks.

They bow, then aim and shoot their long rifles toward the air producing green powder smoke.

Nelson on top of the conductor's car. Wind blasting against his face.

Nelson places his hand on his hart and bows back at his warriors.

The men observe in silence.

In reciprocity, Fritz actions the train's steam whistle.

The July, 1977 BLACKOUT erupts

Moments later.

Train. They listen attentively to the radio station.

CBS RADIO HOURLY NEWS transmitted on the cabin's speaker-box.

Fritz dials the volume knob up a notch.

George Washington Bridge

Night. Hot.

The bridge's exterior lights cascading off in a domino effect.

The Manhattan side of the Hudson River is pitch black.

The New Jersey side of the Hudson River (mostly Fort Lee) is still lit.

Midtown

The Empire State Building's lights cascading off in a domino effect, floor by floor.

Financial District

The Twin Tower's lights cascading off in a domino effect, floor by floor.

Harlem Station, 125th Street

Fritz's train approaching a dark New York from the North.

A far from ordinary starless night.

A demure, crepuscular, industrious New York welcomes the pair.

The city in laden blackout darkness.

Fritz's less romantic train slowing to a halt, docking on Harlem's elevated station.

The cabin's radio frenziedly keeps at it, narrating in kosher detail the blackout conditions.

The men look outside through the front car's side windows. Scenes of people under the blackout biome.

Two gunshots. Glass shattering.

Emergency sirens wailing.

A three-story brownstone burning down at the corner of 124th and Lexington Avenue.

Fire trucks racing uptown. Ambulances rushing downtown.

City residents scrambling - some for cover, others for thrill, and a dedicated bunch for mercantile scores.

Red opens his hidden cabinet door and exposes his prized gun collection.

"Whatever you need." He declares with proud eyes.

Nelson's eyes scan the cabinet in detail. His hand goes for a tin USMC field water canteen.

"This and my Henry are all I need." Nelson explains.

At core, Nelson is still Nelson.

Fritz produces a contented, relieved smile.

An oversized tomato splashes onto the car's front window – its sangria sauce streams down the window.

Welcome to New York City, 1977.

Chapter 22

Grand Central Terminal, Track 37

Fritz's late arrival at Grand Central Terminal.

His assigned train couldn't look more narcoleptic, overworked, and exhausted. But he got them through, unharmed nonetheless, and Nelson is safe, in one piece - a half-true statement, as one can't assume the same for his emotions.

A last, ample shake of hands between the revered compadres at the platform.

"Look after there our old route, will-ya?" Nelson pleads.

"Nelson, don't forget, you'll be out of your element here - just another man. You understand you can't change things here? So, gloves off. And I mean it!"

Nelson gives Fritz a firm jab on the shoulder, then walks out of Platform 37 into Grand Central Terminal. He halts for a beat and turns back at his brother in arms, shouting candidly. "But I *am* just another man!" A beat, he turns, then to himself, "Fool! E*very* man has to die."

Our protagonist stands firmly in front of Grand Central's central timekeeper, who informs us it is "9:13 PM."

Somehow, Grand Central does not feel alien to him.

He stops for an instance and looks up, his eyes run Grand Central's ceiling frescos. The stars glow harder. The Gods nod. It's been some time. They welcome the man.

Different Suns.
Different Worlds.
Only one Nelson.

Grand Central's Lost & Found Department

Minutes later.

Dim, shivering light. Grey tones.

Lamps.

Garbled emergency radio transmissions.

Flashlights.

The smell of kerosine.

Stranded New Yorkers looking lost scattered around Grand Central's golden clock.

Nelson walks towards the Lost & Found Department.

The "Lost & Found" carved into Grand Central's marble wall.

He approaches cautiously and leans into the department counter to speak to the busy-looking MTA employee, aka Leprechaun.

"Excuse me, looking for *a* knuckles." Nelson inquires.

"What-man? Ohhh, you mean you're looking for..." Leprechaun is hastily interrupted mid-sentence.

Knuckles in loud, heavy, unmistakable Brooklyn accent. "Yooow! Who calls my name!?"

Come to meet Knuckles, an imposing, a true Brooklyn native. She emerges from behind the back of the *Lost & Found* file cabinets, holding a large-size Cracker Jack box - her right hand entirely inside it. She wears traditional pinstriped MTA uniform and black-rimmed glasses. Street thugs think twice before jumping this character.

One does not mess with Knuckles. Period.

The stocky, red-haired Leprechaun, excusing himself, points at Nelson as if *not my problem*.

Nelson is taken aback as he follows this impressive personage approach the counter from the inside of the *Lost & Found* cabinets.

She holds, turns her head towards Leprechaun, takes a deep breath, fixes her glasses, and nods condescendingly at him with a shrug of eyebrows. He looks down to his shirt, to his unleveled MTA name badge. His eyes are a proxy of embarrassment.

"Leprechaun!" She yells commandingly.

He acknowledges the reprimand and immediately levels the badge straight.

Knuckles to Nelson. "Yow man, I'm Knuckles. What've you lost?"

She offers Nelson her Cracker Jack box with reluctant body language. Nelson nods a "no" with his hand.

Knuckles munching Cracker Jacks waiting for Nelson's answer.

"I am. . ." Nelson attempts to tell his name.

Knuckles' inquisitive eyes scan Nelson from head to toe. "Yeah-yeah, the old-Fritz, yes, he told me you're comin, but he didn't say when. And you definitely picked the wrong day, pal. Blackout! It's a bag of dicks out there. We are really lucky we got the old D-2 generator running. Man, shit is so bad out there, even wise-guys are tucked-in eating their mama's meatballs."

"Wouldn't be my first." Nelson trying to engage.

"Your first what?! Meatballs?"

She looks side-ways to make sure no one is listening then grabs a small, green top-bound spiral note-pad from inside her shirt's front pocket, and back at Nelson. Less loudly. "Listen, man, we'll simply have to figure it out. You can bunk here for now until I get you better shade. This is neutral ground; nothing can happen to you here, you hear?" She looks to the side. "And you just might like it."

She blinks at him.

A random, well-dressed commuter arrives looking for a lost personal item. Knuckles takes no prisoners and shouts at the commuter. "YOW, man, can't you see I'm in a conference call here?! Jeeesus! Come back in ten minutes, OK, man." The commuter scrams. Probably forever.

Nelson and Knuckles walk together to the back of the *Lost & Found*. It's a huge labyrinth, a universe of miscellaneous eclectic objects. It feels like falling straight into *Alice's* kaleidoscopic crawl space.

A Long Corridor

The couple is welcomed inside the corridor by H.G. Welles' loud vinyl reproduction of the 1938 infamous *War of The Worlds* radio broadcast on the loudspeakers.

They walk through the long corridor covered with theatrical posters of *The Godfather, Coffy, The Exorcist, American Graffiti, Mean Streets, Enter the Drago, Friday Foster, JAWS, Dog Day Afternoon* and *Taxi Driver*. Nelson's eyes grab each poster with amusement.

"Listen, I appreciate what you're doing for me." Nelson says.

In steady voice, she articulates. *"No-problemo*, My-man Fritz told me you're kinda something-special. I owe him big. He saved my dog *The-Deuce* from castration, you know. Poor bastard; suffered like hell. The Penicillin regime only made him hornier. But, shit, the little stinker is now banging anything with legs and a pulse. The nasty puppy thinks he's a tiger! That's what this city will do to you!"

Lost & Found, Deposit Warehouse

As they walk through the *Lost & Found* warehouse, Knuckles places her Cracker Jack box under an office cabinet. She pulls her green notepad from her front pocket and a pink pencil from her left ear. She licks the tip of the pencil, then back at him telegraphically bossy. "You gonna give me trouble, man?"

"No Ma'am."

"You into speed, blow, or booze? Ain't no quarter for any of that shit here, got that? Lights out at ten. No *hanky-pankying* with the women neither. And keep your pickle inside your pants. Your pants, you hear?!"

She makes a quick note on her notepad, keeping hawk-eyes on Nelson.

She hands him a blue key to the *Lost & Found*.

"You smoke?" She asks in a whim.

Nelson figures he has the correct answer this time. "No!" He says.

"C'mon, man! Are you sure?" She points to a smiling Ronald Regan *Chesterfield* smoking poster advertisement.

Nelson nods confidently.

"Too bad! You should! It's good for you; it calms the nerves, you see."

Nelson can't compete.

She makes a second quick note on her notepad while looking at Nelson.

As they walk deeper inside the gigantic warehouse, they stumble onto a light green Philco Predicta tube TV adjacent to a small anteroom.

The Anteroom

"Call this home, cowboy!" She shouts proudly.

They come to a confined space divided by an antique Egyptian room-divider greeted by a common man's walnut bed. Plain white cotton sheets, a side table with one simple, clear glass, a Bible, a copper lamp, and a Baroque water jar. This diminutive portion is minimalist and warm.

Welles' dire radio transmission is cut off abruptly by a screeching of the LP.

They notice a dash of legs moving through files. They can only see its shade.

An aged Cello timbers to the ground on the opposing corridor. The Cello produces a disturbing inflection sound. The "shade" vanishes in opposite direction.

Knuckles yells at the shade. "Yow, Bad-Card, not the Stratovarius! Not the Strat, man!" Then at Nelson. "Bonehead playing with fire!

He's real lucky it wasn't my Les Paul. Real lucky!" She shows Nelson her knuckles.

Two seconds later, our ominous "shade" indemnifies his audience, engulfing the sepulcher with Dvořák's transcendent *B minor, Op. 104 – II*. Adagio, cello solo.

Knuckles holds a beat to admire the grandiose eulogy. "Boy, this guy really knows my soft spots."

Nelson's perplexed, but content, eyes agree with her.

Another question from Knuckles. "Are you sure man we haven't met before? I mean, don't take me the wrong way, and sometimes I am not myself after a beer or two, or a whole pack, you know, but. . . but you look remarkably. . . familiar." A pause from her. She nods. She inspects him from head to toe, now more suspiciously. "I'm sure, am sure we met, man. . ."

Nelson shakes his head very delicately not to ignite unwarranted wrath from his hostess.

They resume their tour of the warehouse.

Shimmering amber lights escort the pair.

They finally come to a halt.

A small, modest room.

A long red-pine framed mirror next to a simple bed. Nelson walks towards it, then pulls it to the side as if he knew this particular space, this specific mirror.

A baroque crucifix hangs, hidden, behind the mirror.

Knuckles' eyes pop in awe.

Nelson's eyes slowly grip the crucifix. He stares at it with visible disdain, while shaking his head gently. Knuckles notices his apparent disapproval and inquires briskly.

"You a churchman, mister?!"

A lie from Nelson would work just fine. "Well. . . I. . ." Nelson visibly vacillating.

Knuckles interrupting. "That's a yes-or-no answer, hombre. Go!"

She turns a page with voluntary force and makes a third scribble on the notepad while eyes locked on Nelson. With her head downwards she looks upwards at him. It is evident she doesn't think Nelson is doing well. Nor does he.

"I was. I was a man of faith, so to speak." Nelson tries to explain.

"*Sort-of-speak*! You-messing with me, right?" A disappointed Knuckles.

She makes another quick emphatic note on the notepad.

"Gimme-time." Nelson says.

"Time!? That's it! You're coming to church with me to meet the reverend. If there is anything we need in this dump-of-a-city, that is faith. You hear? Faith!" She is not finished. "Some advice. You-know, man, there is only one game in town. One game!"

Nelson waits for it.

"It's called SURVIVIN'! Yep, the game is called survivin', and you better get your shinny heinie up to speed, pronto. Chop-chop! You need God by you! With you. We all do." A pause from her, for air. "I'm gonna have a talk with m'man Fritz about you, you'll see. . . just you wait."

A cornered, and battered, Nelson pulls a small brown paper wrap from his front pocket and hands it to her. She reacts surprised.

"Here." He offers it feebly.

Now calm, she slowly grabs and unwraps the paper wrap.

The sound of a Celtic flute in the air.

Inside the small, clear Murano jar, a batch of magical saffron. Its red and golden thin stalk glow on its own as if it were alive. This is no ordinary saffron, and she knows it. We speak of a mystical, extremely sought-after, saffron strain. The red and golden tones reflect onto her face, inside her eyes, reaching her soul.

"It's from Belt-Bay Valley, back home." He adds.

Knuckles, thankfully gentle, with eyes wide-open. "Belt-Bay!? Get-out-of-here! And how did you know I like. . .? Never got your name, man."

She makes a last note on her notepad. This time, she smiles positively back at Nelson and gives him a discrete wink. She the places the jar inside, in between her breasts.

"I'm. . ." Nelson tries again at mouthing, pronouncing, his name.

Knuckles interrupting loudly. "Marlboro! Marlboro it is. Let me know of whatever you need, you hear? Will have an accomplice of mine get you a 9-to-5. His name is Bad-Card. The guy is from Mars but knows the city's guts inside-and-out. He'll be lurking around the files; don't be scared."

"I'll stay low and give you no aggravation." Nelson replies.

"One last piece of advice," Knuckles advises.

"Yes?"

"Watch your back out there, Marlboro. This here is Fear City, *capici*?! It'll rip your shinny Belt-Bay golden cowboy-balls off if you let it. So, don't. You hear!?"

A beat.

Nelson looks down at his balls. "I'll look to that, Ma'am."

Knuckles turns left and walks back to the *Lost & Found's* front desk, yelling something at her run-man Leprechaun, who suits a goose-like look.

Deep Inside the Lost & Found Warehouse

Nelson returns to the inside of the *Lost & Found* warehouse. He cross-examines the perpetual myriad of insolvent items as he strolls through its vast outcasted files.

This is without question another dimension - an in-between world of sorts.

Nelson, fixated, looking at himself in a small Andalusian mirror.

Stacks of post-war comic books, a spooky Hungarian doll, a circus clown costume, a prosthetic leg, hundreds of metal lunchboxes, an eerie armless one-eyed manakin, ornamental festival hats, a stuffed black Jaguar, boxes of overflowing leather garments, LPs, fur coats, a brass tuba, a magician's velvet whip, an old McIntosh M78 Tuner, a Santa Cruz wrestler's cape, a 1958 green Philco Predica, a STAR WARS poster, and an infinite number of Pisa-angled ten-foot book towers.

He turns the tuner's knob on, and the radio's abating blue and orange bulbs courteously light the room. Nelson listens silently to AM radio *Musicradio 77 WABC's* frantic narration of the ongoing blackout.

Nelson stumbles upon a shunned crate of *Little Rascals* Super-8 films and a Noris-8 Synchrometer projector just under a sizeable Polish teddy bear.

He carries a few reel boxes with him along with the projector to the warehouse's far edge.

He takes his time in the stroll, speculating on every lost item. It is necessary.

Monolithic Mirror

By the warehouse's far corner, a small space completely empty with only one solitary, monolithic, upheaving mirror suspended in the ether. Nelson fluently walks to it with no strange feeling. He strolls around it, stopping in front of it to register his reflection. There is none. The omnipresent Senior can't see himself through it. Indeed, he is lost.

But it makes no difference.

He walks back to the anteroom, through the long corridor, placing the projector on the floor, on top of a dark Caspian, azure rug.

Lights go off ephemerally, then come back on at half strength. He looks up to the warm light as if he could fix the issue.

Meanwhile, the Noris-8 holds its end of the trade and projects a silent *Little Rascals* B&W episode.

Our shade-runner, Sean, stands immediately behind Nelson - interrupting his inertia with a shy. "The episode where Alfalfa sings, *I am in the Mood for Love* is my favorite. It's the third one from top to bottom." Sean's face is lit with balmy tangerine flickering light.

Sean wears blue lipstick and munches an over-sized pretzel. His pet Leica IIIc strapped around his neck. Our pretzel-eating, pigeon-hating, pale-faced character proceeds to awkwardly pull that specific *red* film reel from Nelson's hand. Note Sean is color-blind.

"Here; this *blue* one. Oh, I'm Sean. Knuckles calls me Bad-Card." With a roll of eyes.

Sean's voice is muted, and Nelson focusses on Sean's silent mumbling.

Nelson staring at him, impressed with his uncharacteristically abnormal monotone complexion.

"Thanks. Have we met before? You look quite; you look remarkably familiar." Nelson remarks.

"I *ghiet* that a lot, you know."

Sean adjusting the Noris-8 while rattling. "Where're you from?"

Sean offers Nelson his pretzel. Nelson replies by nodding *no*, putting his hand on his heart.

"That's swell then. I don't have too many friends, I guess. Winnie and, well. . . But I like people. I like people a lot, really. The Cracker Jack lady told me you need a job that's low-profile and plugged in. Correct?"

Nelson nods.

Sean turns the Noris-8 tape sound on, and they hear Alfalfa and Darlene talking to each other.

By the Wall

Nelson journeying towards the wall, against the projector's light, producing a shadow mixed with that of the 8mm projected images. The Norris' mechanical tap-dancing joins Alfalfa-Darlene's dialogue.

"Yessir. I'm looking for someone," Nelson says, while placing his hand on the wall and caressing Alfalfa's and Darlene's superimposed image as if he could journey back in time or somehow join them.

Alfalfa's projected face superimposed onto Nelson's stone face.

A quick Black and White micro-flashback of a nine-year-old boy with similar "Alfalfa" complexion wearing an age-old butterfly catcher vestment, and corresponding gear, flashes on the screen.

Senior holds his hand there, on the wall, for a long beat, reflecting on another moment in time. Over another Nelson. Over another life. Over what he lost.

The Noris-8's staple chronometric mechanical sound provides the air with the much-needed density.

The inculpable Sean has no clue over this arch and speaks innocuously. "Yep! Me, too. Me, too. Yes, looking for someone. Someone, yes. Well, I can introduce you to folks at the Morgue. They've published three of my photos this year. That is, so far."

A long beat.

Nelson's eyes fixed at the wall.

One loud gunshot echoes inside the *Lost & Found* interrupting the men.

"The Morgue?" Nelson leery, inquisitively suspicious.

A female's frightened scream.

A second commuter screams a hair raising "HEEELP."

Another loud shotgun-type blast travels more violently - this one is closer.

Rushing footsteps sound.

"We need light! We need to do something about this light situation. Take me to the city's main power substation?" Nelson commands.

"*I-AM-SORRY*? Whoowhat?!" Sean interjects.

"Where the energy is distributed." Nelson explains.

Sean thinks for a short second. "Out-side!? Are you high on junk cowboy-man? Do you know what hell looks like? If you don't, you will! And what can you do anyway?"

"Do you have wheels?" Nelson asks.

Chapter 23

New York, 1977 Blackout

The city is boiling hot.

This is a societal pressure-cooker ready to be set ablaze. And it will. It finds its stage in the heart of darkness - in the summer of 1977. It only needs a trigger - and it comes in the form of a full-blown Dantesque blackout.

Fire Hydrants

There are three types. The ones used by firefighters to combat arson. The ones used by New Yorkers to cool the city down. And the decommissioned, waterless broken ones.

During this specific hellish evening, "community hydrants" provide a spectacle like no other – aimed upwards, they produce a fountain-like atmosphere. In some instances, lunar rainbows are witnessed.

The wet streets also produce an unusual phenomenon – a refraction on the black tarp. Streets resemble urban mirrors. Faceless images of urban contradictions.

Chrysler Building

Wrapped in blood, Cole on top of a steel gargoyle eagle. His Oxford's on, he sits quietly, yoga-style simply observing the city burn under him.

The eagle's eyes cry blood.

His view is of a New York under fire.

Zhain's Limo

CBS radio-cast voice describing blackout conditions.

Zhain inside his black limo, looking out the window, peacefully delighting a red lollypop while strolling down the blackout streets. "Where is your bearded guy now, hum!? Burn baby. Burn."

Zhain's vision is distorted by his Dantean desires. He can only see a New York burning in inferno flames.

Ash rain blankets the limo.

Brooklyn, Amanda's Outside Garden

Amanda, Beth, Claire, Chris, Winnie, Fatima, Janis and seven other borough friends calmly dine under the pergola table. The table is lit by dozens of candle lights and copper lamps.

Amanda's Kitchen

May sits on top of an opened window scouting the ravaged streets.

From the kitchen's wide-opened window, they hear musicians playing on the front steps: a mandolin, a guitar, and a kamancheh produces Far Eastern folk ballads.

Upper West Side, Broadway Avenue

Nelson and Sean wearing yellow night goggles, heading north, on Sean's lime green Vespa, towards Yonkers' West Substation along New York's dark and littered streets.

They are wet from hydrant fountains.

There are absolutely no street signal-lights working – every motorized machine has free discretion. Probably the farthest, lasting sign of civility.

The city is lawless.

Unruly.

Anarchical.

Nelson's views are those of the once-mighty metropolis under Cimmerian Shades.

Sean's views come exclusively through his portable Super-8 lens as he documents the events unfolding on his way uptown to Yonkers through 9A.

The Super-8 at work.

Sean's Super-8 frames become a collection of successive events that follow:

Bushwick

Firefighters rushing inside burning Bushwick buildings.

Residents exiting the structure with personal belongings, many of which were already "waiting" outside.

Masses burst out of a ravaged Saul's Paradise supermarket, driving carts full of canned food, cereal, and shoe boxes.

Next door, a jewelry shop guarded by a few men with baseball clubs and a shotgun.

Seven theatrical posters of *Close Encounters of the Third Kind.*

Loud shotgun blasts pierce the night.

A scent of shattering glass in the air.

Shelterless, deranged, salvation-style, carnival barkers.

More screaming sirens.

South Bronx, 41st Street Precinct, Fort Apache

A chaotically crowded lobby.

There is more cursing than air filling these walls.

A group of half-naked orgiastic Khlysts shackled to each other by handcuffs and chains softly murmuring "redemption. . . redemption. . . ah. . . ah. . . redemption. . . ah. . ."

Cops handling arrested vandals and regular Joes.

Hammer inside the police precinct, commanding a handful of cops punching in from off-duty. One wears a Led Zeppelin T-shirt and baseball pants. Another, a tight Islanders shirt, his belly sticks out.

By the hall entrance, a lanky police officer with a bloody head and ripped uniform helps a senior woman in shock. Her eyes are flooded with apathy, stillness, but mostly fear.

The Bronx

Scorching, rotting brownstones smelling unsanitary.

A men's tailor shop being ravaged, while the senior store owner pleading with patrons to spare his lifetime's work.

Kids playing obliviously happy under gushing hydrants.

Three bus surfers ride on the back of an uptown city bus.

Young artists on the sidewalks of an Italian cantina under candle lights, drinking and smiling. A couple kisses effusively.

Two corpulent women savagely fight over a stolen white fur coat. A little kimono-girl innocently passes between them.

Fire trucks, ambulances, and police cars sprint the city. In all directions.

Teenagers dressed in stolen clothing, price tags still on. Note the sizes don't match - either too big or too small.

Brownstone residents launching bricks and bags of fresh urine down at the Police.

The Bronx, The Hub

The outnumbered police are overrun by a mob of people carrying sofas, TV sets, an Indian cigar statue, a heavy cabinet, a Moose head, and a belt-massager.

A female EMT bandages a woman's foot for deep glass wounds.

Firefighters rushing inside burning Bushwick buildings. Simultaneously, residents exiting with their belongings. Large belongings like fine furniture and TV sets had already been "placed" on the curbside, prior to the fire itself – such hindsight.

Bronx Opera House

Behind a dark alley three street patrons sing ". . . yooo-sa-sa-sa, hit'em in the head with a big-ass kielbasa. . ."

Local patrons of every age, creed, and color bursting out of mom-and-pop mini-markets with carts of anything they can get their hands on. Not surprising, every cart carries loads of cigarette packs inside.

A local jewelry shop guarded by a few men with clubs, flashlights, and rusted revolvers.

Bushwick

Infernal Bushwick.

Sirens wailing.

Francis and Johnny, in full firefighter's turnout gear, battle a set of brownstone fires.

Chief Francis commands the intervention.

The brownstones are engulfed.

Garbled emergency radio transmissions.

A fraternal gathering of local gang youth sitting on a previously extracted long couch listening to Huey's "Hard Times" flowing outbound from a jumbo AIWA TPR boombox, with a $19.99 yellow sale tag still wrapped on it. The front-seat spectacle, less the extra-large popcorn bowl, is priceless. Such plasticity.

Bearing a respectable mustache, Johnny is first inside the smoking building.

One of the gang kids yells at him in generational solidarity. "Don't bother, m'man!"

Johnny and three fellow firefighters are rushed by residents fleeing outwards into the streets. These residents could very well have hit the church - that is how well-groomed they are.

Johnny and firefighters charge attack mode - hose-packs on shoulders, six-foot spikes, and Halligan tools in hands.

Sidewalk

Hours later, blazes controlled - a dozen exhausted firefighters sitting on the sidewalk turf, re-hydrating, gazing at the end of the world.

On the far corner of the same street, half-a-dozen pre-teenagers dressed up in stolen clothing, price-tags still on.

On the other end of the same street, next to a borough butcher delicatessen named Al's Meat Dream, a tug-of-war between a titanic German Shepard and a frail senior Bushwick resident - they battle for a massive full-skinned butcher's cow leg. The canine has the upper hand. Not a surprise, as the luxurious Italian dish *osso buco* is a big deal in Bushwick.

Huey's "Hard Times" commands this block.

Speak of gentrification no more.

Just urban decay. Solo.

Yonkers Power Station

Yonkers Power Station's main gate.
Dark, silent, empty corridors.

Nelson inside with a kid's chrome flashlight looking for the substation's main panel.

Nelson behind the station's main panel working wires and valves.

Nelson handling a GE converter panel.

An intense generator build-up sound.

Some warm yellowish lights turn back on.

Nelson running back towards the main gate, towards Sean, who waits for him like a bank-robbing getaway driver.

Park Avenue, Southbound

Both men ride the Vespa back to Grand Central Terminal.

Sean holds a garbage-can lid as a makeshift shield.

49th Street, Grand Central Terminal

M42 Basement.

Sean and Nelson arrive via a secret access into Grand Central – through the 49th Street, Waldorf Astoria B-7, under Peacock Alley - a Metro North inbound emergency access called Track-12–11. Very few have knowledge of this entrance.

Sean guides Nelson to his hiding place. In truth, his living quarters.

"Nelson, you cannot tell anyone." Sean pleads.

"Of course." Nelson replies firmly.

They come to an underground access to the M42 basement - Substation 1T and 1L.

Grand Central Terminal, M42 Basement Power Plant

A gigantic power plant substation buried under the heart of New York City.

Nelson immediately takes to working on its massive General Electric Cooper Power Panel, changing valves, and cracking leavers.

Sean by his side as his designated First Assistant.

After a full hour's work, Nelson brings light into M42 and, simultaneously, to a good part of the city and the outer train system.

Nelson is covered in oil and grease but looks rather satisfied.

Sean strolls in with a huge smile and a six-pack of Rheingold beer cans he collected from the inside of a turquoise Westinghouse gas refrigerator stashed just behind one of the electrical panels.

Sitting down on the floor with their legs stretched forward, they drink and smile at each other.

Such is life.

New York's infamous 1977 Blackout comes to an end, and what is left of the city tries a rebirth.

Chapter 24

New York Post Blackout
A wrecked New York City.

Zhain's Condo, Alwyn Court, 58th Street

Next Day. Early morning.

Zhain's Study

Zhain sitting comfortably, with legs crossed, on a voluminous leather couch, having breakfast and reading *The Times*. His eyes reveal his pleasure with the blackout-related news.

He holds a simmering Ottoman copper pot and pours freshly made coffee into a light-green enamel mug. He delights in it.

Behind him, a gigantic, wall-to-wall Franz von Stuck's *Sisyphus* (in the realm of Hades) painting alludes to the absurdity of existence.

Zhain gazes at the art piece in contemplation, releasing a satirical. "And don't you dare let go of that boulder, my disrobed Sisyphus." He laughs.

Queens, Above-Ground F Train

Nelson and Sean ride the F train inbound in silence. Nelson carries a red Wilson T-3000 tennis bag slung around his shoulder. His Henry inside.

219 West 40th Street, *New York Times* Archival Library - *"The Morgue "*

Below ground.

A windowless dungeon of our lives.

Sean and Nelson at *The Times'* Archival Library – aka *The Morgue*.

Nelson is welcomed by Mr. Simpson, along with chief clip filer Mrs. Brownstein and a half-a-dozen photo archive specialists.

Nelson shakes hands with Morgue employees, walking to his assigned work desk. They welcome him with warm hearts.

The new hire is visibly impressed with what he sees and has difficulty hiding his satisfaction. Serendipity.

The City's soul is documented and captured by hand, with passion. A time machine of sorts. Invaluable for his mission. It is here, also, that Nelson invests his time to reassess his understanding of the human condition. It's a center for data collection. More importantly, a center for data reflection. It fits his state of mind.

A forum to challenge existence. At least, the one presented to him.

Nelson lumbers through The Morgue's endless maze of scratched, green metal files squared in the old-school Dewey Decimal system.

It feels like every ashtray must have a lit cigarette, regardless of if there is a soul in the room or not.

Contact sheets, rag editions, obituaries, microfilms, cameras, empty paper coffee cups, typewriters, ashtrays, magazines, journals, books, and gobs of rolls of paper - scattered everywhere space available. It smells like tobacco, coffee, aged newspaper and the distinctive metallic-like odor blend of film developer agents.

A B&W Sara Krulwich street photo next to an empty Cracker Jack box and crumbled peanuts shells.

A curious Nelson flips a photo catalogue and sees a negative of Boston Marathon official Semple and runner Switzer fraternizing.

A young female intern, from East Vermont, turns the front-facing German Red ELAC Flip Clock Radio on. She dials a news station, and the room is given commentators reporting on the blackout's aftermath.

Nelson feels comfortable here; after all, he stands to have access to a vast repository of newspaper clippings and photographs beyond any other in the City. Beyond anything, anywhere. But more importantly, this is his best shot at pinning-down Amanda.

He purposely takes on the tranquil night shift.

The Firm

Zhain's Office. Day.

Zhain, Feist, Essex, and Tracker discuss an important, though non-official matter. The men leave while Zhain heads to the Boardroom, strolling through a long corridor reaching the dedicated Boardroom's bathroom hall.

Zhain does not look happy.

Bathroom Hall

This is no ordinary space; we stand on an exuberant pre-art *deco* masterpiece.

Otherwise, an unassuming space, a standard plush bathroom hall with both "WOMEN" and "MEN" bathroom metal signs. As an act of deliberate sarcasm, there are no actual women board directors elected at The Firm. There never was. Nothing but another dark mockery from the creative mind of the Greenwich Hills polo Captain, the distinguished Chairman of the Audit Committee, Mr. Eugene Grace.

Initially, Zhain thought nothing of it. But instinctively saw opportunity in the act. If not to provoke Alexandra, a memento to keep her hungry, sharp, awake. He went along with the chauvinist prank. Anything to keep Alexandra hungry, ahead.

Zhain stands eye to eye, facing the Nineteenth-Century, sycamore, wooden *Mephistopheles and Margaretta* double-sculpture placed between the bathroom doors - purposely in concierge capacity.

An ornate Renaissance mirror juxtaposed behind the double-sculpture allows both sides to be viewed synchronously - the assigned middleman *Memphisto* on one side, and the repentant *Gretchen* on the other.

Zhain hangs his wool jacket on the creature's ear, then to the saluting sculpture. "Everybody has a part to play, even you, Mr. Faust. And don't get confused - you stand on marbles of The House of Accumulation; not some Marxist *bäckerei; verstehst du?* And we emphatically, unceremoniously, disallow any thoughts of self-pity here. Don't you dare. . ."

Halfway into the restroom, Zhain back-pedals for one last re-mark, looking straight into *Memphisto's* muted eyes. He is not fin-ished. "And if you give me that condescending eye again, I will summon Hume's *modus tollens* to solve this problem. How's that, hum? And probably move your derrière to a lesser fortunate hall." He stares at the still statue, then back at it, nodding in agree-ment - in British accent. "Yes, *extraordinary*, I thought so too. . ."

Hall, Women's Bathroom

Zhain enters the "WOMEN'S" (Board) bathroom sliding straight to the counter's wide mirror, chanting *"reductio ad absur-dum, reductio ad absurdum. . . un roi, un loi. . . un Zhain!"*

He stops in front of it.

For reference, this bathroom serves as his de-facto private rest-room and in some instances, a hide-out from the tedious crowd of board directors - the *little-people* as he would, at times, refer to them.

He looks at himself for a beat in the mirror. Left side. Then right.

Red lollypops inside a crystal bowl next to a reisenecessaire against the mirror.

Zhain grabs one lollypop. He looks right, to his left, under the partition box, and then grabs two more lollypops tucking them inside his trousers' pocket pink-pantherishly.

A last lookout with raised eyebrows to reconfirm he is in the clear.

In his late sixties, a cotton-haired bathroom butler, Mr. Thomas, dressed impeccably in whole 20s white outfit and formally stiff, greets our bathroom guest with a light Southern accent.

"Good morning, Sir. All Board Directors are accounted for and waiting for you."

Zhain clasping his hands behind his back, speaking to Thomas with some level of intimacy.

"Thank you, Thomas. And how is the wife?"

Thomas opens a sunflower smile while brushing off Zhain's shoulder with a 20s silver brush.

Zhain looks into the mirror while adjusting his tie.

"Oh-mister-Zhain, she loves her new job. We couldn't thank you enough, Sir."

"Splendid, Thomas, absolutely splendid to hear!"

Zhain is gripped with looking to (into) himself through the mirror while conversing with the bathroom custodian.

"What do you see?"

"Sir?"

"What do you see? In the mirror, Thomas? Look deep."

"I see a champ, Sir!"

"No, Thomas, look carefully. Look deeper. What do you SEE?"

The lights go off and come back on in less than a second.

A confused Thomas zooms his eyes closer into the mirror. A subtle grey wolf shade mixed and blurred with that of Zhain appears subtly on the mirror.

"It's all illusion, Thomas. Illusion."

A French Horn D-Flat.

A monotone beat.

"I can't understand why I can't be loved, Thomas."

"Why-Sir. . .?"

A soft predator's growl.

Zhain still looking deep into the mirror. His silhouette mixed with that of the wolf.

"And this deplorable establishment - with all their predictable pristine dentures, Greenwich colonials, and distasteful ski dens - looking to me; to my pockets, to crumbs, with the corner of their simple eyes, whispering: *What kind of name is that of Zhain anyways? Is it even Christian? European, I'd expect?*" asked me, the distinctly inclusive Chairman of the New York Athletic Club the other day. "*Yes,* I replied, *in fact, my name precedes Christianity,* I countered. He jabbed back with a polished, "*ohh Dear, now that figures, doesn't it? But, look, let us move on with our more pressing matters and, of course, your sincere generosity towards our new racket annex, shall we?*" Zhain borrows a moment, then back at the stoic Thomas.

"And the people, Thomas, the commoner, they don't comprehend my vision for a fair, balanced, and wealthy society. And *The Post*, those jackasses, rattling my garbage daily, trying to pin dirt on me - *The king of LBOs* they call me as if taking risk for the betterment of our economic system, and to correct market inefficiencies, is a sin. Where are we heading to, Thomas? What is the meaning of all of this? And these emotions?"

A beyond puzzled-looking Thomas patiently listening.

Zhain isn't finished. "And money. The curse of it. Our aristocrats and dreamers distracted by it. It consumes them. Everyone wants to make it rich here." He shakes his head in contempt. "Money is a false mirror. Never enough. Never too little. Then, on a cold Friday night, just before hitting the Jitney to the Hamptons, your family physician calls you to let you know the results of your latest check-up. And your Rolex starts running fast. Real fast. You are dead, buried under greed and pride." Zhain's eyes looking deep inside the red lollypop. "Pride trumps it all. You wouldn't believe, Thomas, what I've seen a man do for it."

Zhain spares a long, soul-searching beat looking deep into the mirror with his hand touching his face in a melancholic tone. "I can't see myself anymore."

He turns and walks away towards the Boardroom back door. He then halts. Looks back at Thomas. He zooms into the mirror one last time and professionally succinct.

"Thomas?"

"Yes-Sir!?"

"Please replace this mirror." Zhain commanding.

"Certainly, Sir!"

Zhain is off, lollypop in hand, out the wood-carved back door, and into the far-reaching sumptuous Boardroom.

A fast succession of events at the Firm...

The Firm - Various Departments

The Firm never stops, no matter what. Volatility is welcomed, and it is perceived as opportunity. One trader would say. "Our better days are always the ones with *vola-tunity.*"

Partners go about their job routines.

Zhain's Office

Day. It snows.

Zhain and Alexandra discussing the Media acquisition.

Firm's Elevator

Night.

Zhain leaving the elevator, back-peddling to press more floor buttons than he should.

Boardroom

Night.

Alexandra presenting the IDB's end-of-year results. She has pride in the act.

The remaining Board Directors listening to her, in silence.

Cole pen-spinning. A glass of goat milk in front of him.

Alexandra's Office

Alexandra coaching Josephine, jointly reading a book on strategy.

Alexandra proudly handing Josephine Oda Nobunaga's prized XVI Century Portuguese arquebus.

Josephine bows in gratitude.

Zhain's Office

Ninah walking out from Zhain's office. Artfully.

Zhain's elevated smile. Left eyebrow raised plenty.

Zhain reading a Flash Gordon comic book with his legs stretched over his banker's desk.

Trading Floor

Day.

Zhain walking with Cole through the principal Trading Floor.

Cole proudly showcasing to Zhain the new trading terminals, while introducing him to highly complex spreadsheets and trading market graphs.

A group of seven market traders scootched behind Cole, observing in silence.

Boardroom

Zhain, Alexandra, and Partners commemorate, via cake-cutting, a massive celebration cake that reads "MEDIA BAGGED."

On the massive table, a Wall Street Journal's cover mentioning the landmark transaction: "ANTI-TRUST WHO? Zhain BAGS THE DAILY."

Zhain's Office

Next Day.

Zhain confers with Feist, Essex, and Tracker in his office.

Moments Later

Zhain, in his office alone, drinks Wolfschidmit with pomegranate seeds and looks outside his office window down to the City.

He is at ease. But one can't understand why.

Chapter 25

The years 1977 through 1979 fly by.
But it is still a shitshow.

Gone were the city's moral values associated with American Exceptionalism. 1979 was more associated with economic and social decay.

What to inquire about *equality before the law* and *individual responsibility* is a punch out of its class. Out of tune. These principles are arrested inside a Penn Station holding area; muted, shackled to a sober death desk.

Unwelcome isonomy. The implications will translate into the guiltless sins of greed and obscurity. Eye-to-eye.

Please understand - there are no rules.

It endures.

Chapter 26

New York, Summer, 1979

Amanda's Brownstone, Kitchen

Present.

Amanda wearing a billowy-sleeved dress, in a light-green pattern, flipping through a photograph album, mostly of the years of 1977 through 1979. These photos come alive in her imagination as she swipes her fingers on them.

Photo #1 - Brownstone Steps

Amanda carrying Chris on her back, back from school.

They pass by a theatrical poster of *The Deer Hunter* wheatpasted on the side façade of a Greek Deli.

Photo #2 - Francis' Livingroom

Sharing a winged armchair with Chris, Claire dressed in billowy-sleeved dress in a light-blue pattern reading to him Jules Verne's' *Voyages Extraordinaires*.

Her hair is pulled up and her index finger dictates the reading.

Chris' chin up, eyes glooming principally at Claire's mumbling face, her eyes, her moving of the lips, her curly hair. Her everything.

Chris' toes wiggle a foot-and-a-half from the floor.

Photo #3 - Brownstone's Rooftop

Night.

Hammer holding Fatima as tightly enough to feel safe from reality, but not too tightly to keep her from breathing. They slow-dance Bee Gee's "How Deep Is Your Love."

No nicer place to surf a celestial kiss.

New York City's full moon behind them. She is everything to him.

A beat, he brings his head from her diminutive shoulder and investigates her dark brown eyes. Her hands, behind his neck, softly tangle his hair. Their eyes travel inside each other's finding no place to land - as if love could last an eternity and not have a bottom. Expiration.

Amanda closes the photobook and exits the kitchen.

Front Steps

It smells like recently cut, wet grass and lavender.

Amanda and the Yoldas sitting on the Brownstone's front steps, hanging out, eating Persimmons and sharing the photo album.

Janis and May flipping the album, as photos come to life in their minds.

Photos

Amanda reading Jules Verne's *Journey to The Center of the Earth* to Chris.

Amanda observing people outside her window, contemplating at life, while writing on *The Book*.

Amanda handing *The Book* to Winnie, as Chris observes them through his Steve Austin, Six Million Dollar Man toy-doll's bionic eye.

Amanda at the garden's greenhouse caring for her persimmons.

Amanda's Kitchen table: a seven-year-old Chris writing with pencil and crayons on *The Book*.

Claire and Chris on the couch reading (sharing) *The Making of Kubrick's 2001* book.

Amanda handing out her signature bread sandwiches to Francis as he is on his way, late, to the Firehouse.

The Yoldas keep at the album, as Amanda returns to her condo.

Amanda's Kitchen Window

Present. Day.

Amanda, by the window, observes Chris on the back of

Hammer's Honda Lucky-7 as they approach, from the street, the Brownstone's front curb.

Chris is on the motorcycle holding a Spider-Man comic book.

Winnie sits on the Brownstone's steps with his dog Caruso.

The Honda CB roars in, with Hammer and Chris helmetless.

Chris wears his judo robe and green high-top sneakers.

"Yo, Motown, don't tell your mom." Hammer pleads.

"Right-on." Chris replies.

Chris has developed a robust taste for Motown music. No surprise he is nick-named "Motown Chris." The kid can dance, the kid can sing and spin. The kid can move and embrace. He can unite.

You will hear him reiteratively - in his own universe - across the corridors singing Marvin Gaye's "What's Going On" to Hammer's evident disapproval.

He has special gusto in singing *My Girl* to Claire regularly - his smile too contagious for her not to fall in love with this half-her-size over-confident *Chump*, as she would recurrently refer to him. The metric system has no place in the orders of love. If anyone is to blame, Amanda is probably it. If anything, Chris is Amanda's son - he is all heart.

Chris blinks an okay back at Hammer.

Amanda at the window, looking at Winnie, Hammer, and Chris with a warm smile. She looks at Hammer and shows him her floured white hand and gesture. "I see you. . . you be careful." Hammer shrugs warmly back while Chris plays with Caruso.

Brownstone Steps

Hammer is off to work on his bike. His Honda CB roars out.

May and Janis sit on opposing sides of the steps scouting the surroundings.

Winnie and Chris interact on the lower steps of the Brownstone, delighting in Italian ice.

Winnie's obedient dog Caruso sits by them.

Winnie's shoes are untied.

Chris with an adult-like demeanor asks. "Uncle Winnie, how come Caruso is always like this?"

"Like this what, kid?" Winnie asks.

"He never hesitates."

"Hum. Caruso smart?"

Winnie calls Caruso's attention. The dog looks back at him. "Caruso! Chris wants to play." The dog gets a bit excited.

Chris is not impressed.

"You know, Chris, Caruso loves to play. He is self-aware."

Caruso can only deliver an abstract mewling.

Chris notices Winnie's untied right leather shoe and proceeds to tie it without asking for permission. Chris is on one knee while slowly tying Winnie's shoe. He is slow in the process; after all, these are adults' shoes. By the look in Winnie's eyes, he finds the gesture uncommon but not surprising for a son of Amanda and Nelson. Chris is special, expressed in the tiniest of acts.

Chris still unimpressed.

"What do you mean, Uncle Winnie?" Chris sneered.

"Well, he has very clear understanding of his *true-self*, especially when he steals my, well, our donuts... he has no hesitation. No ambiguity."

Caruso shakes its head in disagreement.

Chris fails to produce an acceptable shoelace, but he keeps at it patiently.

"Ah. You mean he understands stuff in their natural order."

Winnie is impressed, and his eyes are wide open. A blue morpho butterfly lands on Chris' shoulder, and they both stare at it.

"Uncle Winnie, why do you and Mom care so much about *The Book*?"

After three failed attempts, a triumphant Chris, finally done with the shoe-lace ordeal. "Now you can get married, Uncle Winnie."

Winnie looks at him and places his hand under Chris' chin, thanking him for the deed. "Thank you, my child. It is just possible there is hope, still, for this world."

"Hum, I was expecting this. Chris, this isn't just any book, young man. One can say this manuscript, or book, or whatever you want to call it, created everything, see." Winnie points with finger. "Like this curious grasshopper crawling up your sneakers."

The clueless insect seems to follow the conversation.

"It created the wind, the ocean's waves, Caruso's D-flats. Ah, Caruso! Not this one," pointing at the dog. The dog looking clueless.

Chris interrupts him. "And pain?"

"Hum, pain. . . Well, pain is a by-product of living, you understand?"

"Can you run and not sweat?" Winnie asks.

Chris just listens.

"Gotcha, but can it still create?" Chris back at *The Book* theme.

"Yes, yes, it can, Chris. Yes, it can. But you knew that already, right?"

A shy nod from Chris.

"Even the future?"

"Yep."

"And the black wolf?"

Amanda and Claire - both smudged in white baking flour wearing aprons - standing behind them smiling maternally. "Who wants jelly-bread?!" Amanda asks.

Winnie looks up to Amanda in relief.

"C'mon, boys, Mr. Motown, let's go up before it *coldens*." Amanda commands.

Claire smiling at Chris equally bossy, calling for his obedience with her tiny index flour coated finger. "C'mon, Chump!"

A trying-to-be-cool, Chris flexing and looking at his diminutive, toned biceps, pipes in, "Right-on, babe."

He floats.

There goes a kid in love!

That innocence - no sweater ballad.

Lefferts Street, Chris' Room

Night.

Chris turns the McIntosh tube radio on. It gives us Bee Gees' *More Than a Woman*. He dances; pretending Claire is paired with him.

The kid can move.

Woolworth Building, Rooftop

A rainy starless night.

Meanwhile, Cole standing up, soaked in rain and blood, wearing his Oxford's and "ears-necklace," on the edge of a Gothic "Gargoyle" (*skeuomorphism*).

One less dark soul off the bullpen - in his account.

Chapter 27

Brooklyn, Flatbush Avenue

Day.

After school hours.

Chris and a half-dozen energized elementary school colleagues walking down a busy Flatbush Avenue back home from school.

They stroll by a theatrical poster of the *Midnight Express* wheatpasted on the façade of a Portuguese bakery.

The Opposing Street, Hotdog Stand

Janis eating a hotdog while stealthily keeping a close eye on little Chris.

Department Emporium, Balch, Price & Co.

Street level. Store facade. A *Saturday Night Fever* poster glued on a window of *Balch, Price & Co.*

Chris halts the cadenced street stroll. Note that Chris has New

York bones and has groomed a proprietary swagger ("swag") - a confident raised chin, an erect posture, a slight *skip-hop* to the left as he walks. Nothing too extravagant. Just enough to perpetuate confidence.

With his commanding little hands, he signals his friends to *keep moving*. "I'll catch up!" He shouts.

The kids wave him goodbye. They know Motown Chris - it will be a while.

Store Window

The movie poster is aligned with his height.

Travolta's confident, *torero* pose does not intimidate the young-ling. Instead, it inspires him. Chris places himself precisely in front of Travolta. Their eyes meet.

Chris' eyes thoroughly dissect Tony-Travolta's body, hairstyle, posture, and outfit. *I can be that* is what crosses his mind. His only inquiry is, *what cologne does he use?*

He combs his dark hair backward, puffing it, and nods slowly, confidently.

Chris and Travolta's symmetrical reflection on the glass, on the poster.

He pretends he wears an identical shirt.

Inside Balch, Price & Co.

Chris inside the department store.

Stayin' Alive playing in the loudspeakers (*would it not?*).

He, and his inquisitive eyes, groove all the way to the back of the Men's Department.

Curious, entertained eyes shuffling men's shirts on a tall rack.

He pulls one light blue polyester shirt out. His eyes catch the shirt's tag labeled "*SMALL.*"

A tall, handsome Brooklyn Man in his early thirties, wearing a fedora hat with a peacock feather, shares the rack with Chris. The man looks down at Chris, appreciating the good taste and the swagger. He nods at the kid.

Chris looks up to the man as a partner in their objectives. Chris nods back at the man.

Probably knowing the answer, the man casually still asks. "Special occasion?"

Chris answers just as casually. "I got a woman, you know."

The man back at him, showing the necessary respect. "I bet you do, kid. . ." He nods. "I bet you do."

Behind Chris, in respectful silence, a Brooklyn Woman with an enormously welcoming smile.

He looks straight at her with a smile and frustrated eyes, evidence of his condition – an unsupervised nine-year-old inside an adult's department store.

She gently leans and whispers something in his right ear, then calls him, *come with me,* with her index finger.

Deep inside the Department Store

Jackpot, a rack populated with everything a nine-year-old boy in love, could ever wish for.

With proud composure and an *I-knew-you'd-dig-this* smirk, the peculiar store clerk extends her right hand sideways and opens her palm.

With a smile the size of his confidence, the kid smirks back in joy and slaps her a solid "five," joined by a poetic. "Daaaaamn, Woman!"

The store clerk smiles at him and shakes her head in amusement.

His body wants to dance.

His hips swaying.

Fitting Room

Minutes later.

The underage stud inside the fitting room with a stack of pants and long sleeve collar shirts. A white vest.

One by one, he tries on the assortment of clothing at the sound of the effervescent Bee Gees. He joins singing.

A blue one.

He combs and poofs his hair backward.

A red one.

Chest out. Nothing but smooth skin.

A mustard polyester shirt.

The kid is happy just by himself, swapping the booth's lights on and off as if he were disk-jockeying Disco57!

His hips swaying more intensively.

Travolta cannot compete.

Finally, a dark-green long-sleeved. Jackpot!

A beat.

Chris delivers a daring finger-pointing dance pose to the sky.

No superlatives are required to describe Chris. A young stud exempt from *letters of marque* to conduct his hustle - the street hustler of love.

What is childhood if not an act of faith.

4 Times Square, *Music Factory* record shop

Next Day.

Saturday Night. 5:57 PM.

It rains hard. Not dark yet. Getting there.

The store's JBL speakers shout The Clash's *The Guns of Brixton*.

Claire dressed in pink, *Grease* Sandy manner, shuffling colorful, glittering, 45s Disco LPs next to our "Motown" Chris.

Although he still stands half Claire's height, Chris is dressed up like a proper 70s gentleman for the event. He certainly felt old enough; nine years and twenty-seven days old.

He wears a cherished black leather, pointed-toe, winklepicker boot, with red inner insoles and Cuban heels - for the extra stretch.

His white Wranglers held by a tailor-made cotton rope belt. His green, bell-sleeve shirt steamed pressed the previous night by his own hands. And finally, cologne - Faberge Brut leased from Hammer's precious stash, hidden behind an olive-green Volume 49, *Darwin*, Britannica Great Books.

The kid will not surrender to chance. Not this Chris - he is loaded.

For clarification: Chris considers every encounter with Claire a date, regardless of the fact he sees her multiple times a day. He could spend the Earth's stock of time next to her, and it would still be insufficient.

The kid means business.

Chris is plucking, fingerpicking through a couple of Soul and Motown LPs starting from O'Jays, Hayes, Funkadelic, Billy Paul, The Commadores, Cole, Aretha. Hold! He stops, sacks out a The

Delfonics album, and stares at it for a beat. Then stares at Claire. Then back at The Delfonics. Claire again.

The Delfonics returns to the stash behind ABBA's latest release. Almost!

It is clear he has something specific in mind.

He keeps at it.

A new shelf, more fingerpicking - The Spinners, Smokey, WAR, Wonder, Curtis, Womack, Earth, Wind & Fire, Roberta, Rufus. The Manhattans.

Another halt to admire Claire.

She mutters with the side of her mouth (without facing him), with her eyelids closed. "Chump! Stop looking at me and go find whatever you're looking for. Gosh!"

He laughs with his eyes and resumes.

She smirks back.

These two can go on like this forever. And do.

He keeps going, Cornelius Brothers, Ruffin, Wright, Holloway, Al Green, Sly, Knight, then finally, he pulls one specific *single* hidden in the very last file. Jackpot! He conceals the single behind his back, under his shirt, with the subtleness of a genuine urban pickpocketer, and walks towards the Manager-DJ top booth, all the way to the back of the store - a place he would typically avoid, unless completely necessary. Correction, he does not walk - he grooves towards the DJ's tall stand.

Behind the DJ, a theatrical poster of *Halloween.*

This is Motown Chris, and confidence salutes *him.*

"What's goin-on, kid?" The Music Man rasped with ponderous voice.

Chris back at him as if an equal partner to the enterprise. "Please slap this bad-boy for me, ma'man."

"Right-on, ma-brother." The DJ back at him, in synchronicity.

The DJ extends his lasting right hand sideways. They give each other a routine, smooth, quasi-silent low *five-to-the-side.*

"I owe you one, ma' man."

DJ points at Chris, nodding up and down with velvet enthusiasm. "You're the man, Motown. You're the man."

Oblivious, Claire continues hunting for newly released Disco-like types of vinyl and incoming Baez folk disciples' rare finds. She takes pleasure in reading the LP's fine lines.

Lights unexpectedly fade half-notch.

The rebel Mick Jones and Simonon's *Pressure* Fender P-Bass are muted through an awful scratching of the needle. Such lack of etiquette from the Manager-DJ (business isn't exactly thriving). It must be important.

A beat.

The store's rotating disco globe is turned on.

Lights fade another notch, this time on its own.

A crying organ joins, flowing outbound from the wall's JBLs, a shivery, metallic guitar followed by a dry drum.

Motown Chris strolling down the corridor towards Claire.

The set-up is revealed - the Stylistics' *You Are Everything* fills the entire store, every inch of it. Every crack. Every dream ever crafted inside these files. Every wish of loving. Nothing escapes these notes.

The half-dozen customers notice and hold for what is to follow.

Claire can sense her Chump is up to something (as always) and looks to her left and observes him walking towards her with a lion smile. The kid can smile, too!

He sings along, in perfect rhythm, in tandem with the wondrous quintetto Thompkins Jr., Love, Murrell, Smith, and Dunn.

The kid floats.

A full stop. Eyes on Claire.

He bows nobly and extends his daring hand petitioning a *slow-dance*.

She candidly whispers to him with the softest contralto this little piece of New York has ever endorsed. "Chuuump. . ."

She consents, bowing back half-degree holding her dress to the side as an authentic Duchess would. She, too, is all smiles. Her cheeks bend to azalea-pink, matching her candy pink dress. They hold hands.

He gently, but commandingly, pulls her to him. He dives into her eyes. Their innocent bodies touch each other on their own discretion. His face leans on her maternal shoulders. Sweet Honesty perfume fills his dreams.

His extended arms wrapped around Claire's waist like a Tiffany lace.

With shut eyes, they dance unhurriedly under a simple order. Globe lights on them. Every single muscle in Chris' body loves Claire just as much as his soul.

The elements don't dare compete.

The rain needs to stop. And does.

The giver-of-light is granted free entrance and willingly produces a sunset like never before - *Manhattanhenge* is born. In such grace. As it should.

Eternity slips in unphased and embargoes Chris' Mickey Mouse Timex wristwatch - the *seconds hand* halts. It marks 6:13. Seconds become a whole life. One of beauty.

Claire cannot handle such an undertaking, collapsing into loving this unruly, swaggering kid.

She holds him closer to her fragile body.

Such power. Probably the happiest day in their juvenile lives.

The Earth spins.

Yes, it does.

But around *them*.

What is love if not an act of innocence.

Chapter 28

Boxing Gym, Brooklyn

Day.

Layers of cigarette smoke float still in the air.

A busy gym. Men only. Borough patrons of all creeds.

Two worn-down rings and much-dated workout equipment inside the Gym.

The air is heavy.

Speed Bag

With eyes closed, a focused Hammer warming up on a waned-out black speed bag.

Johnny by his side wearing his Judo kimono pants and a dark blue FDNY T-shirt.

A makeshift martial arts tatami behind him. Thirteen kids in Judo kimono *Gi* practicing *handori* drills on it.

Johnny turns to the boys and yells a firm. "Hajime!"

A loud unison, "Hai, Sensei!" back from the disciplined pupils. The boys bow and commence sparing in pairs.

Main Boxing Ring

On the main boxing ring, a group of police officers from Newark's 102nd Precinct congregates around a tall fighter, who is warming up, stretching in neatly pressed, white silk sweats.

Five half-empty, light-green boxes of donuts, half-eaten Sloppy Joe's sandwiches, and dozens of coffee cups are on top of the ring's canvas floor.

The contender is Second Lieutenant Antonio Martinelli (aka Spit-Tony), who spars with an equally fit training partner.

They hear and feel the enthusiasm. Tony's high-octane corner behaves as if they were at the *Garden's* main stage, a WBA world championship title on the ballot.

Tony is a twenty-something, lean, muscular cop with dark grease-ball hair and a pristine smile. His golden polyester gloves are fresh out of the box.

Tony's cigarette-smoking corner looks at Hammer from a distance with excitement and contempt.

Tony's cousin, Sticky-Gigi, stuffing two donuts inside his big mouth while supporting an uncredited, gold-and-green, league champion's belt on his wide shoulder.

Tony's second, yeti-build cousin, Sal Junior (Fat Sal's son), takes photos of his admired cousin Antonio Junior. He is infatuated with the Kodak Hawkeye Instamatic X's rotary flash cube.

From the tightness of their white V-neck T-shirts, it is hypothesized that "Size XL" T-shirts never crossed the limit borders of Jersey.

By the ringside

A group of circa three dozen excited men placing bets.

A bookkeeper wearing an olive fedora hat taking cash and making score notes in his purple notebook.

Against his family's approval, and especially against Chief Francis' advice, Hammer is back into underground street fighting after a long hiatus. Although money is involved and in short supply, this isn't Hammer's principal motivation. Nor is recognition. Rage is the culprit.

Punching Bag

Hammer takes to the half-mended, duct-taped punching bag. The same punching bag his father Francis ripped and stitched in the fifties.

Wearing black trunks, socks, and flat sneakers, he is already sweaty from the short warm-up. His bruised body reveals three gun wounds and a sway of scars. His tattoos are fading. His 82nd Airborne insignia is less dark green than when he had it first commissioned in a Saigon prostibule by the steady hands of a French Legion veteran, a former diplomatic Charge' d'affaires, gone AWOL due to insanity. The Popeye tattoo still holds firmly.

Hammer is a beaten-down man struggling to stay sane.

One gym old-timer, aka Seven-Hell, stands beside Hammer.

"Come-here Little-Francis. I got my lunch money on you, brother. Round two, K? Don't let me down, kid. Just be careful; this crazy cat put down the old Irish Bomb; you remember him, hum? The slick who looked like Brando, from South Philly, 27th, Narcotics, hum? You know *what-I'm-sayin*? Just keep your jive up, man, and watch out for that left hook!"

Hammer just nods procedurally. A loud spit to the side.

Gym Entrance

In Judo *Gi*, Chris strolls in, head-down, late for practice. Two indicators reveal something is out of place. First, Chris is never late for Judo practice. And second, he absolutely never (never) has his head down.

With commanding eyes, Hammer signals Johnny to investigate.

Johnny leaned towards Chris, who is uncharacteristically shy and guarded. Johnny crouched, inspecting Chris' face further with his hands.

Chris' hair is undone, and he has a bruised eye.

Ring

Tony's brash, golden-tooth trainer yells out loud towards Hammer's corner. "Two minutes, old man!" Laughter and anticipation from that corner.

And Sal's cube flashes still at it.

Tony stretching his front thighs.

The donut boxes are empty.

Punching Bag

An indifferent Hammer sees the events unfolding and walks toward Johnny and Chris.

Gym Entrance Hall

With frowned eyebrows, Hammer asks Johnny. "What's up here, John?"

Johnny back with a circumspect. "Nothing, bro."

A mad Hammer talking to Johnny but looking at Chris. "Nothing?! Fuck nothing! What happened, kid?"

Chris' eyes, a short flashback, and his soft words trying hard to dilute the issue. "Nothing, Uncle Drew, nothing really. Street stuff. Well, you know." Inside little Chris' mind, *of course Uncle Drew would understand.*

Chris' Flashback

Chris and two borough friends fencing off five older street gang kids in front of an *Ice & Pizza* joint.

Ring

From a distance, Tony jumping up and down inside the ring, punching the air, and yelling at Hammer. "Your days are over, Veteran. Let's go!"

The over-confident Tony makes the "neck slice cut" with his shiny golden glove. In his reality, there is a new kid in town.

Gym Entrance Hall

Hammer's stoned eyes looking back at the excited Tony. Then back at Chris. Kneeled on one knee in front of Chris, looking up at him. Composedly to Chris. "Hear me out very closely." A beat. "I, *we*, didn't come to this planet to sit on the fucking bench, man, or on the stands. Nor did you! You understand?! Nah! No sir! I, *we*, came to play! Play fucking hard! Kid; life is short. Everybody is born with a pre-set number of years. Call it *life receipts*. So don't go on spending yours on the sidelines of life. Wake up early. Work hard, put your metal cleats on, and come to play with blood in your eyes, kid, and nothing less!"

A beat.

Hammer looks to Johnny but speaks to Chris. "You're gonna need to pick a side, kid. Pick a side. You understand?" Eyes back at Chris. "There ain't no space for the rescue Saint Bernard puppy here. Not in these streets." He looks at and points to Johnny. "You hear?! This is Wolf Town, kid! Eat or be eaten. That's the contract, kid. That's the contract."

Johnny shakes his head covertly. Obviously, the siblings have a long-lasting disagreement when it comes to this specific topic.

Chris' eyes are a mixed of spooked, excited, and saddened. But mostly excited. Chris releases a loud. "Roger that, Captain!"

A proud tap on the shoulders from Hammer's beaten-down black glove.

As Hammer is about to turn and leave to face Spit-Tony, thinking he has the last word, Chris takes charge and introduces his agenda. "Uncle Andrew?"

Hammer turns.

Chris with an innocent but daring plead. "So, does that mean that if I do everything you said and kinda be like you, that I can marry *you know whommm?!*"

Chris' candid eyes expecting, praying for something good. For consent. For acceptance. Consecration.

Those words are enough to break down a hardened man. And they do. Such beauty in life.

A beat. Hammer's eyes want to deliver a tear. But don't. Can't. Not now. But later, maybe. Instead, he chokes. He looks to Johnny then places his hand firmly on Chris' bold shoulder. He leans on the little frame. His mouth an inch from Chris's left ear. Hammer whispers with a broken voice. "I never doubted you, kid. I would be blessed. But earn it!"

Chris nods, then crafts a wide, relieved sunshine smile.

A brotherly hug.

Chris' hands trying to meet around Hammer's torso. But they can't reach, can't close the loop. He is still nine years and nine months old.

This relationship is like no other. Their fates intertwined in the books of life.

A man who has experienced the horrors of war, the real streets of New York, and one with a black-painted heart, Hammer can read a soul. He knows what Chris is. No doubt in his mind, Chris is all heart. All love. And precisely because of this perceived *hand-icap*, Hammer feels his obligation to Amanda, to a kid whose father is a mystery, and to Chris himself. He needs to toughen up the minor – *prepare him for all the shit life will throw at him.* Hammer cares deeply for Chris. Deep inside, Hammer thinks that if he can save Chris from the traps and horrors of life, that he can save himself in the process. He sees a young Hammer in Chris. This is no ordinary relationship.

Hammer back at the kid. "Now let me take care of business."

Hammer stands up, turns, and leaves towards the ring. On his way, he looks at the Eastern corner of the Gym. Another senior gym employee, aka Memphis Jack, hits the stereo.

Behind Memphis Jack, a large green board with "scores" notes and Hammer's name on it among three dozen other ranked street-fighters.

The cassette tape rolling. The Rolling Stones' *Painted Black* takes over.

Hammer saunters mutedly to the ring. A prayer in his mind, "*I shall not impair. Hurt only. Save me, Saint Augustin; don't let me impair. But let me play. Let me play! Bless you. And keep an eye out for the little stinker over-there.*"

His pals from the Precinct just as calm. They know how this ends.

Boxing Ring

Hammer inside the ring.

Five measly push-ups followed by four shabby, short military jumping jacks.

Stretching his neck. His back. His arms. He aches loudly. He adjusts his balls to the left side.

Seven-Hell stuffs a black mouthpiece inside Hammer's mouth.

Hammer kisses his crucifix, the David Star, and hands it to Seven-Hell.

Johnny and Chris join Hammer's Precinct assembly.

The excited and testosterone-rich Tony can't contain himself.

Hammer walks side to side like a hungry, caged tiger.

The men in the center of the ring.

A makeshift referee calls the rules.

Hammer simply stares at the excited Tony.

The bell rings

Tony launches himself like a bull.

Tony's jabs flowing, fast as a whip, electric, three per second.

Hammer *slipping*. Once. Twice. He is hit a few times, jabs. He takes a straight to the side of the head. He *slips* some more. Left. Left again. Bulldozes Tony's body backward with both hands.

A separation.

A beat.

Tony yells. "Am gonna cut your head off, old man."

Tony plunging back.

Hammer *slips* every other way he can. He lets Tony hit him twice in the body. And again. His thoughts, *"Damn, this rookie is fast. Gotta finish this quick, or won't make it to the third. Move soldier! Move soldier!"*

Hammer is in the corner taking blows. An elbow to the temple from Tony, and Hammer bleeds profusely.

A left hook from Tony's golden glove and Hammer's mouth-piece along with every drop of head sweat, flies into the air. The mouthpiece lands on the center of the ring.

Hammer kneeled. Aching.

The referee taking the count.

Tony's law-abiding crowd cheering.

Hammer's corner is predominantly kosher.

The Bell

Round One is over.

Hammer ambles to the center of the ring and grabs his mouthpiece while listening to Tony's entourage call him everything besides *charming young man.*

Hammer telegraphs the group nothing but a still, indifferent face.

Hammer by his corner

Hammer breathing heavily. Clearly, he has been in better shape.

An upset Johnny jumping on top of the ring. Under the ropes. Now inside by Hammer's side.

Johnny and Seven-Hell are by the corner.

Hammer sitting on the tiny three-leg wood bench catching his breath.

An upset Johnny. "Fuck Drew, what's wrong with you, man?!" What are you doing?!" Getting hit like that!"

Seven-Hell yelling to Hammer. "Keep your jive up, man, up! And watch for the left hook! Left, kid." Note Seven-Hell says *left* but actually uses his *right* hand to mimic a left hook.

Hammer's immovable body, his still eyes seem oblivious to the well-intended coaching instructions.

A dissatisfied verbal output while scratching his unshaved face. "Fucking polyester gloves. . ."

Hammer back on his feet, breathing deeply, while Seven-Hell attends to the bleeding temple.

Johnny back at Seve-Hell but with eyes zoomed onto Hammer. "He's allergic to polyester."

Chris's extended arm delivers Hammer a Crush soda bottle.

Detective Hammer downs the Crush soda. Spits blood and orange to the side. A loud burp. He looks at the Seven-Hell and blinks. A nod back from Seven-Hell.

Hammer looks down at Chris, kneels on one leg, and speaks. "The wolf, kid. The fucking wolf!!" A smirk, his bloodied teeth, from Hammer announces his intentions.

A proud Chris yells. "Put him down, Uncle Drew!"

That's all Hammer needed to hear and feel – Chris' excited blood flowing. His animal spirit raging.

His love.

Ring Side

Round Two.

Tony plunges towards Hammer before the steel hits the bell.

Hammer pivots his body in a Judo-like sway (*slips*) of the torso and corners the elegant Tony in the ropes.

A massive punch to the stomach, street-style, from Hammer.

Tony didn't see that coming.

Hammer pounds. Captain Fleming hammers Tony as if he were his back-yard punching bag.

A satisfaction smile from Hammer as he inflicts his leather fists onto Tony's worked-out, gym-sculpted body. His thoughts, *"I shall not impair. Not impair."*

Tony tries to free himself from Hammer's ravage control and the ropes.

Tony's corner frantically yelling. "Get out the ropes, Tony! Swing out! Swing out! Slip! Slip!"

Too late.

Hammer, now drilling his prey, one body blow at a time.

One final right hook to the liver.

A towering "urgh" from the young stallion, who collapses to his knees in unspoken pain.

Hammers snaps his neck left and spits orange towards Tony's stunned, silent corner.

The cousin duet wants to invade the ring but are contained by the remaining meatball-eating uncles.

Tony's trainer and cousins rush towards Tony's fallen body.

Memphis Jack etching another "cross line" to Hammer's track record, twenty-seven, five-lines-squares. He begins a new one (box). The total sum now records 136 knockouts.

Ring

Hammer turns and gives his back to Tony, knowing that *that is the last of that.*

He then walks out of the ring, under the ropes, a-matter-of-factly.

Tony on the floor groaning like a boar calf being chewed by a pack of wolves.

His embarrassedly looking entourage around him helping him stand on his own two feet.

Seven-Hell tosses a towel on top of Hammer, hands him a half-full bottle of Jack Daniels and says. "Man, you've made me more money than my 401k. Fuck yeah."

Hammer downs five long gulps of the whisky, then elevates the bottle upside down over his head. He tilts his head backward and empties the last quarter of it down his face and body.

A last shiver.

Chris and Johnny are observing, unsurprised. This is routine.

Hammer's compadres collecting their scores with the bookrunner.

Johnny is not exactly happy with the events unwrapping. But this is Hammer, his big brother. And that is all that matters.

Off the Ring, by the Judo Tatami

Minutes Later.

Chris proudly attends to Hammer's bloodied open cut. He is gentle and meticulous. The kid wants to be as tough as Hammer. As caring as Johnny. As loving as Amanda. As inquisitive as Winnie. As protective as Chief Francis. As brave as the Yoldas. As humble as Fatima. But ultimately, what he doesn't yet know is that he is Nelson's son. Something greater. And that his mission may be beyond human constructions.

Chris, in a clean pitch shaking his head. "This is nothing, Uncle Drew; I got you. Just a scratch."

Hammer back at him with a smirk. "Do you think the Chief will let this one slide?"

Chris with spooked eyes. "Holy smokes. Holy smokes. Slide!? Not a chance! He's not gonna like this. Not one bit."

Chris feeling proud to be a Fleming.

By the ringside

Empty donut boxes and towels flying in the air.

In revenge, and in disgrace, Tony's boxing duet cousins run towards Hammer with fists up.

Watching the inevitable accounts, Memphis Jack knows the drill and hits the speakers with Rolling Stones' *Give me Shelter*.

Hammer and Johnny have their backs to the disgruntled cousins and can't see what's coming.

But not Chris. Born with Nelson's genes, he can sense danger. Born with Amanda's genes, he is protective.

In a split second, Chris launches forward, bulldozing Hammer out of Gigi's striking range. Gigi's donut-powdered fist swipes a hair from Hammer's chin. He can smell Gigi's cheap cologne.

Hammer falls back on the ground, on his behind.

On Gigi's heels, Cousin Junior's knuckles don't miss Johnny's left eye. He takes it dry and falls to the ground just beside Hammer, equally on his butt. The Brooklyn brothers stare at each other, as in *how the fuck did we **not** see this coming!*

Chris intentionally stands halfway between the enraged Jersey boys and his two fallen brothers. He grows.

The two imposing cousins, now three feet from little Chris. Daring him. "Get outta the way, weasel!" Gigi yells.

Instead, Chris takes one step forward. Spits Crush to the side, snaps his neck left, and charges at the Newark duet.

Hammer and Johnny's eyes catch flashes of Chris flipping Cousin Junior with his signature *Uchimata*, followed by a textbook neck choke hold on the Sicilian descendant.

Hammer and Johnny looking at each other stunned but elated. Then yelling MACOH!!! (their childhood gloves-off code).

The gym employee raises the stereo volume to its max, and The Rolling Stones take over the concrete city.

Johnny, Hammer, Chris, cousins Junior and Gigi, plus a half dozen officers from either side brawling such as one would expect inside a bar on a Saint Patrick's after-hours night.

Flatbush Avenue, Sidewalk

Moments later.

The three brothers walking back home. Kicking cans. Battered, but together, as such.

They stroll by a theatrical poster of *Alien*.

Chris sandwiched between the brothers while holding their hands. Tony's belt hanging on his tiny shoulder.

Chris proudly to his eye-bruised brothers. "Shoot, Chief Francis ain't gonna like this. No sir."

Such is life.

Chapter 29

Lefferts Street, Fleming's Condo

Moments later. 8:17 PM.

Supper at the Fleming's.

Lasagna and green salad. Tomatoes and olive oil. Prosciutto and Bolla Cheese. A massive challah bread. Butter. Two large water jars. Three bottles of red wine and one Portuguese Green Mateo next to Winnie.

Candles.

At the table

Night.

Chief Francis, Hammer, Johnny, Winnie, Amanda, May, Janis, Claire, Beth, and Fatima.

Claire dressed in a light blue dress with a gold necklace, crucifix, earrings, and bracelet.

Behind her a baroque painting of the Pacific Ocean, a sunset, and a rainbow. She serves Chris lasagna.

Chris in Yankees pinstripe pajamas inspecting the Kodak Hawkeye. Tony's champions belt glued on his shoulder. A bottle of Orange Crush soda in front of him.

He sits on a pack of three Encyclopedias books for added height, holding two wooden spoons.

His Steve Austin doll by his plate, probably for added reassurance, just in case; after all, Chief Francis' rants are infamous.

The three boys on one side of the table, with raw steak and ice on their bruised eyes.

Francis scolding the trio. His loud upset voice is muted. His fingers and hands are all over the place.

He points and gesticulates towards Chris while looking at Hammer and Johnny, as in, *"is this the kind of example you grown men want to give to the little guy? Hum?!"*

His fist to the table. The table and everything on top of it tremble.

With cautious eyes fixed on Francis, Chris covertly hides the newly acquired-by-merit Kodak camera under the table, between his legs. He earned it.

Johnny and Hammer with their heads down, taking it in silence.

But not Chris. Although he mirrors his "brothers" and keeps his head lowered, it feels like Christmas morning for him.

A bottle of Orange Crush soda in front of Hammer.

To diffuse the monotone scolding from Chief Francis, May proceeds to the family wall piano and joyfully starts playing the Rolling Stone's *She's a Rainbow*.

It works.

Janis, Amanda, and Beth join with a warm humming of notes.

Winnie takes to scrutinizing the Mateo with his exotic green "analysis" glasses.

Chris is oblivious to the adult's reality and can only dream of Claire at the tune of the piano *She's a Rainbow* notes. This is a special moment for him. His first street brawl with his admired brothers. In his reality, he's been consecrated, and *taking* Chief Francis's scolding is sort of a rite of passage, nirvana in his world.

But most importantly, Chris feels he has earned his chunk of real estate in the family communion. Ultimately, he is closer to Claire.

Holding an uncontrollable grin, and staring fixedly at his "woman", Claire, feeling tough, he subversively pulls the half-pound steak up a notch enough to blink at her with confidence and audacity equal to none.

She first smiles back at him, shakes her head scornfully, sighs, then the pair notice the hushed echo around them, now magnified by Francis's less-than-happy patriarchal eyebrows. It had been minutes. Or more. Who cares? This is Claire and Chris, and time has no business here.

Amanda sees through all the noise and enjoys the moment.

Amanda, Beth, Winnie, May, and Janis can't contain their smirks. Who could?

Love. A conjugated mess of just, simply caring for one another.

This is family. This is life.

Chapter 30

Subway, Number 5 Line

Next Day.

Winter. A cold starlit night.

The subway car smells like piss and beer. An odor unmistakably common inside the subway system - New York's true underbelly. It's true guts and soul.

A graffitied promotion poster of judge-jury-and-executioner Charles Bronson, *DEATH WISH* motion picture pasted on the subway car's wall. His character, Dr. Kersey's *vigilante alter ego*, flashing his four-inch barrel .32 caliber nickel *Positive* revolver. There is no doubt the film depicts an inner desire society craves deep inside. To the regular subway commuter, it is layered bare on one's skin.

A hospital nurse in light blue scrubs calmly reads the *Times*. On its cover, a photo of the deposed Shah of Iran Reza Pahlavi fleeing and walking on JFK's airport tarmac along his wife Soraya, who is properly dressed in all the fur, diamonds and lack of shame an exiled Queen can support.

Nelson wearing a denim Wrangler trucker-jacket standing up - back to the subway car door. He drinks whisky from a brown paper bag. He observes his surroundings and catches his eye on Jojo, who reads a *Post* daily. Its cover reads "PEN KILLER CLAIMS NEW VICTM." A graphic photo of a bloodied, earless, mid-age priest with a long fountain pen jammed inside his left temple.

Nelson's dire eyes glance absently at the photo, then panning up to the newspaper holder's skittish eyes. A last glance at the Death Wish poster.

Jojo sits immediately under the Death Wish poster, five feet in front of Nelson. She wears her hair up, heavy boots, military coat, and an Islanders jersey. She is reading a *Survival Pamphlet*. Her hockey jersey on just to make a point – *think twice*. Her competition rollers are strapped around her shoulder. They are beaten down – and this is her only pair.

Next to Nelson, a vintage Marlboro "Won't anybody cigarette me?" and a "5-1 The Game is Broomsticks" poster ad. Both signed in elegant graffiti.

14th Street Subway Stop

The subway car stops brutally on 14th Street. Not exactly a surprise, as subway car conductors have a thing for making you shake like loose chickens in the back of a farmer's diesel truck. For what they make, who wouldn't?

Half-a-dozen Catholic-School teenage students, girls, and boys returning from school, also board the car *wilding*. One of the girls reads a fashion magazine and mouths. *"The only men who should wear open-toed shoes or sandals are gladiators and Jesus."* Her head nods in agreement. She then looks at Nelson, who wears leather sandals.

Astern, a regular subway junkie sleeping inside a rusted supermarket cart - his life's belongings contained and strapped inside this urban four-wheeler. It reads. "Don't bother. Leave TENS inside tin can."

The scent inside the train is not exactly ideal. It's part of the composition.

One teenager sprays his red gang insignia on a window (looks like a Skull) - the metal ball shaking up and down inside the spray can. Visibly it's Rusto.

A tough-and-rough city Filler wearing a dirty Yankees hat, diagonally, purposely hands Nelson a *FEAR CITY* pamphlet, then grotesquely spits to his side. Intimidation 101. The street teaches you whom to fear and whom not to fear. This is clearly an antagonist not to mess with.

In some instances, subway robberies are an established means to finance southbound club excursions. In this case, it's just anger.

A second high-school teenager reads a black cover book. Her hair is shaved on the sides, military style. She wears long feather earnings and attentively reads Victoria Pineda's *"ECFRASIS, EXEMPLUM, ENARGEIA"* book.

A beat.

She raises her eyes away from the book and gazes gravely at her surroundings, then, after a few seconds, a subtle comment to the ginger hair colleague sitting to her right. "I guess angels or the *thy-holy* son wouldn't be enough to fix *this* mess. Look. Look around you." A contemplating beat from the teenage girls. Her colleague tries to process the comment but can't; she, too has been desensitized.

The short-hair teenager fixes her sight on Nelson, then adds introspectively. "What we *really* need is *the man* himself. No disguises. The de facto aesthetics of evidence." Her voice dying down. "Chop-chop."

Her eyes still on Nelson's sorrowful eyes staring fixedly at her. He may have been observing her for a while or forever. He nods. She nods slowly back. A sense of peace and grace soaks into her skin. Into her soul. Her aura is elated.

Predestination.

Back at the Filler

The Filler's feet backpedals. He is now in Nelson's face, as intended.

A few passengers anticipate the inevitable and disperse.

The angry Filler threatens Nelson loudly, aggressively. "Fighdolla for the poster, pops."

Nelson doesn't move a muscle and stares back cold at the mugger.

Everyone else knows that careless words can get you stabbed, at least, and wait for Nelson's reaction.

The chemical smell of fear is real and swamps the car.

Terror is another story.

A beat.

"You deaf, mother-fucker?!" The Filler seconds.

Nelson does not blink.

The Filler pulls a snub-nose 0.44 revolver – with duct-taped grip – and presses its cold muzzle against Nelson's left temple. The gun barrel pressing hard against Nelson's temple.

The urban Filler pulls the trigger slowly. Forcibly. A careless mistake he will pay for, but doesn't know it.

A controlled Nelson mutters. "Kid; you don't wanna do this. I have some fine Kentucky whiskey, how-bout-that instead?"

Nelson extends his paper-bag whisky.

The Filler doesn't seem interested in alcohol. Perhaps a conscientious teetotaler.

Impatiently back at Nelson. "What?! Give me the green man or am going to blow your fucking head off. . . and then, I'll drink your whisky; how's-about that instead, mother-fucker?!"

The train car goes dark for a beat.

Tracks metal-to-metal loud lightning sparks flashes like a disco strobe onto Nelson's face.

A loud bang! Muzzle flashes in the dark. A second, more deafening bang! A third flash. Train lights flickering back on.

Jojo's eyes and mouth are wide open as she ducks to the ground like a lizard.

A beat. Lights back on.

Filler on his knees. Nelson's hand on the Filler's forehead.

Nelson crouches on one knee and looks at him in the eyes. "You can go now, son."

The embarrassed Filler, standing up gently. He turns and leaves, head down, opposite to Nelson.

Nelson stands up and notices the shattered window behind him.

Two bullet shot holes on the car's door windows behind Nelson's head. One on each side.

A relaxed Nelson holding the revolver in one hand and the brown paper bag in the other.

He takes a composed sip of the whisky.

Nelson has some blood on his face from the glass recoil. Nothing but a bullet scratch and the uncaring memory of fresh gunpowder.

Car passengers dazed, looking at Nelson.

His eyes disallow empathy to drench outward. His mind pulsed vaguely with what he actually wanted to do and couldn't, shouldn't – summon the steel and pound his aggressor. He could only but transcend to his regrets about what humankind has become. Failure.

Had this particular Filler known he was face-to-face with a man no armies could not, would not, dare fight. A Nelson that had no enemies.

But the man known as Nelson Senior now struggles to comprehend such primitive construction.

But why bother here, anyway.

To relinquish his mission to find Amanda and *The Book* in lieu of helping this dimension would be to surrender to his failures. Does this *construction* deserve any acquittal, or *energeo*? Or extension? Not on his mind. In the least.

These thoughts caught him for a beat. Perhaps he could be on even terms with himself. But *no*. He was done with. He is left with the bourbon bottle for now. And he takes it. Empties it all.

Nelson takes a last, long sip of the whisky, then tosses the Yankees hat to the short hair student. She smiles back a "thank you" and gives him a relieved, supportive thumbs-up, followed by a muted. "How great thou art, my Lord?"

He replies with a fatherly wink. Deliverance.

The train car stops.

Doors open.

His legs carry him onto the desolate, half-lit, litter-infested Bleeker Street platform.

The train departs belligerently.

Two youth subway surfers riding on the back of the downtown subway car.

Bleecker Street Platform

A stunned Jojo exits on Nelson's heels, staring transfixed at him.

An ordinary homeless lay on the cold platform floor, by his hungry three-legged black-and-white mutt, back to an overloaded trash can. He holds a sign that reads, "WORK FOR FOOD." Behind him, a Seven Up poster ad with a baby drinking a soda bottle, "*We have the youngest customers in the business – Nothing does it like Seven Up.*"

Nelson and Jojo lock eyes. He nods at her, and she nods back. He opens the revolver's barrel, unloads the bullets, and throws the revolver into a garbage can. He takes a last sip from the paper bag bottle and tosses it into the can too. Cursing, he turns and leaves up the stairs.

Jojo follows his ascent with mesmerized fixed eyes.

Jojo shuffling inside the garbage can for the 0.44 revolver, then holding it upwards while looking at Nelson as he walks up the stairs dropping the bullets behind him. And cursing some more.

Nelson's silhouette fades amongst unruly New Yorkers pounding down the dirty, dripping-wet, and grimy stairs.

A dazed and confused Jojo somewhat loudly, with glowing eyes, certainly cheering, to herself. "My-man!"

A White New York

Night steps in.

It snows heavily in silence.

Nelson strolling Alphabet City.

Vapor from the city's massive underground steam system flow outbound from every street manhole and foreclosed urban cracks.

New York, covered in white snow, holds its beauty in some regard.

It covers, at least momentarily, the spectacle of street filth, overflowing trash cans, rumbled structures, war-zone street blocks, tract housing, and homeless junkyard-style tents. To our benefit, it equally covers a horrendous, vandalized, four-door, haphazardly designed Brown Chevrolet Chevette hatchback abandoned on the corner of Avenue B and E 4th Street – just a few blocks from Katz's Deli.

Notoriously, the slum-like Alphabet City is color blind. Ungentrified.

There is no money here.

Grand Central, Lost & Found

Night.

A Little Rascals episode, *In the Mood for Love*, with Alfalfa's voice singing to Darla.

A wet-from-snow Nelson sits by his bed scrolling through a reel microfilm reader, researching depressing B&W city pictures searching for Amanda.

By the side table, a beaten-down Gordon Park, *Flavio*, photobook resting at ease – albeit, if *at ease* it can ever be.

Nelson's Bed

Moments later.

3:16AM.

An invisible angel's hand closing the *Flavio* book.

Nelson sleeping, then waking up after a dreadful nightmare.

He sweats.

Half asleep. His only words. "Boy, I need my girl. . ."

By the Bed's Edge

An invisible *Angel of Light*, standing up, looking after Nelson.

The angel is crestfallen because it is powerless against whatever it is Nelson has fallen to. It can only summon its thoughts as an attempt to wane its own grief. And no more.

Our *Angel of Light*, feeling ill-equipped, subpoenas music to fill the empty vague room with some warmth. It's the least it can do for Nelson.

Victor Jara's melancholic *Cancion de Cuna Para Un Nino Vago* LP spins on a 78 vintage Victrola. Jara's calm, embracing voice calls for peace. Calls for truth.

The elements respect the moment.

The Angel's thoughts are whispered in a mellow ballad

His heart, in scraps, hard as stone. Colorless as a final breath.
Dark as the vague beyond.
His eyes once deep blue. Just a shallow ash.
His hands, once mighty. Light. Left to hesitation.

His soul once bright. A mere after spark.
His mind once awake. Blind in doubt.

His body once impregnable. Can't lessen the ache of death.
Once a giant in human stature. Now feeling small.
Legendary lyrics written to honor his gallant victories. Now forgotten.

The air he breathes is no longer the same.
The sun's summer rays can't warm his back any longer.
Every day is a cold day.

The ability to feel anything. Gone.
Sadness has no space to compete. Nor sorrow. Or repentance.
Regret comes close. The cruelest of all human feelings.

The man is broken under the gun of dismay.
No sun, or light has measure here.
And worst of all – he knows it.
The idea that time can heal. Another fallacy. Illusion.
There are no last days.

It is sunrise and the nightmare reveals reality.
Repeat. Repeat.

Chapter 31

New York Times, *The Morgue*

2:13 AM.

A cold, rainy night.

By a large meeting room, Nelson reading through a colleagues' research material on the Middle East. He flips a spiral photo-logbook and sees the following B&W photos:

- 1930's, American Standard Oil led executives on an oil expedition in East Saudi Arabia, on the Persian Gulf.
- 1945's, a proud Saudi Arabian construction builder handing over the recently constructed Dhahran Airfield to a U.S. Air Force officer.
- Iran's Prime Minister Mosaddeq and parliament Majilis voting to nationalize Iran's oil industry against Anglo-Iranian Oil Company (AIOC) and British-built Abadan Oil Refinery interests.

- 1953, Iran's Mosaddeq arriving for trial in Tehran.
- 1953, a celebratory Kermit-Eden's Operation Ajax-Boot, post-Coup photo of Secretary of State John Foster Dulles and then Vice President Nixon greeting the Shah Mohammad Reza Pahlavi in Washington, D.C.
- 1953, the signing of the Mutual Defense Assistance Agreement between the U.S. and Saudi Arabia.
- Monarch Reza Pahlavi arriving from Rome to his newly assigned Shah post.
- December 1979, Soviet invasion of Afghanistan.
- Soviet presence in Syria, Kazakhstan, Libya, and Algeria.
- President Carter's financial support of the Mujahideen rebels against the Soviet Union's Afghan war.

Nelson feels he has had enough and closes the photo-book. He strolls towards a metal cabinet and pulls out a whisky bottle stashed behind a French Larousse dictionary.

His eyes now follow the tak-tak sound of a typewriter (from afar).

Nelson pours bourbon into his coffee mug as he walks through file corridors while coming to an obscure glass room, chasing the sound.

The mug is full to the top and a few drops of coffee fall to the floor.

Nelson reaches a glass room where the sound is produced.

Door unlocked.

Glass Room (War Room)

He is inside.

Cold white lights flickering – signaling the times.

He looks around and notices that this particular room resembles (and is) a research *war room*.

Nelson sees at the far end of the room a young woman typing on a sage green Olympia SG1 standard typewriter. The eye-sparkling, Tisch research intern, Lailah, pulls her paper out of the typewriter with contentment and yells, "Done!"

She then grabs her loosely knit Navy backpack, a 35mm FTb Canon, and springs out, granting Nelson a wink. "All yours, Pops! But I will lock you down here in this dungeon for eternity if you erase anything." (looking at the board). She then sighs gingerly. "What a wonderful decade, don't you think?"

The fringes from her cow-girl leather jacket dance in all directions as she "speaks" with her hands.

The short-hair intern tosses him a spellbinding Chester Higgins *Drums of Life* photobook and departs, as optimistic and thrilled as a mortgage free, twenty-three-year-old, *Times* researcher living in The Village, can ever be. It only happens once in a lifetime.

Nelson can only nod, deliver a pleasant smile, and appreciate the courteous expression. He has no business (nor wants) to answer verbally and just follows her with officious eyes and a slight nod of the head. And that is all she needs.

He sits by the ill-kept, disorganized, large, team-group working table. It's a mess.

Apart from food leftovers, half-eaten sandwiches, pizza crusts, Kodachromes, paper coffee cups, C-prints, and empty pink donut boxes, it also affords hand-written notes, paper clippings, B&W photos, scrap paper, and cut-out articles – all scattered in no proper fashion.

Clearly, a dedicated team is working on an important group project.

On the left side wall, next to the table, two oversized chronological blackboards randomly showcase events specific to the 70s. Written in red marker, a hand scribble reads "THE SEVENTIES, THE AGE OF ENLIGHTENMENT."

Taped on the boards, patches, groups of names, photos, sketches, scribbles, expressions, editorial cartoons, and dates.

Nelson pacing side to side, his eyes flash through the board, piece by piece, photo by photo, note by note. And this is what he reads:

THE BOARDS' NOTES
. . . It is said that depression leads to creativeness. . .
. . . So many metanarratives. . .
. . . The *end of confidence* 70s, a turn of era for the arts, culture, and *détente science*. . .

Row One. . . Zappa, *Led Zeppelin IV*, Warhol, Morrison (both), Iggy, *Moondance*, Bee Gees, *Bel Canto* Pavarotti, John Williams (both), *Harvest*, Mitchell, *Blood On The Tracks*, *Born to Run*, Pink Floyd, *Maggie May*, *Sitting*, *Piano Man*, Bowie, *Wild Horses*, Springsteen, Rocket Man Elton John, *Survival*, The Clash, Talking Heads, *Da Ya Think I'm Sexy* Ross-Supremes, CBGB, Wonder, Summers, *The Velvet Underground*, Aretha, Maceo, Talking Heads,

Parliament, *Exile on Main St.*, Miles, Jackson, Dripping Springs Nelson, Denver, *Jolene* Parton, Burdon, *WAR*, Veloso, Sosa, Jara, *El Condor Pasa (If I Could)*. The fabulous Bob Marley. . .

Row Two. . . Punctuated Equilibrium, Ashkin, Hawking, Louise Brown, Black-Sholes, Sloan's Professor Wallace, Biolinguistics, *Reflections on Language*, Voyager-1, Jarvik-7, Mariner 9, Landsat-1, The Venera Program, Sagittarius A, Sagan, Skylab, Gravity Probe-A, *USS Enterprise*, the *Selfish Gene*, Phi X 174 Genetic Engineering, Sanger Sequencing. . .

Row Three. . . KENBAK-1, Commodore PET, Altair 8800, Apple II, Cray-1, WOW, UNIX, tf–idf, Hewlett Packard's HP-35, 12-C, Gödel's Ontological Proof, DynaTEC, VCR, LCD, Magnavox Odyssey, Pong, Atari 2600, Philips' CD, NP-Complete, Monstrous Moonshine, E-Book, Computer Mouse, Ethernet, the e-mail, the lighter, Word Processor, Fiber Optics, the Silicon Microprocessor, Silicon Valley, Route 128, Intel 4004, Soft Contact Lenses, UPC, MRI, CAT Scans. . .

Row Four. . . Synthetic Insulin, Taser, Laser and Ink Jet Printer, VHS, the Cell Phone, Digital Camera, Rubik's Cube, Sudoko, the Floppy Disk, the Walkman, the 747 Jumbo, Concorde, Have Blue, Heimlich maneuver, Tommy John surgery. . .

Row Five. . . LED, Lotus Esprit, Bowerman's Waffle, Margaret Court, Fagundes Telles, Murdoch's *Sea*, Cheever's suburbs, *Dr. Seuss*, Marge Piercy, *The Ascent of Men*, the aluminum beer can,

Title IX, Title X, Clean Water Act, *Our Bodies Ourselves*, Pele's *Jules Rimet* 1970 World Cup Dream Team, Fred Lebow, *Baabaas* Edwards, Mr. Olympia *Pumping Iron* Schwarzenegger, Perfect-Ten Nadia Comăneci, Bird vs. Magic. RAP music. . .

Row Six. . . Copolla, Lucas, Kubrick, *Alien*, Garcia Marquez, R. Crumb, *Airport*, Friedkin, *The French Connection*, *The Exorcist*, *Rocky*, *Monty Python*, *Sesame Street*, Wilder-Pryor, Bertolucci, Scorsese, *Saturday Night Fever*, *SNL*, Belushi, Murray, Radner, Chase, *Star Wars*, *M.A.S.H.*, *JAWS*, Sellers, *Colonel Steve Austin*, *Cotton*, Knievel, Linda Carter, Welch, *Dirty Harry*, Brando, Travolta, Pacino, Jason's hockey *Halloween* mask. . .

A beat.

Nelson to himself. "Hum. . . maybe not all that lost, after all."

The sound of paper being detached shifts his attention to the darker corner of the war room, by a tall, cracked, green-glass mirror.

He notices an old, yellowish newspaper clipping falling to the ground like a bird feather. The clipping is a January 9th, 1966, *Religion* section of the New York Times, which reads "GOD IS DEAD."

He reads it with saddened eyes and head down.

Now holding the paper clip, he looks at his reflection in the mirror for a beat. There is no reflection.

He whispers. "What have I done?"

Table

Moments later.

He calmly sits on the table, stretches his legs on top of the paper-crowded desk, and takes to flipping Higgin's B&W virtuosity with the compulsory gusto it deserves.

315 Bowery Street, CBGB

Moments later. 2:13 AM.

Sidewalk.

It rains lightly.

Three hot-dog and pretzel carts.

Five-dozen wet patrons in line anxious to enter an alternate dimension.

A strong whiff of cannabis and pretzel.

CBGB's Entrance

Sean standing on tall black military boots, dressed in punk rock leather, wearing black squared sunglasses eating a giant pretzel, and escorting Nelson inside the buzzing CBGB.

Inside CBGB

A dazed-looking Nelson entering, strolling inside the loud and anarchic culture-setting New York incubator as the underground Nico, garbed in light blue kimono, sings *The Fairest Of The Seasons.*

A long beat.

A calm-faced Nelson drifting inside CBGB's rows of poets admiring, contemplating Nico's velvet voice.

A pale, bald, short, young lady wearing green swimming goggles and a wolfskin coat halts in front of Nelson. Her left hand on his right shoulder. She looks deep into his eyes and snugs a white rose on his right ear. On her toes, she lands a kiss on his cheek. An innocent girlish smile. She bows gently.

Nelson knows this is a freethinking spirit that understands life's subtle under netting. An essential element in the balance of life. Of existence. You take that away, and the world will submerge.

Sean lays his long arm on her shoulders. He kisses her on the lips. They have identical facial complexion and texture.

Sean and his pair are off.

Nelson alone, looking lost, wondering if dreams are finite. Colored lights swirl around him and blanket his dimension for a beat.

He hoists his right arm against the flashing lights, then stares at his aged hand, wondering if he is the same man.

His body wants to cry, but his eyes are too tired.

Time.

Time is not a measure. It is a language.

41st Street and 9th Avenue

Moments later.

5:01 AM. Still dark.

A metal trash can as firepit. Tall flames.

Nelson and Sean peacefully eating lotus root and pork soup with a group of two-dozen homeless.

New York Life Building, Rooftop

Meanwhile, Cole standing up, soaked in blood, wearing his Oxford's and "ears-necklace," on the edge of the Gothic *grotesque* and gold leaf roof.

A fallen star rips behind him in the sky. Note the "fallen star" counterintuitively rips upwards.

Subway

7:27 AM.

Empty, dirty scooped-acrylic seats.

A tall man in full Gucci suit reading the Wall Street Journal. Stamped on the front cover, a photo of Babrak Karmal - the exiled leader of the Parcham faction of the Marxist People's Democratic Party of Afghanistan (PDPA) - grabbing government.

A lonesome Nelson riding an even more lonesome subway car towards Grand Central. His car companions are a lesbian couple dressed in hippie white, a group of Polish immigrants and a Vietnamese woman playing a sad melody on her mandolin.

The couple gently nods at him as if they knew him. He nods back the same.

New York subways – the real America represented by every single ethnicity and personal inclination, preference available. Such poetry.

With an air of contentment, Nelson, in his own way, seems to welcome and appreciate the diversity.

The car carries on raging to its next stop.

Queens, City Morgue

An artless clock on the tile wall reads 6:13 PM.

Mozart's *Magic Flute* flowing from a Marconi's tube radio.

Competing with Mozart, the loud voice of a methodical pathologist describing the body dissection of a stabbed female victim billowing out of an RCA portable tape-recorder.

The pathologist's recorded voice is deep, soothing, and unassumingly academic. Almost pleasing. Almost.

Zhain inside the expansive cold room by the door entrance.

The Morgue Man's index finger is on the stop button. He presses it down to "stop". One would expect a hard stop. But this tape recorder has a malfunctioning stop mechanism, and the pathologist's voice stretches progressively in slow motion for about five seconds before completely halting. Then a loud click.

The walls are relieved of the eerie voice, just as Zhain is.

Mozart endures.

Zhain serenely toddling inside the eerie forensics room. He stops midway, next to a corpse lying on a metal dissection table. This body is dry and carved open. Zhain can see its internal organs, and its exposed rib cage.

The Morgue Man stands a bit further, by the metallic shelves, closing a black notation book.

On top of the Morgue Man's metal desk, a copy of Goethe's *The Sorrows of Young Werther* opened on page 316.

Zhain can only see the Morgue Man's curved back and his oversized white gown. He hums. "Papageno. . . Papageno. . ."

With his kyphosis back to Zhain, the Morgue Man asks, in a professorial tone. "Did you know that your fingernails continue to grow even after death?" A beat. "Really, they do."

A half-step to the side. Zhain's astounded eyes gazing at his left hand's fingernails. Another step back from the awkward Morgue Man, who is equally fixated on his own elongated fingernails.

"I see," is all Zhain offers back to fill the space between them and their realities.

A beat, and they look at the disfigured body.

The Morgue Man asks somberly. "Are there such things as sins?"

A beat.

Zhain looks fixated on the bluish body while speaking.

"Sins, you speak of. Yes, my friend, there are. I can assure you there are." Zhain replies in a deep Medieval voice, thinking that this ends this conversation. But it does not.

The Morgue Man takes to sharpening his precision medical scalpel, referring to the tortured body. "I am an admirer of his work, you know. Such craft. Steady hands. Precision, my friend, *precision* is everything in our business. A modern-day Privateer." He salivates a notch. "And this one knows exactly what he is doing. An artistly colleague."

With spooked eyes, Zhain takes a third half-step back away from the Morgue Man. Evidently, he has learned his lesson and will not dare try to fill the silence a second time. He just nods slightly.

A last remark from our flesh-cutting Renaissance Man. "People are afraid of what they don't understand, you know. But not me."

43rd Street & 9th Avenue

Sunday night.

Rain patterning.

Ambulance sirens wailing.

A man wearing large, metal airframe glasses strolling 43rd Street and Ninth Avenue carrying a black garbage bag with what appears to be two watermelons inside. The bag has smudged blood on it.

Firehouse

Monday.

Firehouse clean-up night.

On the radio speakers, the standard dispatch orders and *tones*.

Kitchen

Francis and one short firefighter cooking.

Francis smashing tomatoes. Johnny peeling potatoes.

Chris lying on a couch reading Bradbury's *The Martian Chronicles*.

The remaining half-dozen firefighters cleaning the kitchen and setting up an Italian-style dining table.

Outside, the world is raging.

515 West, 42nd Street

Same day. Night.

Hunting season.

Aboveground madness.

A man wearing large, metal airframe glasses comfortably

strolling the bright and loud Deuce sidewalks hunting for wounded buffalos.

The sex-charged, pornography-engulfed 42nd Street - ground zero for the sex trade. For raw pleasure. For transgression. And violence. Of every kind.

Illicit pleasure establishment.

Municipal orange "CLOSED" stickers are taped on the front windows of busy, functioning emporiums.

Burlesque clubs.

Quarter-peek machines and lenient *booths*.

Master and Slave Suburbia Family Men (MSSFM) roaming unceremoniously in turtle-neck sweaters and weekend golf boxers.

Sex workers of all races, and all genders. For every (and any) preference.

Dozens of walking street billboards shouting, advertising, "Wall-to-wall-pussies! Come-and-have-it!"

A victim's pool.

Travel Inn Motor Hotel, corner of 10th Avenue

Next day. Day.

Inpatient horns honking loudly.

Firetrucks, ambulances, and police cars about.

A fire ladder truck parked, extending its ladder out, reaching the building's fourth-floor window. Thick smoke streaming outwards from shattered windows.

Rescue Company One - engines and ladder trucks.

Firefighters carrying packs of houses, slogging up the stairs.

Inside the Travel Inn Motor Hotel, Fourth Floor, Room #417

A room fully engulfed with thick dark smoke.

A Firefighter performing CPR on a lifeless, headless, handless body. No, not a *Resusci Anne*.

Inside the Hotel, Room #417

Moments later.

A burnt "DON'T DISTURB" sign hangs on the door knob.

Bloodstains on the carpet.

Women's clothes piled neatly inside the room's enamel bathtub.

Patrolmen in blue, ambulance personnel, and homicide detectives from the 10th Precinct in beige and green London Fog overcoats.

A Forensic Photographer flashing his camera at the horrid body parts.

Life. A painful prose.

Insanity.

Chapter 32

42ⁿᵈ Street, RHOPE's DINER

It is Saturday night in 1979.

Starless, muted skies.

The cold, gritty streets produce a loud polyphony of sounds and rhythms.

Two hundred and twenty thousand heroin addicts waltz New York streets.

The repetitive, bitonal, cocaine-chopping metal sounds from a Gillette blade.

The diner facade has only a few pink neon letters lit.

Only "R___'S DINER" lit. The letters "H-O-P-E" are not lit.

The neon letters flicker.

A theatrical poster for *Apocalypse Now* wheatpasted on the diner's left façade.

A sign on the diner door reads, "LONG-HAIRED, FREAKY PEOPLE MAY NOT APPLY."

Gillette chopping cocaine endures.

Sidewalk

Yellow checker cab drops off a young, blond prostitute along with a short, stocky municipal pander.

Random, paradise rag-tag pimps hustling the litter-infested streets.

This corner translates into a central clearinghouse for hookers, *tricks, flashers* and *Johns* - the usuals. It fills the bill, along with acute resentment at the callousness of the authorities and inept government officials.

There is no drama here.

Reality reigns.

RHOPE's DINER

Zappa's *Bobby Brown (Goes Down)* playing inside the convoluted urban restaurant.

This diner - a metaphor for the American Dream. One of those institutions to work long hours and make very little money.

It smells like grease, wet clothes, and naphthalene. And negligence. And depression.

Essex, Tracker, and three unshaved paramilitary Goons eat T-bone steaks, mashed potatoes, and gravy.

The men watch with on-and-off attention the "Sugar Ray vs. Wilfredo Benitz" Caesar's Palace, Welterweight title fight on a top wall TV.

In yellow-lens glasses and a Daniel Boon coonskin cap, a stoned

Tracker smokes a thicker-than-average joint. He pours loads of bottled ketchup over his steak. A MAD magazine by his plate.

Goon-Two, aka Mustard, "reads" Farah Fawcett's August Playboy edition.

A *Jacki Curtis* type waitress catwalks by the diner's vaulted corridor making sure she is accounted for.

Mustard follows the well-adorned *type* with the side of his brown eyes with clear, however, discrete interest. As our glamorous waitress walks by him, he pinches her derrière unassumingly, abashedly.

The waitress turns violently with a kitchen knife in hand, threatening Mustard. For real. Their intentions are unclear. Perhaps theatrics. Perhaps they have shared more than tips. Perhaps it doesn't matter – it's the 70s. Her chromed knife on his jugular. It may (or may not) be their *thing*. They lock eyes. She resumes her catwalk down the corridor. Mustard smiles contently.

Goon-One, aka Roach, reads the Village Voice and mocks the *Stonewall Inn Pride March* photo, showing it to Essex and referring to the image. "Can you believe this shit!?"

Essex abruptly snatches the newspaper from Roach's unsanitary hand.

Meanwhile, Mustard snorts a line of cocaine from atop the diner's menu book. With bulging red eyes, he proclaims. "Man, I miss the China White, damn this Mexican Mud garbage. . ."

"Gimme-this, knucklehead." Essex with force.

The March Parade photo shows a blurred May and Janis holding hands while entering a Brooklyn-bound subway Green Line entrance.

"God-damn. . ." Essex shouts out loud.

Essex shows the picture to Tracker, who immediately recognizes the women from their train exchange. He nods.

Mustard's wide-opened eyes and cocaine powder smudged face blend in.

A welterweight rat under the table scouts for leftovers. This is *its* assigned booth, corner.

Sidewalk, by the Diner Window

Juxtaposed to the gritty diner booth window, a gutsy Homeless in a ragged-Army coat sprays dirty water from a fading pickle green *Pinaud Clubman* bottle onto the window. He composedly spreads the *Eau de désespéré* on the window with an even more soiled rag in comprehensive circular cleaning motion immediately in front of Essex, who sits by the window.

In orange dhoti, a half-dozen shaved Hare Krishna strolling down the street, holding candles, chanting the *Hare-Krishna-Hare-Rama* mantra.

The Homeless has no more than a pair of functioning teeth and smiles at the Goons, hoping to collect a coin or two. Anything.

Essex's patience runs thin, and he bangs abruptly on the window, giving the Homeless *the finger*.

As the Homeless attempts to reattribute *the finger* gesture, an all-out brawl of two random intoxicated junkies erupts out of nowhere, smashing into the laborious homeless. He goes face-first into the window, sliding down glued to it like a desert lizard.

Our street civil tenant is back up exchanging fists with the intruding junkies.

The Diner

The men inside the diner could hardly care - it's the street's in-difference that hurts. Just another savage, starless New York City Saturday night.

Tracker pours loads of ketchup over his steak, immune to the outworld violence. He, too, has been desensitized, as every breathing New Yorker.

Essex back to the men. ". . . as I was saying - listen up: tomorrow zero-six-hundred, we meet at this subway entrance. Pointing at the picture. "Got that, Westie?! Zero-six-hundred."

A garbage can flies across the diner window. Loud, muffled brawl thumps pound the window. The brawl fades out of scene.

"And the third one?" Tracker asks.

"Dude, she can be anybody." Essex explains.

Tracker makes a gun sign with his hand to Goons. "Bring your shit with you. *All* your shit!"

Tracker empties a bottle of Sriracha hot chili sauce over his steak.

"Roger-wilco!" Goons back at him.

On the Dinner's TV

The diner's cook on his toes switching channels.

The ten o'clock newscaster frantically announcing a breaking news – militarized college students (Imam's Line) participating in the Iranian Revolution, jumping fences, and storming the U.S. Embassy in Tehran. Others burning the U.S Flag.

A new order in the making.

Chapter 33

Next Day.

Brooklyn Subway Station

Sunday, 06:01 AM.

A windless morning.

The men - Tracker, Essex, Westie, Roach, and Mustard - huddle behind a black van with their loaded backpacks. They check guns, radio comms, and ammo.

Brooklyn, Booth Pay Phone

Essex speaking to Feist. A visibly collapsing brownstone behind him.

Hell's Kitchen, Phone Booth

Feist on the phone, reacting surprised and agitated.

Brooklyn, Booth Pay Phone

Essex's verbal remarks about Feist. "Fuckin-*knuckle dragger!*"

Essex hand-signals his men to move ahead.

The men disperse out into Brooklyn streets.

Zhain's Condo, Alwyn's Court

06:07 AM.

Alwyn's Court front facade - and its sinister Gothic *grotesque.*

Muffled moans of pleasure.

A window blanketed in condensation. The Empire State building behind it emitting purple light.

A beat.

A reclusive Villa-Lobos' aria from *Bachianas Brasileiras No.5* rehearsed on a string instrument echoes inside the massive room. Although solitary, it captures empathy.

Spacious Living Room

Moments later.

Zhain tuning his rare, Neapolitan, five-course mandocello. The affable Zhain - a virtuoso.

Ninah's articles of clothing scattered around the living room's marble floor and red velvet chair.

He switches instruments and straps a Medieval Celtic Bouzouki and commences a folk Foggy Dew arrangement while gazing out in soul-searching contemplation out the city skies. Perhaps a premonition, an omen.

The unfairly sexy Ninah appears on the far stern of the room, under sfumato, in stilettos and pearls only, to join the ensemble with her own, a rare, 1920s Aluminum Pfretzschner up-right, Double Bass. A Renaissance painting of *The Abduction of Psyche*, in purple tones, behind her.

The double bass fills their lungs. Her talents are unaccounted for. They are vast, and some argue they may not be from this world, deserving a chapter on its own. Multiple ancient royal Yolda tattoos printed on her dark-skin mystic body - these tattoos hold battle passages and a spell no man can unbind - a mystery better left to obscurity.

It is rumored she is the only daughter of surviving Anastasia, Czar Nichola's mysterious missing daughter. On her left hip, a dark green Faberge Egg tattoo.

The bewildering ensemble declares independence and extends beyond the physical. It prevails in the air. In a reflective continuum.

A beat.

Zhain wonders uncomfortably inside the infinite-size living room, pealing a pomegranate, and looking outside the window to the Manhattan's horizon. A black leather whip hangs on his shoulders.

His eyes sense matter, presences, out of place.

With tense eyes looking out the window he sees a blue butterfly land on the window right in front of him. His hand on the window glass wanting to feel it.

He retracts his hand briskly and looks straight at the phone (before it rings). The phone is silent, and he stands firm, locking the phone with his eyes.

Pomegranate seeds fall to the ground.

A porcelain vase next to him, by a small coffee table, tips over and shatters on the floor. Not a blink from him. He is indifferent. He feels a chill run down his spine.

The phone finally rings loudly. His eyes catch Ninah, and she nods at him. Then back at the Baroque clock next to the phone - it reads 6:08 AM.

It is time.

Zhain listens on the phone's handset.

He hangs it up abruptly, storming to the private elevator. On his way out to the elevator, by a dedicated hall, he stops to stare at "THAYER'S, A VIRGIN" painting for half a second. Then blasts out to the door.

Zhain inside the private, velvet-and-silver elevator, repeatedly pressing the "L" button. A substantial, blue butterfly painting hangs on the elevator's back wall.

As the elevator's inside mirror-door closes, an apprehensive Zhain and his tense eyes.

Ninah by the window, where Zhain had placed his hand. Contrasting with the condensation, she sees not the palm of a man, but one of a wolf.

The Foggy Dew duet lasts and follows across all chapters.

A Scottish bagpipe now joins in.

Amanda's Kitchen

06:09 AM.

Today is Claire's birthday. A big day at the Fleming's.

Amanda is alone in the kitchen tossing flour and baking bread.

Outside, on the sidewalk, a Little Cheyenne kimono-girl looking up to Amanda's kitchen window.

They look at each other in silence for a few seconds, then nod gently.

To herself with a relieved smile. "It's time."

A relieved, lasting sigh.

The Garden

Minutes later.

Amanda now setting-up a breakfast table outside at the Garden for her guests - the Flemings, Chris, Winnie, May, Janis, Fatima and others.

Persimmon cake engraved with Oreos smiley-face reads "Happy Birthday Claire." Tons of white flowers.

Seven books wrapped in pink and blue birthday paper.

Amanda holds for a second and looks to the blue sky. She stares at the infinite.

New York Times, *The Morgue*

The Morgue's ELAC radio clock *flicks* 6:13 AM. A slow TAK.

Nelson, wearing a white Jets jersey, a magnifying lens in hand, slogging through packs of photos, mainly probing people and events that may raise attention (robberies, murders, mugshots, etc.).

He notices a thick stack of photos labeled "WHITAKER, S., UNTITLED ARCHIVE 13.6-76," on the edge of his desk next to Chester Higgins' *Black Women* wide-opened book. He respectfully closes the B&W work of art, grabs the Whitaker stack, and reviews it carefully – what he sees are photos of decadent New York and human misery.

He flips a picture of Lucy Komisar having a drink at McSorley's. Then a photo of Soviet ground troops mounted on top of BMD-1 infantry vehicles and T-62 tanks entering Kabul, Afghanistan.

He stumbles on a photo of Amanda's side profile inside her Brooklyn kitchen. The photo is a blurred B&W still of Amanda tossing bread flour in the air with Chris and Winnie happily observing.

Nelson recognizes Amanda and Winnie (Don) but not Chris. Ecstatic, he grabs the phone and calls Sean at his day job, the Red Caboose.

Red Caboose, West 46th Street

6:17 AM.

Phone ringing.

In a granted Williamsburg accent, the Caboose's Manager voice echoes loudly with a lit Camel in his mouth. "YOW, Bad-Card! Phone!" Note the Caboose Manager wears a yellow Crazy Eddie T-shirt stamped *HIS PRICES ARE INSANE.* Then back to taking the business of the day.

Sean passionately reads R. Crumb's "MR. NATURAL #3" *comic* book (hardly a comic, but undeniably comical) with his feet on a small corner table. He feels proud with his new look: black military boots, black leather pants, black lipstick, and a The Clash *London's Calling* white T-Shirt. His nails are painted green. He wears a black head scarf and hair net.

Sean walks towards the plum color desk phone cluelessly and timidly answers it, hesitantly, with a clogged. "Hellooo?"

"Sean, where did you take the photo of the lady in a kitchen, Don, and a young boy?" Nelson impatiently asks.

"Cowboy-Man?!" A confused Sean asks.

"Sean, pay very close attention: where did you take that picture?" Nelson asks in instructing tone.

"You mean Winnie. Oh, it's probably his friend, the bread-lady."

"The address, Sean, what's the address?!"

"Yeah, it's over at Winnie's, Lefferts-12-23; why?" Sean pipes, light on details.

Nelson hangs up, grabs his tennis bag, and blasts out.

Brooklyn Gospel Church

6:37 AM.

Knuckles fully dressed in Gospel green robe, playing a Foggy Dew solo on her prized Les Paul.

Four of her church accomplices, along with Leprechaun on the bass, join her, pounding along their Irish drums.

Behind them, a complete choir softly humming Foggy Dew lyrics on stage.

Chapter 34

Brooklyn Shootout

Brooklyn, 1223 Lefferts Street

6:13 AM.

A bright sunny day.

The air is clear, but not for long.

Tracker alone scouting Sterling Street.

Essex and Goons scouting Bedford Avenue.

Amanda's Brownstone

7:27 AM.

Johnny's early morning solo bagpipe rehearsal takes over from Zhain's Irish Bouzouki and Double Bass duet, now joining Knuckles Foggy Dew version.

Street

Tracker spots May from a distance crossing Lefferts Street jogging towards Amanda's Brownstone.

May waits for Janis, who is running late and carrying a flower bouquet. A beat and May enters Amanda's Brownstone alone.

Tracker to Essex on the radio. "Kilo-1, Essex, jackpot! 12-23 Lefferts. Over. Repeat. Jackpot on 12-23 Lefferts, you read? Over."

"Copy, kilo-2! Gheeme two-mikes." Essex excitedly back at him.

Tracker discreetly pulls out his Desert Eagle, cocks it, and hides it inside his jacket. A DOUBLEMINT to the mouth.

Amanda's Garden

7:47 AM.

May enters the Garden area.

Johnny's bagpipe Foggy Dew solo is louder. He sits by the garden's entrance wearing a Kilt and FDNY blue T-shirt. The rhythmic tap of the sole of his boots to the ground as percussions drums.

Everyone else sits at the table under the pergola, enjoying the day, except for Chris and Claire.

Stairs

Chris walking up the building's stairs to the Third Floor, APT 3C, to surprise Claire with *his* present. It is a fancy, professional hair blower wrapped in red bow (box). It took the kid four months of running errands for Winnie to save for the gift. Worth every cent saved.

Claire proudly brushes her long, thick shining fawn hair and sprays on Avon Sweet Honesty cologne. It's her birthday, and she is the happiest.

Claire's Room

In silence, Chris stands by Claire's room, by the door, box under his arm, looking passionately at her. He does not want to interrupt her contemplation.

Claire turns her head back gently, sensing (knowing) Chris is in the room.

She recites Oscar Wilde out loud. *"Man is least himself when he talks in his own person. Give him a mask, and he will tell you the truth."*

She stares at Chris with her luminous eyes, then opens a big strawberry smile. "But not this man. *My* Chump needs no mask, Mr. Wilde. And that is a fact of life." Her candid remarks delivered in a passionate, affirmative voice.

Chris' eyes mellow. And one single tear dives to the ground. This tear built on passion. On that innocence of such magnitude able to fix all the wrongs in this dimension.

Chris takes one, then a second, step inside her room, slowly as if waiting for authorization, proudly holding the wrapped present with his arms and tiny hands extended like a robot. Herbert's *Dune* wrapped in pink bow snugged under his armpit.

The present box is wrapped in light heather paper and silk-like lace, fitted with a solitary cherry rose. He drives a slow-motion smile back at her, placing the box on the edge of her Norwegian wood bed, then tacking to the window.

He sits on the window's frame, body half out the window, like a watchdog admiring his crown princess. He observes a green beetle crawl placidly on his arm.

Claire walks towards the edge of the bed with her curious eyes fixated on his.

She grabs, shakes, then unfolds the wrap knowing the whole ordeal has one culprit only – that daring little boy.

She can't believe her eyes – holding, in dismay, the precious hair blower. She follows, looking at Chris, shaking her head sideways in utter *how-could-you* elation, "Chump. . ."

Claire places her portable turntable needle into *The Three Degrees* LP's crevices as it spins. The apparatus twirls slowly, giving us a confined, *When Will I See You Again*.

An imperceptible sway from the closet door. Possibly airflow. Most likely, the elements scooching covertly not to forfeit this act of love.

Lefferts Street

7:51 AM.

Janis is running late and sprints to Amanda's Brownstone holding two bottles of Mateus Rosé. Her wooden mule spits out in the middle of the street.

As Tracker advances to a closer corner, he is caught cold by May who is hopping back to retrieve her mule.

And so, it begins.

A solo, Shaman battle drum gains body.

They lock eyes, and Janis abandons the shoe, rushing back to Amanda's Brownstone.

The wine bottles fly in the air, then smashing hard onto the ground loudly.

Brownstown Steps

As fast as lightning, Janis retrieves a picnic bag loaded with guns stashed behind the boxwoods. She pulls a 0.44 Colt and May's Walther WA2000.

Janis cocks, aims, and shoots fiercely at Tracker until empty. She reloads just as quickly. Her act is brutal. Physical.

Tracker ducks and returns fire instantly. He takes one to his chicken-plate and falls into defensive position behind an abandoned station wagon. Two rounds blast on one of its tires, producing a dreadful explosion blast.

One dozen Shaman drums join the scene in anticipation.

Garden Table, Breakfast

7:58 AM. Guns Fired.

Hammer and May pull out guns. Hammer a Beretta and May a Ruger. They both yell out loud in unison. "Janis!"

"The kids!" Amanda yells.

Amanda, Beth, and the petite Fatima rush to the Third Floor to safety and to be with Chris and Claire.

Breakfast chairs fly upwards, falling hard to the floor.

The cake smashed on the grass.

"Everybody, stay inside! Pops, call the Precinct!" Hammer orders out loud.

Beretta in hand, he cocks it and storms out.

Francis neglects and commands Johnny, "*You* call the Precinct!"

Francis goes for a baseball bat behind the column corner and rushes behind Hammer.

Lobby

Johnny inside the lobby, speaking into the wall phone. He is conflicted between helping Francis and running to the Third Floor, to the kids.

Lefferts Street, Brownstown Steps

7:59 AM.

Janis ducked behind the steps' cement low sidewalls, reloading while taking fire.

Essex and the three Goons run to huddle up around Tracker.

Hammer comes out to the stairs and sees Janis pinned down, under a haze of bullets.

Bullets ricochet inside the lobby area.

"We're sitting ducks here! Move!" Janis commands.

Hammer runs down the steps, turns North, and takes position behind a pimped El Camino. As he does, he takes fire from Tracker. Essex joins in the shooting. The bullets wreck the orange El Camino, blasting windows and igniting a gas-tank fire.

Hammer now runs toward his AMC.

May jumps out of the Garden into Winnie's backyard shop. Only a low fence separates both lots in the back.

She reaches the top of the shop and takes suppressive-fire position. She grips a Bren LMG out of a stashed cache of weapons and rips at Mustard and Westie, pinning them down with her heavy gun.

Janis opens fire and holds the assailants momentarily from advancing.

Building Stairs

Amanda, Beth, and Fatima reach Claire and Chris's, hiding them deep inside APT 3F.

Amanda uses her silver wood cane to punch out the apartment's metal number plaque (3C) in one swift move. The metal plaque falls to the ground face down producing a distinctive cling.

Stashed inside a small room, Chris and Claire are confused.

Chris pulls Claire behind him as her protector and shield.

Beth is inside APT 3F, holding an imposing butcher's knife.

She trembles and prays to herself.

Fatima runs down to the second floor to take guard also holding a kitchen knife.

Her Crescent Moon & Star pendant swings violently as she desperately races down the stairs.

Lefferts Street, North-West Corner

8:01 AM.

The wrathful sound of thunder. Lightning.

The horizon is grey. Winds raging. Leaves blown in the air.

A storm to come.

One thousand battle drums provide density and escort Nelson in his charge. He grows. He is transformed. Nelson is Grand.

Nelson sprinting from the North-West side of the street smack in the middle of the shootout like a lion - pitching towards

Hammer, drawing out his short-barrel Henry from the tennis bag, cocking it, and shooting at Tracker. Nelson speeds to the East side of the Street. His speed and agility are unnatural, especially for his age.

He surveys the scene and sees Amanda and other folks on the Brownstone's Third Floor. Amanda is shutting the blinds.

Nelson sees Tracker exchanging with Hammer.

Roach notices Nelson and charges, then shoots back at him. Roache's M16 jams. He tosses it to the side. He sprints on foot with a .45 pistol spitting consecutive rounds.

Nelson darts out of nowhere and knocks Roach flat on the floor with a massive superman-punch to the jaw. Roach is out flat on the sidewalk.

Hammer captures Nelson's actions and is puzzled.

As Nelson approaches the burning the AMC, Hammer points his Beretta at him but holds his fire. Nelson yells. "Don't shoot! My lady is up there."

"Hey, Namath, keep your head down!" Hammer shouts.

Although puzzled, Hammer welcomes the hand, and both men return fire at Essex, Tracker, and the Goons.

While ducked, Hammer opens the AMC's trunk and retrieves a shotgun and a 0.38 revolver. He then reloads and pushes covering fire as Nelson comes closer to the Brownstone's side wall. He looks up at the rusted fire escape as the shortest route to Amanda.

Nelson takes a round that ricochets on his Henry's barrel.

Up he goes.

Third Floor Corridor

Amanda stands determined in the Third-Floor corridor with cane ready in hand. She can see the living room window, corridor, and stairs from where she stands.

Lobby Area

8:13 AM.

Winnie running out from Amanda's kitchen, hiding *The Book* inside his Flash Gordon T-shirt. He rushes out into the street and is met with a haze of bullets.

Janis notices Winnie trying to pass. "Get your butt outta here, Winnie!"

Winnie retreats to the lobby area faster than a scared rabbit.

A beat, a small door that leads to his shop - a secret passage. The passage is engulfed with ancient lamps. Winnie takes one and proceeds through a narrow Probation-era brick tunnel holding *The Book* under his shirt.

Zhain and Feist approach via the South-East side

8:17 AM.

Feist spots May on the shop's rooftop shooting toward Sugar and Westie.

Feist signals Zhain that he is going after her. Giving a quick nod in agreement, Zhain resumes walking firmly. He moves determinedly towards the Brownstone feeling immune to bullets.

Lefferts Street

Roach on his feet behind a white VW Beetle, shooting at Hammer.

Francis sees Hammer being overrun. The Chief grabs the Walther, stands up, and shoots fiercely at Essex and Tracker, who notice and fire back.

The load is off Hammer as he feeds his last magazine.

Roach notices a frightened mom-and-daughter pinned down behind a garbage can and cowardly goes in their direction for safer cover. Hammer shoots Roach twice in the torso before he reaches the innocent civilians.

Francis takes a shot to the leg and is down. Johnny sees it and rushes to help him while under intense crossfire. Chief Francis directs, "Get-outta-here, John, it's just a scratch. Go with your sister!"

Johnny is now pinned down, too. He looks up and sees Nelson climbing the back-end fire escape.

Hammer tosses the revolver to Johnny. He then climbs the crippled fire-stairs speedily to the Third Floor, immediately behind Nelson, like an Alpine speed-climber.

Nelson senses he is being followed.

Tracker shoots multiple times at Johnny, but bullets don't hit him. Tracker finds that odd. He would never miss such a routine target. He looks at his gun scope and readjusts its sight.

Hammer joins Francis to cover Johnny's ascent, now with the shotgun.

Hammer and Francis maintain gunfire, shooting to protect themselves and Johnny, who is rushing up the fire escape.

Hammer pulls out his .38 ankle throw-down and tosses it to Francis.

Winnie's Shoe Shop

Feist sneaks from behind Winnie's shop unnoticed to May, who is pumping lead. Her body quivers from heavy gun recoil.

He creeps behind May.

Feist stands still behind her, in eerie silence, takes a long breath, and shoots point-blank, from close range, in the back of her head.

May falls slowly to the ground, face-first.

With May down, Zhain proceeds unchallenged.

Lefferts Street

Tracker and Essex moving forward, closer to Amanda's Brownstone as bullets haze past them.

Brownstone's Stairs

8:47 AM.

Janis notices that May has stopped shooting, and shouts towards her direction. "May! May!?" No reply.

Janis swaps firing position now with a M1-Garand hoping it will help May. "Talk to me!" She senses (knows) May is gone and cries angrily while still shooting. Her sweaty face trembles. Her eyes turn red. She is in rage.

Janis provides covering fire so that Hammer can get Francis back into the lobby area. She hits Sugar in the neck, killing him instantly. He lays flat in the middle of the street.

Hammer and Francis are cut off purposively by Tracker.

Essex moves ahead and is closer to the brownstone's steps.

Tracker and Westie provide covering fire while Essex

approaches closer. He reaches the steps, shooting his shotgun repeatedly. Buckshot explodes car windows and boxwoods.

Janis, out of ammo, retreats to the inside of the lobby for cover. She is hit by buckshot on the back of her shoulder and lungs. She falls flat (not dead) - spitting blood out of her mouth.

Lefferts Street

Hammer retrieves Roach's M-16 and unjams it. He shoots to protect Francis and the building's entrance equally but cannot do both. He chases after Essex.

Essex reaches Amanda's brownstone steps. He sees Janis crawling her way inside, but takes fire from Hammer, which prevents him from killing her.

Janis crawls behind the lobby's stairs. Winnie drags her into the secret passage. Her blood stains the floor.

Fire Stairs

8:53 AM.

Francis shoots the .38 and limps. Limps and shoots.

Nelson, by now, reached the Third Floor and enters through the fire escape window.

Amanda sees the incoming silhouette entering through the fire escape window and launches her cane spear with full force.

Behind the curtains, Nelson senses and grabs it with an easy, quick motion.

He is in. Cane in hand.

They see each other for the first time. Amanda opens a wide smile. Nelson follows. Wind blows her hair in all directions.

A beat.

Amanda firmly to Nelson. "You're late, Sweetie. Again."

They smile at each other as if it were their first date. And love resumes just like that.

He returns her cane to her.

Nelson hugging her *not-wanting-to-let-go* wise. "Darn hard woman to find. Shit you're damned beautiful. Ain't nothing slowing me down-none."

Tracker shooting at Nelson hits the inside of APT 3C. Wood splinters from the wall, and glass shatters, hitting Nelson's face. He bleeds.

Nelson takes another shot to the back of his shoulder. He stumbles but gets inside the living room.

Amanda ducks laterally while keeping her eyes locked with Nelson.

Police sirens wailing from afar.

Lobby Area

Tracker tries to keep Hammer pinned down by launching himself back inside the building.

Francis unloads covering fire while Hammer pushes closer to the entrance door.

Tracker needs to fall inside for cover, and does.

Johnny plunges inside the living room, Judo-style, right behind Nelson. He sees Nelson. They lock eyes. Johnny is evidently puzzled.

Essex and Westie enter the gun-smoked building, then dart up the stairs. Guns drawn.

Westie is badly hit in the left leg by Hammer, and tumbles inside the building entrance.

Street Level

Garbled emergency radio transmissions.

SWAT units and Hammer's Special Crime Unit approaching from oposing ends of the street.

SWAT helicopter roaring in the backdrop.

Firetrucks incoming.

Apartment 3C

A wounded Essex and Westie enter APT 3C and open fire.

Nelson fires back. Out of rounds, he launches the cane at Westie hitting him in the arm.

He puts himself between Essex and Amanda. Nelson is hit seven times. In full rage, he kicks Westie in the chest then charges toward Essex. If this were any other mortal man, he would not have survived. But this is Nelson.

Amanda kneels to the ground, and coughs.

A beat.

Gun smoke engulfs the room.

She looks for Nelson.

Johnny jumps out on top of Essex's back holding him from behind with a neck-choke, then flips him over with a textbook judo *uchimata.*

As Essex lands, he recovers and pulls out an ankle .32 S&W and shoots at Johnny, but Nelson jumps in front and takes two more bullets to the side before striking Essex to the ground with his fist.

Nelson kneeled, moaning.

Essex is out for a beat.

Police sirens approaching, louder and louder.

Zhain proceeds to the Third Floor. He coldly walks over Fatima's dead body. Her engagement ring lying in a pool of blood.

Zhain, in front of APT 3F's door, senses something odd. He holds for half a second and notices the missing apartment metal plaque. He feels something unusual inside – something out of place.

A loud bang; a bullet ricochets on a fire extinguisher blasting away the edge of the door molding, right in front of Zhain. He shifts his attention to his left side, to APT 3C.

Johnny kneeled on one knee, by Nelson's side, providing covering fire with the revolver, shooting at Essex who is ducked next to the room's door.

A lost bullet hits Zhain in the neck, passing through his flesh. Another bullet hits his torso, on the left side, violently punching him backwards. Neither wound is lethal. With his hand applying pressure on the neck graze, he enters APT 3C.

Nelson at the opposite end of the room from Amanda - unconscious, face covered in blood, face down on the floor.

Johnny inspects and cares for Nelson's wounds.

Zhain dives inside the living room and picks up the .32 S&W from the floor (he is oblivious to Nelson).

SWAT sirens louder and louder – the sirens shake the room.

Zhain finds the scene odd. He ambles over the rubble and blood. He observes closely and approaches Amanda. She is flat on the floor, supine. Her hair covers her face.

Feist enters the room, storming. "Boss, we have to leave! Now sir!"

An indifferent Zhain kneels and gently handles Amanda's hair to the side. Amanda softly opens her eyes and sighs. Zhain notices she has one small entry wound close to the heart. Nothing but a bit of clotted blood on her white shirt. A beat.

Zhain recognizes Amanda. He holds her hand and caresses it in utter kindness. His heart pounds irregularly. He sweats. His lower lip trembles.

A cloud of blue butterflies invades the room placidly.

One lands on Zhain's shoulder.

Amanda's breathing is labored. But she still settles her hand and puts pressure on Zhain's neck wound.

With his eyes fixed on Amanda's, Zhain gently covers Amanda's hand with his own (on his neck).

They both release their hands, and we notice the graze stopped bleeding and is fully healed, only a scar as evidence.

The drums and sirens pause.

Zhain is at the epicenter of disillusion, knowing he has no recourse to this outcome – to death.

An Irish flute resonates inside the room.

Amanda's glowing eyes looking deeply at Zhain. She attempts a smile, followed by a shy nod to the side. She places her warm, soft palm on his face and whispers a tone into his ears. "I see you. . ."

A distraught Zhain.

He loses his senses.

Time halts.

The universe is dead silent.

Zhain holds Amanda's hand firmly, then hugs her inconsolably. Tears come out of his sore eyes. Zhain, still kneeling next to Amanda, looks up to the sky and yells an unbearable, "NOOO!"

It may take Zhain an eternity to overcome the upsurge of rage that has installed inside his soul. If ever.

Time resumes. . .

A French horn cracks in, followed by one thousand angry Taiko drums.

Zhain erects himself, lethargically languid, and in utter rage points the .32 S&W at Essex and unloads it viciously.

His immobile red eyes.

He empties the chamber and keeps shooting, although the barrel is empty - the metallic mechanical trigger dry click. . . click. . . click, but no shot sound. Smoke fuming out of the .32 S&W. With a cold face, and empty heart, he robotically lowers the .32 S&W, then slowly opens his hand. The revolver falls flat on a pool of blood.

Silence.

Zhain is immune to fear and stands there by Amanda's side - forever if he could.

Building Stairs

SWAT team charging inside the building, busting doors, and clearing apartments.

SWAT team reaching the second floor.

A purple smoke boom fills the first floor.

Opposing Brownstone

9:16 AM

SWAT Sharpshooter adjusting his elite rifle scope.

Sharpshooter on the brick walkie-talkie. "Eagle-Two in position, two-six. I have visual! Copy."

Firefighters spraying the El Camino.

Corridor

SWAT Team agent and seven heavily armed agents. "MOVING!"

Apartment 3C

Feist is behind Zhain, pulling him to egress as the SWAT charge up the stairs.

Random SWAT on the radio. "CLEAR. MOVING!"

Repetitive gunshots in the backdrop.

Loud coughing.

A tactical SWAT agent launches a diffusion smoke bomb inside APT 3C. A defining BANG. The sound of coughing.

Bullets swarm inside the room.

Sunbeam from the exit window joins gun smoke to illuminate and fully cover Amanda's body.

The blue butterflies calmly exit the room just as they came.

The room turns pitch black. A long silent beat.

Chapter 35

Inside the Ambulance

Moments later. 9:47 AM.

New York cobblestone streets.

Loud sirens. Bumpy ride.

Garbled emergency radio transmissions.

Busy EMTs doing what they do best.

Ambulance Stretchers

Amanda and Nelson lay side-by-side on stretchers inside the busy ambulance.

Two EMTs and Johnny's views of events differ from those of Amanda and Nelson.

Nelson's labored breathing.

Nelson with tears in his eyes and a cracking voice to Amanda. "...how can you be this beautiful? (he coughs) Am sorry, couldn't... Hanna... am so sorry..." He cries (finally).

Amanda's hand holding a *mailbox key* by a light blue string.

"I'll join her. . . almost there. . . but we have no time now. . . you need to be Nelson again for me. . . for the boys. (she coughs) Little Nelson needs you, babe, for all the boys. . . and the one to meet. . ." Amanda gently with fading voice.

Amanda coughing blood. "He likes to dance, like you?" A beat. ". . . but he is actually good at it." More laughing with coughing. "He's the answer, Nelson. . . and you will need help from. . . Trust him, he is here. And he too needs you. . . Time is thinning, but you already know that. Give them a chance, babe. They should not have to pay for our mistakes. . ."

"Amanda, babe." A beat to catch his breath. "I'll get this right this time. . ."

"Don't change my fate, Nelson. It needs to be done. Don't be long. . . I will miss my garden. . . see you on the other side, babe. . ."

Amanda's EKG is flat - EKG sounds and monitors.

Flatline on the monitor, BEEEEEP. . .

Amanda's hand falls to the side of the stretcher. The mailbox key moving like a clock pendulum.

Ambulance whips through city streets.

Johnny helps EMTs with the oxygen mask on Amanda.

Nelson, also on an oxygen mask, turns his face and clings Amanda's hand by the tip of her fingers, a delicate three fingers release. A beat and Amanda blinks lovingly, yet conscious, at Nelson.

EMT-Garcia looks at Amanda's tranquil face, then to EMT-Mariam. "She lost too much blood. She ain't coming back!"

EMT-Sarah looking at Nelson, "I got eight bullet entries so far. He's in God's hands now."

Nelson's EKG monitor goes flat, too – another extended BEEEEEEP. . .

An inconsolable Johnny swaps position with EMT-Sarah and performs dramatic CPR on Nelson.

"No, he isn't!" Johnny says.

Nelson's EKG remains flat. He still holds Amanda's hand.

Their faces are turned to each other.

Amanda closing her eyes gently, pianissimo - purposively.

Their hands untangle and fall, slowly, in their separate ways.

Johnny commanding the EMTs, while looking at the ambulance's defibrillator.

"Light it up! Light that fucker up!"

The electric, charging sound. Johnny's voice, "CLEAR!" Then the brutal BLAST. Nelson's body pumps upwards with the joules of energy. The ambulance becomes engulfed with intense bright light. The EKG still flat-lined. Johnny's voice, "CLEAR!" A second BLAST. Johnny is unrecognizably distraught. This is personal.

The joules of energy bounce back from Nelson's body blowing up the defibrillator and the EKG monitor. Electric sparks and smoke decommission the equipment.

Spooked, desperate eyes from the EMTs.

EMT's in disbelief step aside as Johnny takes charge and continues his brutal CPR on Nelson. Overwhelmed and angry, he shouts. "Come back! Come back YOU! By-God, I *will* bring you back!"

The busted ambulance charges ahead and disappears into Brooklyn streets and into a torrential storm.

All comes crashing down.

Brooklyn Gospel Church

9:53 AM. It rains hard.

Requiem.

A Foggy Dew sung by one hundred and thirteen children's choir.

Voice and drums only.

Knuckles conducting.

And it lasts.

Chapter 36

Brooklyn Hospital

Next Day.

A silent morning.

A rundown, decrepit public hospital.

Cold fluorescent lights sizzling undramatically.

Seventh Floor, ICU Ward

Knuckles and three of her stalwart church associates dressed in green-and-white gospel robes guarding Nelson's ICU room.

Heavily armed cops from Hammer's unit stroll the same defunct corridor.

Loud back-and-forth police radio exchanges.

Through the door window, Knuckles observes Nelson's Jets jersey covered in dried blood on top of a red chair. He is stretched in a bed, in a coma, kept alive by dozens of archaic ICU equipment.

She carries the weight of responsibility over Nelson's well-being and will honor her pledge to Captain Fritz. But more importantly, she has grown incredibly fond of the mysterious cowboy man. His silent magnetism. His rightful mandate. His bona fide eyes. His simple manners. His silence. She is not ready to part with him and will take no prisoners to protect her special guest.

A significant, worn-out respirator moves slowly up and down, its white enamel paint fading - a clear indication of the public health system's lack of resources.

Sunbeam coming from the room's window blankets Nelson's body. And nothing else.

Knuckles' hand immersed inside a Cracker Jack box, and her eyes fixed inside the room, on Nelson.

"Have faith, Knuckles." Gestures Mohammed, aka *Brother-Med*, Knuckles heavily armored church associate.

A discontent Knuckles eating while protesting back at him. "Faith, man?! C'mon, *man*! You kiddin-me?! Faith wants nothing with this here-town. It's on us, man! On us. . ."

ICU Unit, Room 316

Nelson wearing the mailbox key around his neck entangled with Amanda's bloodied white-and-blue silk scarf. A green, desolate grasshopper settles on his bloodied Jets jersey.

Nelson appears to be in peace.

Chapter 37

Prairie Cemetery

Two days after the Brooklyn shootout.

Early morning. Blue skies.

Green fields.

A cool breeze.

A foggy mist gives space to a beautiful sunny day.

A small gathering to bury Amanda, May, and Fatima.

Six men dressed in ceremonial-white carry Amanda's humble balsa casket. Amanda's signature blue stone seed necklace on each of their necks.

The athletic pallbearers are her sons.

On the West end, Hammer's unit guarding.

On the East end, Knuckles Church accomplices along with Sean and Leprechaun.

Hammer, Beth, Claire, Chris, Johnny, Janis, and Winnie by the burial site.

Claire and Chris holding hands.

Chris wears the same *ceremonial-white*, such as his *brothers*.

Hammer is the only one dressed in black leather and dark sunglasses.

Prairie Hill

Far from noticeable view, from the vantage of the green hill, Zhain looks down at the gathering. Behind him, Alexandra, and Cole.

Further out, Feist waits by the limo holding a black umbrella. A patched-up Tracker stands behind him, surveying the scene with binoculars.

Zhain too is dressed in *ceremonial-white* and wears an Amanda blue stone seed necklace. He is silent and in pain. He barely moves. He holds APT 3F's metal door plaque - blood on it.

Alexandra and Cole simultaneously, symmetrically, nest their hands behind Zhain's shoulders in solidarity. It comforts him.

Burial Site

Amanda's six sons approach Chris and kneel compassionately in front of him.

The eldest brother, Lorhenz *Heart of Lion* takes a knee in front of Chris and grabs his little hand, then places a blue stone seed necklace around his neck.

Lorhenz to Chris. "Remember this, Chris: you're not alone. She is always with us."

Chris looks up to Lorhenz with the saddest of eyes.

A second brother, the valiant Ihanz, holds Chris' hand. "Our father will come for us. You will meet him. Shouldn't be long."

"My. . . my father you say?" A dazed Chris.

A third brother, the Hercules-like Mharthinz, answers. "Yes, Chris. *Our* father. *Your* father. He will come. Until then, tender your path, your own way, brother."

Lorhenz, Ihanz and Mharthinz stand up in sibling synchronicity.

Claire gives Chris a consoling bear hug.

All other brothers, while proudly standing up, gather around Chris, placing their hands on his slight shoulders.

Lorhenz remains low on one knee holding Chris by his upper arm.

Prairie Hill

Zhain slowly extends his arm forward.

A blue butterfly lands on his forearm.

He stares at it. Then holds it on his palm.

Burial Site

A white butterfly lands on Chris' shoulder.

Prairie Cemetery

Same day. Hours later.

Empty of people.

Just silence.

Amanda's wood casket lays on the grass in solitude. A white rectangular Boulder next to it.

A Little Cheyenne Girl stands in front of Amanda's casket,

holding a bouquet of Plain's Lavender flowers. She places a Cedar bucket of persimmons and oak seeds next to the lonesome casket.

The wind picks up and blows her hair wildly. She kneels and places a large oak seed in front and under the Boulder. She stands up, looks at the Boulder, and turns in its opposite direction, skipping towards the last rays of sunlight.

It rains. Mostly around Amanda's casket.

Dusk arrives.

From afar, the little girl enthusiastically dances with rain drops, the mercury Sun, and the always feisty Wind. She jumps and cheers as if completely immune to the world as is.

It is dusk. Skies turn dark blue and orange.

It's a full moon.

The Boulder and casket burn inside a massive bonfire.

A Requiem bell from afar shutters the scene.

Night steps in dressed in a mystic purple mist.

Amanda's Brownstone

Next Day. Early morning.

Lobby.

Mailbox Cabinet.

Amanda's apartment mailbox-letter box panel area.

Winnie opening a vertical metal letterbox door, APT 3F. His hands opens the letterbox's metal door and unveils *The Book* resting solo inside it, intact, lit by warm golden light.

Winnie's face lit in golden light.

Liberty Tower, Rooftop

Dawn.

Sun raising behind a cloudy screen.

Cole standing up.

The agnostic Sun hits Cole's bloodied face, he enjoys the touch of warmth.

Chapter 38

The Plains, Train Station

Next Day.

Dusk. Tangerine skies.

The day is dry and hard.

A bronze plaque reveals the station's designation - "ORIGIN'S EDGE".

Platform

An Elder dressed in beige leather plays a Funeral March folk ensemble on his ancient bass tagellharpa cello.

A dark body walks by, in front of the Elder.

The folk ensemble follows Zhain all the way to the Farm House.

Farm House

Outside the Farm House, by the mailbox *01 Aboro Street*, a red train key swings on the mailbox ear flag.

Zhain stands firm outside the Farm House yard with bloody hands, holding a still-smoking shotgun. His face bleeds.

A wheezing Red lies bloodied on the floor behind him.

"Big Pants. This is not. . . right. Your father will not let this. . ." Red pleads distraughtly.

"Don't call me that!" Zhain back at him. He gazes at the twilight. "How could I have forgotten this sky? That narrowly singular gap in time and space where light cheats the dog and promotes the wolf. Ahhhh, isn't it just, absolutely, beautiful?"

Zhain's wet eyes. He is clearly in pain and possibly not exactly in his best senses. A tear creeps down his cheek. With broken voice. "My *father*, you speak of?! I have no *father*! There is no *father*!"

A blue butterfly lands on his forearm. He gazes at it. He changes tone. Now softer. "You were always good to me, Doctor Hooker, always. The going was that I was brought to this world through your hands, and that my mother tipped over for a few minutes, and you brought her back. Yes, I was *occasionally* reminded of that; that my birth could have killed mother, more than a few times, you see. . . And again, now, I will be reminded once more - *it is all his doing, his fault, him to blame, and no other*! It is my time now. This is my world. Not his. *He* failed us. *He* failed you, too, Doctor. *He* failed us all!"

"Nelson can't be destroyed. *The Book* can only be rewritten by. . . but you knew that already, kiddo." He struggles with the words.

"You wanna bet?" Zhain says.

"Little Nelson. . ." Red back at him, pleading kindly.

"And we never really finished our *immortality* conversation, did we, Doctor? I miss that time." Zhain asking, contemplating, now more caring.

A tall, massive fire burns the Farm House down. It collapses. Zhain proceeds to the Bur Oak tree next to the House.

A sizeable speck of red, flickering flame lands on his shoulder (burning him), yet he is indifferent to it. He crouches by the oak tree and digs down the Earth with his hands.

A sizeable old cigar box. The cigar box being opened. Inside, an original Jules Verne's *Voyages Extraordinaires* edition, Nelson's hunting knife, a comic book, six dried butterflies, a wolf's tooth, and a photo of Zhain and Hanna as young kids.

He wipes dirt off the photo - Hanna (seven), sitting on top of Zhain's (nine) shoulders, looking damn happy.

Origin's Edge POSTLUDE

Zhain's Flashback Begins. . .

Farm House

A long, long time ago.

A tall-haired, young Zhain (eleven) wearing a Thayer's style green cape, at the Farm House's back yard, fighting a massive black wolf by the oak tree. Young Zhain down on his back, under the tree swing, with the wolf forcibly on top going for his neck.

Zhain musters his butterfly net and his sprinter's legs - like a pair of coiled springs – and fends the wolf off. For a beat. He rolls. He wields the swing's wood bench as shield. He handles the hunting knife, puncturing the wolf's neck, then kicking the beast in the mouth. A bloodied canine tooth spits to the air.

But this is no ordinary wolf. This is a vicious killer, accustomed to sparring for survival. Equally, this is no ordinary child.

The wolf pulls back, countering with a side hook of the claws that produces a deep cut to Zhain's smooth face - now covered partially in blood.

The wolf pins him down, hard. It salivates profusely over him. Zhain can smell the beast's putrefied breath and read its intent – death.

They've been fighting for a full hour now.

Having lost plenty of blood, young Zhain passes out for a beat.

Surprisingly, the beast exits from atop the injured Zhain. It has another target in sight - the House. It locks its sight on the Farm House's half-opened back door and proceeds towards it with all the killing thirst a beast of prey could ever whirl.

Dirt Road

A sudden, loud ballistic shot from Nelson's Henry zooms past Zhain's head. He sees the bullet's trajectory whipping, cutting through the galvanized air, then he turns his head and sees the inside of the gun's smoking barrel.

In full thick beard, a younger Nelson running viscerally, Henry in hand, from the dirt road towards Zhain. They make split-second eye contact. A lasting muted second. One with its own psychology.

Oak Tree

Our young Zhain tries but fails to stand up.

Nelson cocks and shoots his rifle again at the beast while running. The bullet hisses over Zhain's head, who looks helpless and yells desperately to Nelson head-pointing to the House.

"Hanna!" He yells.

A second attempt from Zhain to stand up. He can't. He is left with a military crawl toward the House.

The black wolf gazing back at Zhain while leaping forward towards the doorsteps, gaining ground, almost inside.

Nelson still in rapid motion, doesn't stop and acrobatically, desperately jumps over Zhain, while in hot pursuit. The wounded wolf looks back at Nelson as it walks limping towards the House's back door.

The beast bleeds but keeps going.

Another blast of the Henry.

The wolf's torrential growl. The wolf's cry. Then a bestial, horrendous awl.

A young Amanda over Zhain, cane by her side, maternally caring and protecting him. She is barefoot and wears a light, full-body Greek drapery dress. She presses a shred of her dress's cloth against his face wound.

Tears escape Zhain's tiny dark eyes, falling solemnly into the fertile dirt. His shallow voice, "I couldn't. . . I'm sorry, Mom. . ."

Hanna, Zhain's soul-bond sister.

The elements are unsure of what has just unfolded.

End of Flashback.

Farm House

Present.

The battering sound of Taiko drums and dark skies arrive abruptly.

It rains torrentially.

The rain and ashes produce a distinguished scent. One of sadness. And sorrow. The Earth exhales steam smoke upwards from its pores.

A fuming Zhain soaking wet, standing up. Mad as hell. Holding the hunter's knife in his bloody hand as he looks to the burning House crumbling down.

Thick, post-fire smoke plume blankets him. Drops of water mixed with blood and ashes threading down from his knife.

Zhain's unforgiven, red eyes turn South to New York. His hands covered in ashes. His heart wrapped in rage.

A wolf's howl.

A solitary sunbeam far in the horizon challenges the dark and cuts through the heavy clouds.

Zhain gazes at the defiant sunbeam and squeezes his grip forcefully onto the knife, then speaks out with unbound anger. "Father! Is this your work?! (he fills his lungs with air) I am waiting for you on the other side, Old Man!"

The drums halt.

Silence.

Love – an act of rage.

Brooklyn Hospital, Room 316

Same moment.

A soft, lasting Mandolin ensemble plays *The Sound of Silence.*

A diagonal ray of light from the window illuminates Nelson's battered hand.

Fade to black.

End of Book One,
Origin's Edge

With Gratitude

With unbound love and deep gratitude to my father and mother for absolutely everything. And especially for being there, always. Even when they shouldn't have.

***

And thank you Tim Morrison, my brilliant editor, for not tolerating my numerous shortcomings.

***

To my beautiful family and faithful friends, which are so many. How fortunate am I.

***

In memory
Graceful souls Dani and Vo'-Theo.

***

My love to All.

About the Author

A.C. Coelho is an award-winning screenwriter and the author of *The Book of Men* saga – *Origin's Edge, Ashes,* and *Ascent.*

A graduate of MIT, a faculty with New York University, and a by-product of New York's public school system, A.C. Coelho lives and works in Manhattan.

If you liked this book, I invite you to join my mailing list and Newsletter for updates on the saga and on future events through my website: www.authoraccoelho.com.

You can also follow me on social media. Instagram: @authoraccoelho

Thank you!